Endless Days of Summer

Stacy O'Steen

Supposed Crimes LLC • Matthews, North Carolina

www.supposedcrimes.com

This book is typeset in Goudy Old Style, licensed by Ascender Corporation.

Dedicated to my husband, who is my greatest supporter, and to my betas, for this book would have been far less with out you. You loved them like I did.

Preface

THERE ARE moments in life you expect, then there are moments in life which expect *you*. Crazy, you say? Not quite, but close. Bear with me. Everyone expects puberty, and everyone expects death, but on the top of the hill there is your first break up expecting you while you dream of everlasting love.

Now, there is a lot of argument as to what love is and when it really happens for the first time, but I'm not here to argue semantics—although I will say, if it hurt in the end then that's enough to convince me. I *am* here to argue that there are moments which had to wait longer for me than either they or I expected. My name is Penelope; I'm twenty-two and asexual. Cue theme music...

Chapter One

I MET Clayton through a mutual friend, at the end of my sophomore year of high school. She liked him and wanted my approval, but he only wanted me. I can't say I was proud of myself; I can only say it happened. We started hanging out, and in my naivety, I assumed we were on the same page. I assumed he was falling as much in love as I was. If you talked to him, you would have believed it, too.

He was my first kiss. He was the first person I threw caution to the wind for. He was the first person I loved, and he was the first guy to hurt me. I fell for him fast and hard. He told me he loved me in August of our junior year. Some people told me things were moving too fast, but I defended our love, telling them "it was just meant to be." I thought we were falling together. We didn't have any of the same classes, but I saw him during passing periods. He would walk me to class, hand in hand. What I didn't know was during class, he was flirting with someone else, asking *her* to be with him.

After six months, Clayton told me we couldn't be together anymore. The other girl had finally said yes but had made it clear she wanted to be his one and only. I didn't realize this was something which had to be specified. Consider that lesson learned. Apparently, she was worth an exclusivity clause when six months of exchanged "I love you" weren't enough for him to commit to me. Hate her, you ask? Oh, did I! Until I met her... Gah! I mean, I didn't know what was happening. The girl's name was Summer, and we got along from the start, even though it was completely awkward.

She was tall for a girl, like me. She had a pale complexion and a small, button nose. Her red hair could only have come from a box, but it looked good on her. She walked with a graceful awkwardness, which made people notice her, but she never gave them a sideways glance. She never thought she was anything special, but I knew she was from the beginning.

We both knew who the other was by our first meeting, yet we tried to piece together an unlikely friendship. I fully believed Clayton probably never even mentioned me before they were together, but by all teenage drama rules, I was within my right to hate her. She had taken what I had claimed as mine (forget the details), and I should have wanted her head on a pike—but what happened was truly the opposite.

We became friends rather quickly and soon spent a lot of time together. My time before and after school was all filled by Summer. My old lunch table crew wondered where I went because I was with her every day. I wanted to be near her always; the only free time she spent away from me was when she was with Clayton.

I found myself talking about her all the time, trying to make sense of what I was feeling. My other friends probably thought I was obsessing over the girl who took "my man," but I knew it wasn't that. I felt like I had finally found someone who I could truly be myself with, a friend who would always be there.

Chapter Two

"Hey, are we going to get together this weekend and look at college applications?" I asked Summer, holding the phone to my ear with my shoulder. "I need to know what SAT scores I have to get to qualify for our top selection schools."

"I want to, but Clayton and I are back together...and we're supposed to hang out on Saturday," she said, guilt lacing through her voice.

"Well, then I'm coming over on Sunday, no excuses," I said as I rolled my eyes. Their break up had only lasted three days this time. "Whether you stay with him or not, we need to go to college together."

"Of course I'm going to stay with him." She huffed. "Maybe I'll invite him over on Sunday too, and we can all look at applications."

I rolled my eyes so far back into my head it hurt.

"I suppose if that is what you feel you need to do but I will not spend the day watching you two make out. It's gross," I admonished, annoyed that I would have to spend any time with him at all.

Since the dissolution of Clayton and my relationship, also known as the start of his and Summer's, I had felt less and less inclined to be in his presence. It had nothing to do with jealousy or heartache and everything to do with what a jerk he was when he was no longer interested in me. In a relationship, Clayton was kind and caring (at least in appearance), but once a girl was no longer "the chosen one," it was easier for all parties if she disappeared. I did not have this luxury as I had irrevocably hitched my wagon to Summer's.

"I know, I know," she replied, her voice taking on an exasperated tone. "Hang on, someone's calling.—Oh! It's him, I've got to go. I'll see you at school tomorrow."

"Okay, bye," I said, hanging up the phone. "I wonder how long they'll stay together *this* time," I cried, flinging my phone on the bed.

It was the first Tuesday night in August before my senior year. School was imminent and so was my eventual explosion if I had to endure much more of the Summer-Clayton saga. They were constantly fighting and breaking up and getting back together...and fighting and breaking up...and getting back together. Sometimes the periods between were minimal; once they were broken up for only two hours but other times, like when Clayton was on summer vacation in Florida, they were separated for almost a month.

It's not like I could reason with her. When they broke up, she was close to inconsolable. When it happened the first time, I almost wished them back together to stop her tears, but I learned better because now he was slowly torturing her.

I had my theories about why they broke up so often and it had little to do with them as a couple and everything to do with him being a jerk. He had his own personal code. For him, if he was single, even if only by a few minutes, then whatever he wanted to do was fair game. I had tried to explain this to Summer, but as mentioned, when it came to Clayton she wouldn't see reason.

"Are you off the phone?" my mother's bellows erupted from downstairs.

"Yes," I called back.

"Dinner is ready. Come eat," she said.

I pulled myself off the floor of my bedroom and looked around at my wallpaper of carefully cropped photos of me and my friends. I had made it my summer project to transform my room into a place that looked like I actually lived in it, much to my mother's chagrin. With her, it was better to ask forgiveness than permission. Although it had been a blow-up fight she hadn't asked me to remove the hundred or so pictures I had sticky-tacked to the wall.

My mother was over-bearing in the worst way, with a need to control everyone and everything. It never mattered what I did—she always seemed to dislike my choices. Her judgment of me didn't even come from love, more like a want to pretend we were a perfect family—which was hard to do considering my dad left us when I was seven. I had given up years ago on trying to please her. Now I was just determined to live a life worth having, even if she hated me for every second of it.

I flounced downstairs and plopped into a seat at the kitchen table. The night's menu included some of my favorites: bread and mashed potatoes. When the whole family was seated—me, my brother Cooper, and my mother—we began eating.

"So, have you finished your college applications yet?" my mother asked with fake cordiality.

"No, Mother, I haven't," I sighed, already tired of the charade.

"When are you going to do it?" she replied with imitation niceness, unable to keep the annoyed edge out of her voice. "I told you, the earlier you apply, the better chance you have before they see everyone else's applications."

"But you don't want me to apply just anywhere, do you?!" I cried, dropping both my silverware and the pretense of having a nice conversation. "You want me to stay here so you can keep me under your thumb. I need to live my own life, Mother!"

Why can't she just be supportive? I mean, a similar conversation with any other mother would have gone a little like: "Hey, mom, I was thinking about going away to college." "That's a big decision, dear, and it's hard for me to let you go, but I will if that's what you really want." "It is, mom, thank you for understanding. Can you please pass the potatoes?" But not my mother, it's her way or the highway, and that highway is at the top of a cliff. I'd fall to my death before taking two steps, and she'd probably push me off the edge.

I took my plate and retreated to my room, her protests echoing up the stairs after me. The same conversation between the two of us played over and over again in my head. It seemed to me, whenever we were in the same room, the only words she had for me were ones of criticism and nagging. When I told her I wanted to look at options out of the state, she had laughed at me. She had always tried to force me to live the life she wanted for me, but the objections had become more frequent as I had gotten older.

Summer and Clayton's mended relationship only lasted until Friday. I imagined he wanted the weekend to do whatever it is he felt he needed to do without a girlfriend. Since Summer now had no Saturday plans and was moping around like she was dying, I headed over to try and console her.

"You need to get past this," I said as Summer wiped her tears away with the back of her hand. "You deserve to be treated better than this."

"I know. I don't know what's wrong with me," she sobbed. "He does this every time, and I just keep going back for more."

"So if he called you right now and asked you to take him back, what would you say?" I asked.

"I don't know," she said.

"Summer!" I screamed.

"I'm sorry!" she cried. "I don't know what to say. I could feed you some bull about how I'll never go back, but we both know it'll probably be a lie."

"Okay, fine. Well, I'm not going to continue to have this conversation over and over again," I said. "I will however, have a conversation about colleges. The sooner we decide the better, *then* I can spend my time convincing you to get away from him."

We decided on three colleges to apply to together, Washington University, University of Illinois at Chicago and the University of Florida. That night I stayed with Summer; we spent it talking and laughing until her parents went to bed. We were asked to be quiet and not wake the whole house with our raucousness. We were both avid video gamers and huge fans of scary games, so around two in the morning we decided to play one. We sat next to each other on the floor in front of her television. Though we were both prone to screaming when startled, we had to be quiet lest her parents woke up.

"Here, you have the controller," I said. "I can't take it when the murderer starts to chase you."

"Haha, that's the fun part of a scary game! The fear," she said.

"I want to watch until you get to actually fight the bad guy," I said.

"Okay, but you have to sit with me. This game scares the crap out of me," she said, patting the floor next to her.

"So, where are we in the game?" I asked.

"I've found the matches, and now I need to go upstairs to light the lantern," she replied.

I sat down next to Summer and watched as she guided the character of the game through the old concert hall toward the stairs. The character went through a door, and the murderer leapt out and attacked with his hammer. Summer reflex paused and dropped the controller. We both jumped and screamed, our hands automatically reaching for each other. Her hand was soft and warm, gentle even while trying to crush my fingers in fear.

We looked at each other, our faces mirrored masks of fear. Summer looked down at our clasped hands then up to my face. My eyes darted down and I began to remove my hand from hers, afraid I had made her uncomfortable, but she just squeezed my hand and began to laugh. It was contagious after the scare of the game and I fell alongside her into fits of laughter. We ended up waking her parents anyway.

At school on Monday, Clayton and Summer were back to being... whatever it is they were aside from obnoxious, if they were anything other than that.

Chapter Three

"Summer!" I screamed into the phone, letters clutched in my hand.

I called her a soon as I had opened the mail box.

"What? Oh my god, what is wrong?!" she cried.

"Summer! Go check your mail!" I exclaimed as I slammed the metal mail box closed with a clang. "We got letters!"

"EEEeeeeee!" she sqeed.

Her footsteps echoed down the stairs, followed by a door slamming open and the thud of feet on pavement.

"I got one too," she yelled, her voice coming out in puffs. "Did you open yours yet?"

"Nooooo," I said, my voice a sing-song.

"I'll come over so we can open them together," she said.

"No, don't come to me. You know my mother is unbearable. This is a decision I want to make without her nagging," I said. "I will be there shortly."

It was March, and Summer and I both had multiple letters to open. We had agreed to only check the mail on the same day each week, so we would most likely get our letters together. Our respective families were banned from touching the mailboxes. The only one we had in common that time was the letter from Washington University in Seattle. We had both been accepted.

"I've been researching this school some more," I said to Summer after we had opened all of our letters. I waved the Washington acceptance letter at her. "I think we're going to have a really good time there."

"Yeah, but what if Clayton didn't get in?" She pouted, pooching her lip out ridiculously.

If I hadn't known that she was entirely serious I would have thought she was mocking him. I, on the other hand, was irritated. I hadn't even known he'd applied.

"Well, we'll just have to find out," I replied, trying desperately to keep my annoyance in check. "Call him and ask."

"I can't call him," she said, still pouting. "He broke up with me again."

I had lost count of the number of times Summer and Clayton had broken up. It was a testament to how often they did that she wasn't even crying this time. One would figure, if the word "again" could be added to the end of a sentence like the one she'd uttered, it would be time to pursue other options, but she was holding fast to their tragic relationship.

By late May, we had received letters from all the schools we had applied to. We were both accepted to Washington University in Seattle and University of Florida. We had decided to go to Seattle together. Summer had agreed in anger one night after another fight with Clayton. He had not been accepted, and I had made sure she meant it for three weeks afterward. She agreed whole-heartedly even when she was not single, and my heart soared. The next four years were looking promising. Now I just had to break the news to my mother.

"You want to *what?*" my mother bellowed, her head snapping to look at me.

"I want to go to school in Seattle," I said, my head held high—determined.

"I told you to apply to colleges around here," she shot back. "We could save money on tuition and you could live at home..."

"That is precisely one of the reasons I don't want to go to college here," I explained as calmly as I was able. "I want to go live a life not directly connected to yours, and I want to learn my own lessons."

"Well, I just don't think that's going to happen." She huffed.

"Don't act like money is the real problem. I know I have a college fund, and I know you have one for Cooper too," I replied. "I know you want me here but that, for sure, is not going to happen. If you don't let me go so I can get a college education then I will run away and be homeless and do god only knows what for my next meal. Is that really what you want to happen!" I glared at her.

The two of us stared at each other to see who would flinch first. Negotiating in my family was almost a blood sport. Arguing was inevitable and usually everyone had to give a little. The problem with this particular negotiation was I wasn't going to give an inch. We had been arguing the same points for at least six months now, and I was simply not willing to stay here, even if I was "allowed" to live on campus.

For a little while, my mother had even tried to convince Summer to stay close to home, thinking if she stayed, I would as well. She had underestimated my desire to leave and the emotional toll Summer and Clayton's relationship was having on Summer.

My mom looked away first; she looked down at her hands and then threw them up in the air.

"Fine! If you want to go off and get yourself killed or worse then I guess I can't stop you," she said.

"Ha! Yes, yes, yes, yes, yes!" I yelled, jumping up and doing a little celebratory dance. I pulled out my phone dialed Summer's number instinctively.

"Hello?" said a deep voice.

"Oh..."

The sound of Clayton's voice brought me up short. I stopped dancing.

"Summer, please?" I said, as politely as I could manage though it still came out with a little bit of snarl.

"She's busy. How are you, Penny?" he asked with a snigger.

"You think you're so clever, don't you?" I mocked. "Don't answer her phone when I call, and *don't* call me Penny. Matter of fact, how about you just not address me at all. I'm so glad you're not coming with us to Seattle." I hung up, fuming.

It seemed they were back together for the moment. I knew Summer would probably pay for my snark, but that boy took pleasure in getting under my skin as often as he could. I was more than happy to have something to retaliate with this time.

Chapter Four

I HELD Summer to me as a tear escaped and rolled down my cheek. Her perfume was light but sweet and wrapped itself around me like it always did when we were close.

"I can't believe you're going so far away," she whispered.

"You were supposed to be coming with me," I choked over a sob.

"I know. I'm sorry," she murmured as she pulled out of our hug.

I couldn't look her in the eyes; I knew to see her upset would be my undoing. I turned to my mom, hugging her goodbye.

"Have a good flight," my mom said. "Call me when you get to Seattle."

"Yeah, sure," I said, releasing her and turning to Cooper.

"Find me a hot girl and bring her back with you," he said, patting my back as we hugged.

"Right, that will be my top priority." I rolled my eyes playfully.

Then I was back to Summer. I hugged her quickly once more and then walked swiftly to stand in the line for my security check. It took a while for it to be my turn, but I didn't look back until I was at the front of the line, when I just couldn't help myself anymore.

She was still there, waiting for me to disappear into the sea of people beyond the checkpoint. We lived in the south where the season was ungodly hot, so Summer had worn a light sun dress to see me off. Her red hair hung down to her shoulders, and she had pale, porcelain skin complete with a smattering of freckles across her cheeks. She was a little chubby but healthy and absolutely beautiful in my eyes.

Summer stood on her tiptoes to wave one last time, her face only barely visible now over the mass which was the line for security. I turned around and put my carry-on on the conveyor belt for the metal detector. I was quite upset to be making this trip alone since we had talked so many times about what Seattle could be like for us. After passing through security and finding my gate, I plopped in to a chair.

I couldn't believe Summer had abandoned me in the choice we'd made together. I had asked her over and over again if she submitted her tuition check, and time and again she told me she had. Then with only a week before we had to leave, she informed me she would be staying home. I could have refused her wish to see me off at the airport, but what was the use of being angry when I was going to be so far away?

I secretly dreaded Clayton was her reason for staying but they had split for good at the end of senior year. She enlightened me she had been offered a full ride to a graphic design school back in May and simply hadn't known how to tell me. So instead of being an adult and telling me the truth, so I would have the opportunity to change my mind if I wanted to, she hid it and left me with no choice.

"...Penelope Van Buren booked on flight 352 to Seattle, Washington. Would this passenger proceed to gate B21 immediately."

My head snapped up as my mind caught up to the present. I grabbed my things from the chair next to me and rushed to the attendant waiting to take my ticket.

"I'm sorry," I exclaimed, handing him my ticket.

"No problem," he said as he scanned my ticket. "Have a good flight, Penny."

"Thank you," I replied as I dashed past him to the plane. "And my name isn't Penny."

I was, of course, the last passenger on the plane. All eyes were on me as I shoved my way down the aisle and into the first available seat, packed between two passengers like a sardine.

The flight to Seattle was going to be a long one. I wanted to use flight time to catch up on sleep, but my mind would not be silent. It kept running ahead of me, trying to figure out what my life would be like at Washington University, and then falling back to the friends and family I had left behind. The effect was dizzying.

When the woman sitting next to me on the aisle side began to snore, I knew there was no hope of me dozing off. I turned instead to try and see out of the window, wanting to catch a glimpse of the world going by. I couldn't see anything but the clouds, but it was better than the back of the seat in front of me.

As the sun began to set, I caught sight of my reflection in the window. It sometimes came as a bit of a shock that I truly looked the way I did. I wondered how other people must see me.

I had dark brown hair, naturally wavy, but only enough to make it unruly; it fell down right below my shoulders, and sometimes tried to attack people if they came too close. I kept it on the short side to avoid a catastrophe. I was a bit overweight but curvy in a serious way: big hips, tiny waist. I had brown eyes, a small nose and full lips. The sun and I were complete strangers, despite my life starting in the sunny south, and I was pale to the point of vampirism.

Yet, when I thought about myself, I didn't think of my packaging but as more of an amorphous blob made up of all the traits squished together making me. When I spoke to someone, I was never hoping they would find my lips irresistible or my hair perfectly quaffed but that maybe they would find me funny or charming.

When the sun was too low for me to comfortably stare out the window, I laid my head back and tried to rest. No sooner had I closed my eyes than I, once again, thought of Summer.

Chapter Five

So, FUNNY thing: in all of the agonizing over my now less than desir-
able, but fairly permanent, decision to attend school in spite of Summer's absence, I hadn't really given any thought to my living situation.
When I had submitted my application to the dorms, as I assumed Summer had, I put her name down as my preferred roommate. It hadn't
occurred to me, until I got my room assignment, I would be sharing my
room with a complete stranger.

"Hey!" a voice called from the bathroom as I pushed open the door
with my elbow. "I'm Alyssa." She emerged into the room, short, blonde
and busty. "I'm your roommate."

"Hi," I said, dropping my luggage on the floor. "I'm Penelope."

"So, which bed do you want, Penny?" she asked while giving me the
once-over.

"I don't care, and it's not Penny," I said, my voice apathetic.

I was used to people trying to shorten my name upon first meeting. I
just corrected them and moved on.

"Well, Penny," she said, emphasizing the "P." "I'm going to take the
window bed and that desk," she said pointing to a small desk at the foot
of the bed.

"I don't care what you do, but if you call me Penny one more time our
semester together is not going to be a pleasant one for you," I growled,

my voice a warning.

"Thank God," she said. "I just wanted to see what you're made of. Make sure you at least had an opinion about something."

"Haha. Great test," I muttered as I began to take my belongings out of my suitcase.

"I didn't mean to make you mad already," she said. "Honest, I was just trying to...I don't know. Penny sounds dumb anyway. I don't blame you for not wanting to be called Penny. I mean, you're not a nine-year-old with pigtails, and you aren't wrapped in copper with a president stamped on your forehead, so..."

"It's okay. Let's start over," I said. At least she had the decency to be sorry. "I'm Penelope Van Buren and I'm not made of metal."

"Hahaha, that makes it worse. Van Buren like Martin," she joked.

"Most people don't make that connection. He wasn't one of the better known presidents," I replied.

"You're right," she said, turning to grab her luggage and throw it on the bed she claimed. "But I'm a history major, so I guess that figures."

"Ew, history?" I replied, also starting on my luggage. "That is my worst subject. I couldn't imagine majoring in it."

"What's your major then?" She tossed her school supplies on her desk.

"I'm not sure yet. Probably something to do with science though." I grabbed my night clothes and retreated toward the restroom to change. I was ready to sleep.

"See, that, to me, sounds like torture," she called out as I changed.

I emerged from the bathroom and looked around at the room I would spend the next year in. Our room was only large enough for two desks and two beds. There was a shared closet and bathroom (consisting of a toilet and a sink), the shower was communal and located down the hall. I glanced at Alyssa, who was still unpacking, and, in spite of myself, wished desperately she were Summer. Then I crawled into bed physically and emotionally exhausted.

When I woke up, I didn't know where I was at first. I wasn't a "rise and shine" kind of lady, but more like a "hate the world until food" kind. After only a moment, I remembered where I was, glad Alyssa's bed was already empty. The full impact of the choices Summer and I had made, both together and apart, hit me full on. I would be spending at least the next five months without seeing her, and I missed her already.

To say I wallowed in my own depression for two months would be an understatement. I missed all school activities other than classes or things otherwise required. There was a lovely dent formed in my mattress in the shape of my body curled into the fetal position. I had, at least, stopped staring at Alyssa's empty bed, wishing it was Summer's. I switched to watching musicals and eating whatever junk food I had.

"I'm not going to let this happen," Alyssa said. She pushed the door wide open and found me in my bed for the third time that day, not sleeping. "I'm not going to sit by and watch you deteriorate. When you missed the activities fair, I thought, 'Don't worry, maybe she's not one for crowds.' When you missed the bed races, I hoped maybe you had become ill, but when you missed free food today, I knew it was time to step in. No freshman passes up free food cooked by someone else, unless they're depressed or rich. Since you are living in the dorms, I know it's not the latter. I don't know why you're all sad and pathetic, but you're not going to get away with it while I'm around."

During her speech, she had stepped into the room, kicked the door shut behind her, stalked over to my bed and ripped the covers off, throwing them on the floor.

"You can't hide from me," she said. "We're going to freshman movie night, and tomorrow you're going to find three clubs to join."

"Like hell I am!" I grunted, my body hanging over the side of the bed, straining toward the covers. "I'm not a club kind of girl, and I was already watching a movie."

"You know, sitting here, crying along with the *Sound of Music* doesn't count," she retorted with blatant disgusted pity on her face. "Don't make me go to the showers with you. Get yourself ready, or we're going to be late."

I stared at her defiantly, but she planted her feet, crossed her arms and stared back. It was a familiar exchange. I had seen that look on Summer's face before. I didn't have the strength to fight Alyssa, so I knew I would lose. I had to throw something into the bargain.

"Okay, I'll go tonight. I might even find *one* club to *try* tomorrow, but if I do, you have to join with me!" I cried, pointing my finger at her and sniggering like I had won.

"Okay, fine. Whatever. Now go shower—you smell like feet," she said, a smile playing at the corner of her mouth.

The following day, Alyssa made good on her threats. She pulled me, kicking and screaming, to the meeting board and made me pick out three clubs to attend.

"Pick one!" she said after I sat there letting my eyes glaze over. "We're going to be late for classes if you continue on this way."

"I don't want to join any clubs," I whined, throwing my head back and letting my arms drop to my sides. "I don't like clubs!"

"You don't know that!" she cried, tapping her foot. "You haven't even tried any."

"It's the same as high school," I moaned, still lamenting my situation.

"Just pick." She scowled and pushed me a little toward the board.

My eyes still facing the ceiling, I swung my hand and jabbed my finger in the direction of the board.

"There, that one." I looked at her out of the corner of one of my eyes. She looked at the board then at me.

"Great. I've always wanted to learn fencing," she said, rolling her eyes. "Will you please at least pretend to care?"

"Uhhhh, fine!" I said, tilting my head back down to look at the board in earnest.

I chose the LGBTQA club, the art club, and the fencing club (purely to annoy Alyssa). The next meeting for the art club was two days later, an experience which almost made me retreat back into my room. The day Alyssa and I attended a meeting, the club members were painting large canvases.

They didn't have any extra canvases but were willing to pair us up with members who were already painting their own, so we were split up and put with different people. This being the first club we decided to go to, I was not sold on the whole adventuring-out-of-my-room thing yet. I got paired with Gustav, who was apparently trying out a new "artist vision." I believe he was trying to channel his inner chicken as he was, alarmingly, dressed in a chicken costume.

I approached Gustav cautiously, afraid he might attack. I saw with surprise he had large, rigid paint brushes strapped to the toes of the chicken feet. As I watched, he lifted one clawed foot and dipped the attached brushes into carefully arranged paint buckets. Then he set off across the canvas with his hands tucked into his armpits and elbows flapping, while his feet shuffled their way along. I waited until he need-ed to reload his brushes to introduce myself.

"Hello. Are you Gustav?" I asked warily, terrified of being pecked. "I'm Penelope, and I'm supposed to collaborate..."

I stopped. Gustav was slowly extending his neck after having made it disappear as much as he could. He wasn't facing me. His face was pointed to my right, but his left eye, the only one I could see from my vantage point, was staring at me. Once his neck was extended as far as *humanly* possible, he tilted his head from one side to the other. I made a mistake in that moment. I took a tentative step back from him and he saw my weakness.

"BAWK!" he screamed, the noise so loud in the quiet room many others dropped their brushes. "Cluck, cluck, cluck."

"Um..." I breathed. My only thought was to try and be a still, like a dinosaur maybe he wouldn't see me if I didn't move.

"Don't interrupt MY METHOD!" he bellowed, raising his winged arms and coming at me.

"What the hell!" I turned, like any sensible person and ran for the door. "You're crazy!" I grabbed at whatever was on the periphery of my path and threw it to the ground in front of him.

I heard him continue to screech but I made it to the door well before him. If it was because I was not weighed down with a fifty pound bird costume, or because he had tripped on the obstacles I had thrown in front of him, I'll never know. I ran through the door and slammed it once I was safely in the hallway.

Gustav tried to open the door, but there was no way it was going to happen with wings. Instead, he screeched and clawed at the door. That was the precise moment I decided. The art club was not for me.

Among the screeches, I became acutely aware of laughter—lots of it—coming from within the room. I waited in the hallway for Alyssa to come out, but even after Gustav stopped bawking and the laughter died down, she still didn't come out. I gave up and went back to our room.

She showed up later in the evening, her clothes stained with paint and a smile on her face. Obviously, her club excursion had come out much better than mine.

"Where have you been?" I accused.

"Out," she said, raising an eyebrow at me.

"I waited for you in the hallway," I said.

"Well, I wasn't ready to leave." She tossed her hair over her shoulder and turned to the bathroom. "I was having a great time. For a little while, I was sure you two were putting on a show for us, but then you didn't come back. That business was funny, though."

"It wasn't funny," I replied, my eyes narrowing. I followed her, standing outside the closed bathroom door. "It was terrifying."

"You should have seen the mess he made on the floor. There was a trail of paint swashes on the floor behind him. He got super mad when the club leader told him he had to clean up his mess, too. I laughed so hard, I fell into my partner and landed in her painter's palette." She opened the door just enough to throw her dirty clothes at me. "See?"

"I'm glad my near-death was funny to you," I huffed, throwing her clothes on the ground. "I'm not going to any more clubs. This experiment was a failure."

"Oh really?" she called, her voice echoing in the bathroom. "How many times today did you think about Summer?"

"I, uh." I stumbled over my words. "How do you know her name?"

"Please, we've been living together for two months now," she said, opening the door dressed in clean clothes. "I might not have the full story, but I would have to be dumb not to know she's who you've been moping about. And don't change the subject. How many times?"

"Not until about an hour after I came back to the room." I turned away from her and walked back into the room to hide my face.

"And that's some kind of record isn't it?" she asked from behind me. I knew that her arms were crossed over her chest by the tone of her voice.

"Maybe," I admitted and flopped face first on my bed.

Chapter Six

I HAD to give some credit to Alyssa for her plan. Without my realizing it, she was making sure I didn't kill my freshman year before I had properly given it a chance. The following week was our first time to go to a LGBTQA meeting. We arrived early, not wanting to be singled out in any semblance of the first time at art club. There were a few members chatting waiting for the meeting to start and a club officer to greet us at the door. After signing in, we took our seats near the middle of the room.

The space filled quickly, and soon I was surrounded by new people. A boy with green eyes and blonde hair sat next to me—I couldn't stop staring. He was gorgeous, if not a little over cooked. I couldn't tell what his natural skin tone was supposed to be, since he was tanned to a nice golden brown.

"I'm gay," he said, after the fourth time he caught me staring.

I blanched but tried to play it off. "That's cool, makes sense."

His eyes narrowed, head tilting to the side. "Does it? So you're with the lovely lady to your right?"

I giggled, the situation going from awkward to bad. "No. Sorry, um... I'm straight."

"I see. I thought we were simply going to assume things instead of knowing."

"Wow. Okay, I didn't mean it like that. Starting over, I'm Penelope."

"Can I call you Penny?"

"Only if you want me to ignore you."

His face broke into a smile for the first time, "I'll remember that. I'm Noah."

I returned his smile as the club officers began to speak at the front of the room.

I enjoyed the LGBTQA club visit a lot, meeting Noah was a large point in its favor. I became a member and got involved. I was instantly immersed in a group of people with similar interests. I was a big supporter of all kinds of love and thus accepting of all sexualities.

When an opportunity came to get involved in fighting for gay rights, I helped to get signatures for petitions and spread the word about proposed laws that were trying to be passed through. I was even part of a protest lobbying for unisex bathrooms.

I spent fewer nights in my dorm, more nights enjoying myself, and less time pining for Summer. I did well in my classes and juggled them easily with my rapidly filling social calendar, while maintaining a good GPA. I was still sad Summer wasn't with me, having new experiences alongside me, but she had made her choice, and I was making the most of mine.

The LGBTQA club gave me somewhere to belong. I felt loved and safe there. I didn't feel judged, and I got along with pretty much everyone, but no one more than Noah. He wasn't necessarily what one would call nice, but he was always honest. We became friends the first day, and he was the reason I was no longer in my dorm room—alone—crying to musicals.

It started slowly, my heart looking for solace, when I began to tell Noah about Summer. The stories started with how she had abandoned me, but then everything else followed and the trickle became a flood as I poured out our relationship history. I had never quit thinking about Summer completely, and with Noah, my thoughts of her escaped my mouth like word vomit. He heard of her probably more than he ever cared to.

"Have you heard from Summer recently?" Noah asked one night when we were watching *Cats*.

"No, I haven't. She's too busy with her new boyfriend," I said, rolling my eyes.

"You mean the guy she mentioned to you like a month ago?" he asked.

"Yeah. They've only been together since a week before Halloween, and she is already acting like she can't live without him," I said.

"I see," he said. "So when did you first realize you were in love with her?"

"What do you mean? I'm not in love with her—she's my best friend," I refuted.

"Right, if she's only a friend to you then I'm a Cocker Spaniel," he said, poking me in the side to make me jump.

"Well, that would explain some things!" I playfully shouted back, tickling him and laughing.

"What are you trying to say?" he asked, moving out of my reach. I grabbed for him as he stood up. "No, but really, you are in love with her." He turned to face me sitting on the bed. "You do know that, right?"

I slapped his hand away from my side as he made to tickle me and replied, "Ha, ha, ha, hilarious. I've told you, I'm straight."

The look on his face said more than words could. He looked at me with the pitying look you give someone who is lost in an open-ended paper bag. I told him to go home on the pretense of cleaning and then showering. He knew I was just making up excuses, but he went anyway, giving me time to myself.

Could I really be in love with her? Is this what love feels like? This isn't what it felt like when I was in love with Clayton, but then again, it's not like I believe love is ever the same from person to person.

I had a theory: you never loved the same way twice. I believed this was true for two main reasons. Firstly, love was between people, therefore it changed with each new person you loved, and second, love changed people, thus every time you fell in love, even if it was with the same person, the love would be different because you were different.

Trying to figure out my true feelings for Summer kept me awake all night. At first I tried to sleep, but after three hours of tossing and turning, I decided I couldn't simply lie there anymore. I determined a shower was in order to try and clear my head and relax my body. All of the "trying to figure out something which should have been obvious to me if it were true" was making my muscles tense and inflicting a skull-splitting headache.

The showers in my dorm were not individual stalls. The bathrooms were separated by gender but nothing more. I walked in, put my clothes in a cubby, and walked into the communal shower area. It was about four in the morning, so thankfully I had the showers to myself.

I turned on a shower head in the corner and stood with the warm water hitting my head and flowing down my back. I could only hear the sound of the water and my own breathing. I thought of Summer again, of the many hours we had spent together, and my depression when I knew she wouldn't be with me this year.

I remembered the night Summer and I played the video game together, our fingers clutching each other in fear. It was the first time our hands had touched in a moment charged with emotion. It was forever long yet over so quickly, but I wouldn't give it away for the world. I lost and found myself in that moment before her mom came to check on us.

How could I not love her?

The clouds of confusion cleared to show a millisecond of shining clarity before crashing in again like the Red Sea.

If I do love Summer, do I tell her? Do I not tell her? Would she want me to tell her? I can't lose her, no matter what happens. This would be easier if she were here. Maybe if she loved me back then things would have happened on their own. Wait, love me back? Did I just admit to loving her? How long had I loved her without either of us knowing? Oh my god, does she know?

I was staring off into space, at war with myself, when I realized there was a girl showering across from me. She was looking at me, probably thinking I had been staring at her. I turned around to turn off the water and went out to my cubby and toweled off.

The other shower turned off and the girl came out and stood in front of me. I stood up straight from drying my legs and wrapped my towel around me. She stood there boldly and unabashed, her hands on her hips, her wet, dark hair fluid down her back. I blinked a few times then smiled a little. She cocked an eyebrow at me, and I quickly turned back to the cubby for my clothes.

"If you're interested, you should just say so," she said with a smirk, slight cockiness in her voice.

"Sorry, I was just spacing out in there," I muttered, my back still turned to her.

"Too bad," she said, then turned to go to her cubby.

I watched her walk away out of the corner of my eye, and while she was attractive, I felt nothing; I had no interest in her. Then I thought about Summer and found myself able to imagine kissing her and holding her hand. Above all else, though, I simply wanted to be near her.

It was this feeling which had fed my depression for two months, a deep-seated desire strong enough to make me consider leaving a school I had worked hard to get into. Yes, I supposed, some would consider it love, but did I?

After my shower, I sat in my room watching the sun creep in the window. I could have sat there and contemplated my feelings all day, but at some point it was blatant denial. I could imagine Noah staring at me, giving me sideways glances and knowing looks. I heard his voice as clearly in my head as if he were sitting next to me. "Girl, you might as well just accept it. This won't get any easier until you do."

As imaginary Noah cocked his head to the side, I cried, "Fine, you're right. I love her!"

This was met with grunts from Alyssa's lumpy-looking bed, which I assumed meant: 'Good for you, now shut up and let me sleep.'

I grabbed my phone and called Noah. I had spent most of the night imagining his voice in my head, so I figured I should at least tell him about my revelation. When he mumbled either a greeting or a cruse into the phone, I asked him if he wanted to grab some breakfast.

Chapter Seven

With the knowledge and help of the LGBTQA club members (and by that I mean Noah), I had identified myself as bisexual. It took a little bit for me to decide to come out to everyone at home, but I was safely lodged in a different state with a support group of people which made it seem like not as big of a deal.

I knew my family probably wouldn't take it well; they kind of agreed with the old military rule of "don't ask, don't tell." I wasn't willing to live my life shut up in a closet making choices based on what would keep my mother happy. However, I wasn't ready for a one on one conversation with my mom which would inevitably include the phrase "why are you doing this to me" either.

"So, are you sure you want to do this before telling Summer?" Noah asked for the fourth time.

"I'm sure. I know it might not be the best way, but it's happening. Summer hasn't contacted me since she got her new boyfriend. With that amount of silence, she doesn't get a personal notice," I said, my finger hovering over the laptop mouse pad.

"Okay, then just do it. Rip the Band-Aid," he replied and waved his hand at the computer.

I tapped my finger and the change was saved. Within a few seconds, my new sexual orientation was showing up in my friend's newsfeeds.

Only a few seconds afterward, I received the first comment.

Amanda Radcliff: Oh, I didn't know this was news... I thought you were with that one girl.

"*I knew it*," I said, staring at the screen. "That's all they have to say... and that's the first comment? This is going to be dumb."

"Let this be the first of many choruses of the 'I told you so' song and dance routine," Noah said, and then proceeded to do a little dance while singing, "Told you so, told you so, t-t-t-t-told you so."

He stopped singing when I got my second message, however.

Steven Kinnley: It's not like we didn't already know you were a sympathizer. Go hang out with your faggot friends, you dyke.

"He needs to wash his mouth out with soap," Noah said, his expression appalled. "Was he always like that?"

"Obviously not or I wouldn't have him on here," I replied, thinking. "But then again I can't really remember having anything to do with him, so...maybe?"

"I think he should be removed from the gene pool," he said.

I couldn't say I disagreed. It took only a few more comments for me to regret my choice and close my computer. Noah and I curled up in my bed to watch another musical. I wasn't really paying attention though; I was running through many of the comments over again in my head.

"How do you not let the things people say bother you?" I asked Noah, pausing the movie.

"It's not like they never do," he replied. "First of all, I don't know any of those people so it's way easier for me than you, but also you know the phrase 'they can only make you feel bad if you let them'? Well, I don't let them."

"How is that even a thing? I can't help how I feel." My voice pitched into a whine.

"Think about it. In order for what they say to matter, you have to care about them or what they think. I try to only care about things which are said by the people who truly matter to me," he explained. "You are the one giving power to the words that hurt you. You are the one letting the words said by other people define you and your actions."

"You're right." I moped and turned the movie back on.

"I know," he interrupted.

"But that's the hard part," I said, rolling my eyes and hitting pause again. "I can't force myself not to care about people judging me for something I can't control."

"You're right," he said. "But you can also try to see it as 'they're missing out.' People like that will never know what an awesome person you are or who you will turn out to be because they're blinded by their hate and bigotry. They've judged you because you don't fit in the tiny box they've shoved themselves into, and frankly, they're missing out." Noah hugged me to him, trying to suffocate the pain I was still feeling.

I wished it was that easy to look at all of these negative comments and consider it their loss. I should've been able to. I hadn't known any of the negative commenters very well anyway. I think most of them added me so they could keep tabs on me after high school. However, if they were reacting in such a harsh, judgmental way though, how was my family going to react?

I loved the idea of his words, but I couldn't shake the feeling of being dumped on. Although many of my friends from high school were more like acquaintances than friends, their comments did serve to bring me back to reality.

The state I grew up in was one of the few actively trying to produce and pass the legislation I was fighting against so fervently in the LGBTQA club. I got a few messages asking me what I was thinking—one in particular from my aunt, whose opinions on such matters were best ignored.

She took it upon herself to try and straighten out everyone in the family so we could fall like ducklings in line behind her, forced into this idea of a perfect family she had made for us which included the unwilling submission of everyone.

The truth was, my immediate family had been messing up my aunt's plans for years. Therefore, I added my Facebook reveal to my side of the tally board and replied telling her to message me when she had something nice to say.

I had never been one to be quiet and shy, keeping everything inside. I lived proudly and strived for a life without regret. This didn't mean I wasn't ever affected by ridicule, but I was less apt to let it change me or my life.

I had discovered new information about myself—I had found out more of who I was. I wanted to share it and not even incredibly dramatically, like over Thanksgiving dinner. Announcing it did not change who I was, it simply gave me a name for a piece of myself. I would still have been in love with Summer even if I had never given my feelings a name; they didn't change the moment I put a label on them. It helped me understand and accept what was already happening within me.

After I had gotten over the shock of some of the rude things people had the audacity to post in public places, I took matters into my own hands. It was time to prune my friends list. I deleted everyone who had made a dirty or hurtful comment on my Facebook. If they didn't want to know me, then I certainly didn't want to know them. I kept my aunt simply on principle, but I deleted her post from my wall.

I wouldn't let the close-mindedness of others stop me from enjoying the rest of the semester. I would continue to meet up with the LGBTQA club and fight for gay rights and equality. I threw myself head first into my social life so I didn't have to think about anything concerning home—Summer included.

Soon it was time to go home for the winter break. Noah's family lived in Washington. He offered to take me to the airport, and I gladly accepted. I was excited and fearful at the same time. This would be the first time I had seen or really spoken to Summer since I had made my huge personal discovery.

I wouldn't hide it from her. I was who I was and wouldn't be ashamed. I was, however, terrified of messing something up. Maybe she knew how I felt, and she wasn't interested, or maybe she wouldn't want to see me anymore. The fear didn't stem from an uncertainty about her sexuality. In the two years we had now known each other, we'd had many conversations about sexuality, including but not limited to our own. Summer was also bisexual.

"But," I whined in the car on the way to the airport, "what if she won't want to hang out with me because she thinks I've tricked her?"

"Tricked her?" Noah said, rolling his eyes while trying to keep them on the road. "How?"

"I don't know. Maybe she'll think I was pretending to be straight so she wouldn't want me," I said throwing my hands up in dismay.

"That is the most convoluted..." He started to turn toward me, and I pointed back at the road.

"What if she was happier when I identified as straight?" I rambled, cutting Noah off. "What if she's repulsed because I love her?"

"How could she be? You haven't even told..." he broke in.

"What if she's been avoiding me because she's straight now and knows she's going to break my heart?" I said covering my face with my hands.

"If you don't quit it, I'm going to slap you," he shouted, his voice ringing throughout the car.

Startled, I fell silent.

"You are being ridiculous, and not even half of the things you are babbling about are even logical. Give yourself some slack and her some credit, gah!"

I had never platonically loved a friend more than I loved that solid rock of a man. We arrived too quickly for my liking; I wished it had taken longer to get there. I was anxious to return home but would miss Noah immensely. It seems airport terminals are meant for tearful good-byes. I hugged Noah and walked to security, my mind still in a panicked frenzy.

Chapter Eight

I STEPPED off the plane into a half hug with my mother—not to be confused with a proper hug, more like a hip bump while she took my luggage. She was never one to show affection freely; my hugs as a child were limited at best. We made it almost all the way to the car before she "slyly" brought up my Facebook post.

"I need to get something off my chest before we can have a good Christmas," my mother said, a smile plastered on her face.

"Oh?" I replied. *I knew this was coming. Does she really think that I don't know what she's about to "get off her chest"?*

"Yes, we need to talk about the phase you are going through and how you're risking everything on some silliness," she said.

"Some silliness?" I said. "What are you referring to?"

"You're facespace debut as a lesbian, of course," she said, stopping as we reached the car. She turned to look at me and set my bag on the ground. "You know, prospective businesses look at people's facespaces now. I saw it on the news."

"First of all, it's Facebook. And secondly, good! I would hate to work at a company that discriminates," I replied, picking up my bag and shoving it in the back seat. "And third of all, I'm bisexual, not a lesbian."

"That's only another way to announce you are harlot, dear," she said, giving me her most chastising look.

"Thanks, mom. I really appreciate that." I opened the car door, hoping to quell the conversation. "It's a wonder I have any self-esteem at all. You know, I always knew you had a problem with anyone being different, but I figured some part of you would have conceded to the fact I was, and would always be, anything but 'normal.'"

"You can be different all you want to." Her voice was now coming from inside the car. "I just don't want to sit by and watch you throw your life away on some girl you met in college."

"Thank you for your opinion, *Mother*, but I am perfectly capable of making my own decisions. And, pray, tell me, what kind of future prospect might I be endangering?" It was obvious this conversation was going to continue all the way home.

"You know, you might meet a nice boy someday, and if they find your little secret on the Internet, it could go badly. You know things on the Internet are never really gone," she explained—a fact I, myself, had taught her. "I knew you should have stayed home to go to school."

"Mother, any man I would venture to be with would not only have to accept the fact that I like women, but also not use it as an excuse for a threesome. Not to mention, you're overlooking the possibility of me not ending up with a man. I might very well end up with a woman, especially since this is not a phase!" I replied, trying to remain calm but raising my voice in the end.

In a stern voice, she urged, "Don't be gross. You know that would never happen. Now, you need to remove that nonsense from your Facebook and make up with your aunt before Christmas. You have to play nice and don't ever mention your mistake in front of your grandparents. The mere idea might kill them."

"Thanks for the guilt trip," I replied, in my most exasperated voice, while rolling my eyes. I couldn't wait to escape the car, and more specifically, my mother. "But you don't get to run my life. I'm an adult and will do what I want. I don't have to fit into the mold of who you want me to be. I only need to be someone I'm proud of, and I can't do that if I'm hiding myself away, pretending to be ashamed of something I can't help."

"Why do you always have to be the most difficult child? Of the two of you, I never would have imagined my little girl would have been the one to cause me the most trouble."

"Geez, Mom! You are acting like I've taken up stripping or making nude videos! I'm merely living my life, and I'm sorry it offends you."

There was no way I was going to let my mother get to me, or at least show her that she had. She was kind of like a crazed wind-up toy when she got going. I couldn't handle her bigotry, and I marveled at how I came out moderately well-adjusted and accepting when I had grown up with her.

When I was younger, there was nothing I wouldn't read. I loved escaping to far-off lands which could only be imagined instead of lived. I got lost in a wardrobe on a regular basis, trying to find my way to a winter wonderland. All in all, I still had a rather reasonable childhood. Strict but supposedly loving, my mother tried to guide me, but before I took anything to heart, I would do my research.

I lived on the Internet, reading wiki and science journal. I couldn't have imagined a life without the Internet. There wasn't anything I couldn't learn, and there was no amount of knowledge that could be hidden from me. I learned at a young age my mother wasn't the authority people tried to tell me she was. She was an acceptable guide—good, even—in the younger years when I was learning right from wrong, but as my curiosity peaked and my questions no longer had simple answers, I needed more than her.

I already missed school, my accepting support group, my friends and Noah. Nothing was going to make the holiday pleasant, I thought, except maybe Summer. She had been wiped from my mind during the cyclone of my mother's tirade, but as she rushed back into my mind, I felt all the blood in my body flood my face.

My mother should be happy for the days I didn't upset her suburban lifestyle with my wild, reckless "phases." It would only be a small matter of time, especially if Summer consented to a relationship with me, before she started worrying about the neighbors. If Summer returned my love, not only would I be all kinds of excited, but I would shout it from the roof tops. I would ignore the stares from whoever threw them our way and enjoy a love I had been silently harboring for way too long.

I had a burning desire to know if she felt the same. There was a part of me, confident in my new found life style, which knew she had to have returned my feelings at some point. But then there was this quiet, but growing ever louder, part of me madly whispering there was no way she would return those feelings for me. Telling me she was better than me, and all I would ever be able to do was stare at her and wish from afar that she would be mine.

I started to run through the next month and a half in my head, trying to see when and where I would be able to see her. She had texted me a few days ago to tell me she was already in town for the holiday. I had no idea if she was seeing someone or not, but I would find out. I had been away from home for what seemed like a lifetime but in reality was only a few months. I wouldn't be truly shocked if everything had changed.

Maybe we would meet up and act like nothing had changed, transported to the months following high school. Or it could be everything would be new and she wouldn't be the girl I had loved for so long. My insides began to churn as my mom pulled onto our street. I sent Summer a text as we pulled into the driveway.

Penelope: Hey, I'm back in town. What are you up to?

I lugged my stuff up to my old room, kicked open the door, and stared around in wonder. I've seen this phenomenon in every movie ever, where the child comes home from college and the room they used to occupy is in a state of one of two extremes.

The first would be a completely unchanged room, sporting everything from pictures on the wall to musty unwashed sheets which were six months without use. The other extreme was the room which had been transformed into some sort of crazy obnoxiousness the parents had been dreaming about since the birth of their child. Mine was the former. I stripped the bed of sheets and toddled downstairs, dropping the sheets halfway down to look at the reply message on my phone.

Summer: HEY! I'm sooooo bored. Wanna hang out?

Summer was in town, free and wanting to see me—*that night!* I shrieked like a prepubescent girl would at a glance from her crush and flung the sheets to the lower landing with my feet. I primped more for seeing her than I had for prom. I wanted to put my best foot forward with this brave new world I was entering. I hadn't made up my mind to tell her immediately, but I would at least see if she responded to a little honest flirting.

We planned to meet at IHOP. I arrived early and asked to be seated in a corner booth—wanting us to have at least a little privacy—and waited for her.

There are those moments in movies where everything is suddenly in slow motion, and you wonder what gives until it is punctuated with whatever they are trying to force into dramatics. Well, the moment she walked into the restaurant was like that for me, only it wasn't needlessly dramatic—it was tension driven.

My choices were laid in front of me, and the universe was giving me more time to decide if I had made the right one. For me, there was no turning back. Even if I was Don Quixote chasing windmills, I had made up my mind. As she walked closer to the table, time returned to normal and I stood up to give her a hug.

She squeed with excitement and scampered toward me. We embraced, and despite the bit of chill in the air, I was instantly warmed. She smelled like home and adolescent nostalgia. She had worn the same perfume since I had met her. It would forever remind me of her and the way I felt when I was with her.

The embrace lasted far longer than one would expect, but then again maybe I was over analyzing. We sat down, and I could tell there was a goofy smile plastered on my face. I couldn't help it and I couldn't wipe it off.

"So, how have you been?" she asked, getting the ball rolling.

"I've been good; things are looking up. I love Seattle, and I love school. What about you?" I replied, trying to get myself under control.

"Good. School's fun. I'm learning a lot, but it's not the same as going away to school. I'm kind of jealous of your freedom," Summer said, looking chagrinned.

"Well," I began through a pang of hurt. "There is an Art Institute in Seattle. You could just transfer." *Why is she bringing this up right away? Doesn't she know it still stings that she abandoned me?*

"Sorry, I didn't mean..."

"It's all good. Let's just forget it."

We fell into talking like old times, me ignoring the old pain. Summer was everything I had remembered she was. My memory of her not bloated or inflated by a wicked mixture of nostalgia and love. We ordered, ate and paid the bill, yet we did not leave. We stayed and chatted. I couldn't find the courage to simply tell her I loved her, nor did I think it was the right time. I didn't want to ruin anything. We were together again. It seemed less important to tell her than it was to simply hold onto the moments we were spending together.

After about two and a half hours spent at the diner, I decided we might want to vacate the seats we had been occupying. Neither of us were ready to go home yet, so I suggested black light bowling. It was bowling lasting from 10pm to 2am, and everyone dressed in crazy outfits and tried to bowl with fluorescent balls.

She agreed, and I followed her back to her house so she could change and ride with me to the bowling alley. I walked in to her house and said hi to her parents. I had known them for two years now and they were really nice. They asked the congenial standard questions, and I answered while waiting for Summer.

She came from the back room, hair in a ponytail, wearing bright pink shorts, knee high white boots and a tight white top. She looked amazing. My stomach flopped like it had at the diner, and I knew every time I saw her was going to be like the first time all over again.

When we arrived at the bowling alley, I had her pick out a ball for me while I rented our shoes and paid for the lane. She was so adorable while bowling. She had a little ritual she did to "give her luck."

She would turn to me and walk backward until she got to the ball return. Then, with her back to the ball return, she would bend over and pick her ball up from between her legs. Bring it forward to rest under her chin, she would straighten, spin in two circles then prance to the line—almost always stepping over it—and shove her ball down the lane.

Mind you, Summer was a horrible bowler. She almost always hit the gutter, but when she didn't, when the ball went all the way down the lane, she would get a strike every time without fail. These, she told me, were the times she had done the preliminary ritual correctly.

We bowled a few games and then found ourselves in the arcade playing *Dance Dance Revolution*. Unlike her bowling prowess—or lack thereof—she could actually play DDR like a pro. She wiped the dance pad with me and laughed me into blushing on multiple occasions. It was late in the night—well, early in the morning—before we headed back to her house.

"What are you doing tomorrow?" she chimed on the way home.

"I don't really have any plans. Matter of fact, aside from some reading and Christmas, I don't really have anything planned for the whole break," I explained.

She beamed. "Well then, I'll see you tomorrow?"

"Sure. Call me when you get up," I said.

"I will," she said as she exited the car.

She turned to smile at me from her front step; I stayed until she was safely inside.

Chapter Nine

CHRISTMAS WAS always one of my favorite times of year. I was a big fan of anything shiny, so having the world light up around me was nothing short of a miracle. I often took nighttime drives into suburbs where putting up lights was mandated by some stuffy homeowners association. They were usually the best, as the occupants of such houses usually had money to spend on the fancy inflating things or even better, lights to music!

Since I'd been home, I spent most of my time with Summer. After spending the day with her, I would travel through lighted suburbs on my way home, giving myself time to think and sort through my feelings. I was now torn between holding onto the relationship we had and trying my luck at telling her how I truly felt.

I wanted more than anything to stay with her; the thought of returning to school caused me endless nights of turmoil. I wanted to return to Seattle, as I felt at home there—I missed Noah like crazy—but they say home is where the heart is, and my heart belonged to Summer. Noah was still in Seattle, enjoying his break. We texted daily, and he harped on me constantly not to lose my focus and to bite the bullet.

He had guided me through my first semester and was personally invested in my mental health. I would drive through the suburbs, lighted as a fairyland, imagining Summer and me living in these houses together. I called Noah. He answered with noise and bustle in the background.

"Hello?" came his raised voice.

"Hey, I didn't want to bother you. Call me later," I said, disappointed.

"Wait, I can't hear you," he shouted. I heard the noise in the back fade into nothing as a door opened and closed. "Sorry, my parents are throwing their annual Christmas party. What's up, Sweetie?"

"Nothing, I didn't mean to bother you. You can call me tomorrow."

"Don't be ridiculous. First of all, you are saving me. I hate making nice with my parent's friends. And secondly, if you think I don't know you well enough to know when you are blatantly lying, then you obviously weren't there for the past four months."

"You don't know me!" I exclaimed with mock indignation.

"Riiiight. So tell me." His voice dripped with sarcasm.

"Why can't I get it out? Why am I so scared? I'm being ridiculous!" I complained.

"You are being ridiculous," he replied, chuckling. "You'll get no argument from me there, but on a separate note—you're scared because you can't control how she's going to react, and telling her is a gamble."

"How do you know I'm talking about her?" I questioned haughtily.

"Only because you've talked about nothing else since before you even went home and with an even higher frequency since you got there!" He cried, exasperated. "Don't try to change the subject."

"Bah!" I screamed.

"You need to make a decision. Don't consider me. Don't consider her. Don't consider school, family or whatever else you are using to put stress on this decision. Only think about you, how you feel and what you want. You can't control anything more than yourself, so you shouldn't even try to."

"I both hate and love you."

"You only pretend to hate me when you know I'm right. I love you too." With that we said goodbye.

Before I could give myself time to doubt, I called Summer. I told her—in tones probably more excited and awkward than usual—I wanted to see her the next day. She asked what we were going to do, and I told her it was a surprise. I would pick her up at 10pm. She hung up sounding excited.

If I was going to regret this, then I was going to regret it big. I went home and started putting together my plan. I would pick her up at ten and take her to my favorite lit up houses. There was a particular suburb that went all out. The families of some of the houses even dressed up and were in their yards throwing fake snow at each other.

You actually had to pay to get into this one, but a few canned goods—which they donated to charity—was totally worth it. Did I mention the display wound through the entire neighborhood? There were six full streets of sparkling wonderland.

I lay awake late into the night fighting with myself about the best way to tell Summer I was in love with her. In some scenarios, she would respond with like sentiment and I would pull her into my arms, kissing her with proverbial fireworks erupting in the back ground. But in others, she would tell me she wasn't interested or some facsimile thereof and I would end up burying my face in my pillow to cover my groans of anguish. I fell asleep at some point in the night and dreams took over where my thoughts had left off.

I was outside Summer's house promptly at 10pm. She came out the front door and I handed her a single origami flower, the shade of green matching her eyes. She was stunning. I had told her we were going somewhere special, so she had dressed up a bit. She wore brown tights under a cream and earth green dress, her pale skin contrasting in a wonderful way with her bright red hair. Her hair was half down and half up in a fancy knot. She wore brown boots and was carrying a brown coat.

She always knew how to look amazing. I opened the car door for her. She squeed, jumped in the air and climbed in. Always the excitable one, her energy was contagious, and I began to get the tell-tale contact high I always got when I was around her.

I climbed into the car with as much grace and spatial awareness as I was capable of. My normal reliable hands were jittery and unsure. I had to mentally chide myself before I lost the nerve to follow through with my plan. I sat in the seat next to her. She looked at me excitedly but held off her questions until the car was started and we were underway.

"Where are we going?" she questioned.

"Well, if I tell you, it won't be a surprise," I scolded her.

Her eyebrows knit together in exaggerated annoyance. "Yeah, but if you tell me then I'll know, and I can stop going crazy!"

"Oh, honey. I don't think that would fix it," I explained, brushing her hair behind her ear.

"AH!" she cried—affronted—and swatted at my hand.

We both fell into fits of giggles as I continued driving into the night, the Christmas lights like stars around us. The moon made only a scarce appearance. I could not have asked for a better night on which to transport Summer and myself to a twinkling landscape. When we were close to the place, I told her to reach into the back and find the canned goods.

"What do we need this much food for?" she wondered, her voice strained from her contortion into the back seat.

"Oh, I'm kidnapping you so I can have you all to myself," I joked. She pulled the bag of cans toward her seat, enough to pull her head back into the front. She raised one eyebrow at me but said nothing, simply pulled the cans the rest of the way.

The suburb was actually a gated community with fairly high walls and an enormous metal gate. This served to only further my ideas of entering a different world. It looked like the entrance to a castle as we approached.

"Oh my god," she said in awe. "If you're going to make me a princess, then you're the best kidnapper *ever!*" She stared at the high walls and the entrance gate with her mouth slightly agape.

I simply chuckled as I turned toward the open gate and the lights beyond. I stopped and handed the bag of canned goods out the open driver-side window to a man who was dressed as Santa, bell-voiced carolers singing behind him. He pulled it from me with a surprised thank you—the entrance fee was two cans per person— and handed a pamphlet into the car.

"Enjoy yourselves, and thanks for coming!" He shouted from outside the car as the carolers reached the peak of O Holy Night. Their voices faded as I rolled the window back up and set off down the road. I looked at Summer. Her eyes were large and bright and her head swiveled from side to side trying to take in all of the lights.

"Would you like to look at the paper?" I asked as I pulled to the side of the road just past the welcome station.

"Why? Does it light up too?" her voice full of whimsy and magic, still not taking her eyes from the few visible houses.

"No, it doesn't, but I believe it has a map and some instructions," I said.

She was always a sucker for the details. She ripped her eyes from the shining horizon and turned them to me and the paper. I handed it to her, and she took it hungrily. I let her read it over as I reached into the back seat for the picnic I had prepared. I pulled a thermos full of steaming hot cocoa from the basket. I had mixed it just the way she always liked it: cocoa powder, half skim milk and half toffee flavored creamer. It made the cocoa ridiculously rich and decadent.

I poured some for each of us into mugs and put a bag of mini marshmallows in the seat between us. I set the two mugs on the dashboard and grabbed a blanket from the back. I covered her legs with it. She, so engrossed in the map, hadn't noticed what was going on around her. She told me to turn the radio on and put it on a specific FM channel.

She lifted her head after reading—more than likely because she didn't start hearing music immediately—and goggled at me. A huge grin spread across her face and she childishly stuck out her hands for her mug. Her smile could move mountains. If I ever had any intention of playing like I wasn't going to just hand over her cocoa, it disappeared as the smile stretched across her face. She took it, sipped it and moaned.

"I love how you make cocoa. It's my favorite!"

I just chuckled and turned on the radio. It was already set to the correct channel, as I had done my research. We sat and listened for a little bit. The next rendition of the music, properly matching the houses, started in 5 minutes. I pulled us back onto the road. It wasn't particularly crowded; I thought we would be paying for our late arrival in the season—only a week before Christmas—but thankfully not.

We drove down the streets, Summer sipping her cocoa and occasionally throwing more marshmallows on top. I hummed along to the music as she pointed me in the direction I should turn next. When we were about halfway through the adventure—Summer had already finished two helpings of cocoa and put her mug down—I was determined to tell her how I felt. Everything thus far had gone perfectly, and after all, I couldn't control how she felt. I could only control what I did about how I felt.

"Summer?"

"Mmhmmm?" she murmured.

"I've been thinking about someone, I mean, something I wanted, err, realized after I moved away to Seattle..." I stumbled over my words.

"Yeah?" She turned her face ever so slightly to look at me while keeping the houses in her line of vision.

"Well..." I paused, starting to feel the fear of rejection and uncertainty clawing its way up my throat. "Well, you see, I think I might be in love you."

Well, that got her full attention. Time slowed, only this time I had made my decision, maybe this was time slowing down so she could make hers. She stared at me, her eyes still wide but for a whole different reason than the magical world around us. I would have given anything in that moment to be able to read her mind and take everything back.

The fear had won out, and as seconds passed like minutes I was aware of a strong feeling of nausea rolling its way around my stomach. Time gathered speed and hurled itself back into proper momentum. I snapped back to here and now as I saw the same wonderful smile start to creep across Summer's face. I realized the feeling of nausea had turned into a feeling of obnoxious relief.

She hadn't responded in kind, but at least the little bit of response I had gotten hadn't been the utter rejection fear made me believe I would have. She grabbed the blanket from her lap and crawled across the seat, nudged my arm with her nose so I would raise it and crawled into my embrace to sit next to me. She pulled the blanket over both of us and cuddled next to me to finish staring at the lights.

I was more than content sitting next to her in this fashion, and while maybe I was still confused as to what it all meant, there was no way I was going to force her to give me some kind of concrete response. It had taken me a few years to work out my feelings for her, and even then I didn't do it on my own. Plus, after I had deciphered them, I still sat on them for a few months before I decided what to do with them. I would afford her as much time as she needed.

I had played my cards, and when she was ready, she would tell me how she felt, however that was. After I drove her home, we both climbed out of the car. I walked around to hug her before we parted ways. I squeezed her close, and she grunted happily. I released her so she could go inside. She turned to go but quickly turned back and kissed me on the cheek. My face lit up like so many of the displays we had just seen.

Summer turned without looking back and ran inside, giggling as she retreated. The small flame of hope I had let live when Summer crossed the car burst into life, growing exponentially until a bonfire raged inside me. I climbed back into the car more hopeful than I would have ever given myself permission to be.

Chapter Ten

I WASN'T able to spend time with Summer between the night of lights and Christmas. I had planned it as such so if things had gone badly, I would have time to figure out what to do, but as it stood I was going crazy. I wanted to see her, spend time with her, and see how things would develop. My only saving grace was Christmas. I had shopping, decorating, cleaning and baking to do.

My family always gathered together on Christmas Eve. I was the first, and currently the only, one in the family to move away from home by any sizable distance. Therefore, everyone from grandparents on down got together to celebrate holidays. I had not made amends with my aunt, despite my mother's ardent requests, but we were not actively fighting. I had accepted long ago this was her way, but there was not a chance I would lie about what I had posted or apologize to her for anything about my life. Everything was going just like any other holiday.

The food was spread across my mother's considerable counter space, the younger generation was upstairs playing a video game, and the older generation was sprinkled around the first floor, drinking wine and watching some sport on the television. I was flitting among groups, not necessarily fitting in any one place.

I stepped out onto the back porch for a bit of fresh air and breathing room. It wasn't snowing even though it was crisp winter evening. We were too far south for snow on a regular basis. The sun was sinking steadily into the horizon, throwing its last shadows onto the ground, seemingly clawing at it to keep its foothold.

My mother, immensely proud of her backyard, had a porch swing overlooking her expertly preened flower gardens, now dormant for the winter months. I sidled over to the brown metal contraption and ensconced myself in its floral-cushion embrace. There was just something telling about a veritable field of dead twigs sticking out of the ground, knowing next spring they would be beautiful and full of life.

I heard the door behind me open and braced myself for another onslaught from my mother, but nothing came. Maybe it was Cooper, come to find out what had become of me. Yet when the wandering foot-shuffler rounded the opposite end of the swing, it was not my tousle-haired brother, it was Grandma.

"Hi, Grandma! Where have you been hiding yourself?" I enthused.

"I've been around, chatting with your mother and them," she explained.

"Oh, I see," I replied.

My Grandma and I were always capable of comfortable silences. She never tried to force an uncomfortable conversation, but she always spoke when she had something to say. Sometimes, I liked to think of myself as the more out spoken, maybe less well-mannered, version of her. We sat quietly, gently swinging for a bit, both of us staring out into the hibernating, tropical oasis masquerading as a frozen wasteland.

"I wanted you to know I'm proud of you," she confessed, her brown eyes shining in the dying light. "I know it's hard to leave your family and travel far away, but I heard you're doing well in school and that's just wonderful."

"Thank you, Grandma. I really love it in Seattle. The weather is really nice, and I've made a lot of new friends. They help me when things get a little tough, and then I'm home again after only a few months." I smiled at her, appreciating her praise.

"Well, you just remember, even if you are coming home every few months, you still have your own life to live, and you can't be living under the expectations of everyone else."

"Grandma?"

"I may not know everything about the Internet," she said with dignity. "But I do know how to read, and Cooper put me on that book of faces after you left for school so I could keep up with you. Don't think I don't know what my daughters tell you about me, but the truth is, I'm not going to keel over from the decisions you make with your own life, as long as they aren't reckless or dangerous. Now your aunt on the other hand..."

Anything which might have resembled an intelligent response or a giggle at the way she referred to Facebook was knocked out of me as my breath left my lungs in a whoosh. This was my Grandma, the fragile one whom I could send into the hospital with my "indecent flaunting of my silly phases," telling me she didn't think my life was offensive or wrong. I had always found support in my friends, never hoping my family would understand enough to be a pillar to build *anything* on, much less myself.

I sat stunned, my eyes welling with tears. I was overwhelmed with a range of emotions I didn't even know I was capable of feeling at the same time. Her aged, fragile hands found my face and wiped my tears from it. Then they moved down my arms to clasps my hands and squeezed them with a reassurance and strength you wouldn't bestow them without knowing the woman they belonged to. She looked me in the eyes and gave me a little nod. She released my hands into my lap and stood to go.

She turned back and added, "Just remember, no matter what you do, I will always love you. This whole family will always love you, even if they are horrible at showing it."

I stayed in the backyard until the sun had set long before and my fingers were numb. The moon was bright but still rising. I couldn't bring myself to walk inside and ruin the feeling my Grandma had instilled in me. It was heinous to think my life up to this point had gone without such encouragement.

There was love in my family but not the kind that was spoken out loud. It was the type theoretically implied in actions and something some seemed to think should be read from their very minds. I reveled in the glory of pure unabashed love and wrapped myself in the internal hug of my Grandma to keep myself warm.

I hadn't noticed my fingers were turning blue or that my throat was dry and parched until my mom stuck her head out the back and cried, "There you are. Everyone's been looking for you. It's time to eat!"

The door slammed behind her as she returned her head to the

warmth of the house. I sat there for a few more minutes, steeling myself against another onslaught from the rest of my family.

The food was delicious. I stuffed myself to the point of explosion then promptly went into a food coma on the couch. Some of the men, I think, tried to move me so they could continue watching the television, but I would not be moved. I groaned and shifted but that was the closest any of them came to getting me out of the way.

Grandpa came and sat near my head, shooing one of the younger generation from his seat.

"What's up, Grandpa." I groaned.

"Huh," he grunted.

"Ah, third helpings of potatoes got you too, did it?" I inquired.

Chuckling, he responded, "No, two slices of your Grandma's pecan pie plus two helpings of potatoes."

"Ah, that'll do it too," I said, snuggling into his leg.

He reached down to pinch my nose and "pulled it off." A game shared between grandpas and grandchildren around the world since the dawn of time, especially in our family, as far back as I could remember.

"You can have that," I told him. "At least that way I won't have to smell the family anymore."

"Ah! Phbbbbbbbbt," He was mockingly shocked and then blew a raspberry at me. I pinched his leg playfully and groaned as the food in my stomach tried to take over.

I was about to drift off to sleep when Grandpa gave me back my nose and said, "I know Grandma has already talked to you, and I just wanted to let you know, I agree with her—well, you—or whoever. Point is, you should live your life the way you want, and everyone else will either come to terms with it or not. Either way, it isn't your problem."

I don't know if you have ever been brought to tears in the middle of a food coma, but I assure you it's not therapeutic in any way. My family was fond of saying crying was good for digestion, but in my mind there was no way to harmonize the pain in my abdomen and the overwhelmed feeling in my heart.

"Grandpa, you can't do that. Grandma's already made me cry once this evening," I whined, clutching my stomach.

"Just trying to help you with your digestion." He laughed. "I love you," he murmured as he turned away from me and back to the television.

He donned a pair of 3D glasses, and I knew the conversation was over for good. I wiped my tears off on his pants and settled back into the post stuffing-my-face coma, ready to sleep until my food baby had disappeared.

Late into the night, the parentals "needed" to make a beer run, apparently needing more beer and, of course, there was only so much the family could put down without being inebriated. This meant one of them had to sober up before leaving to retrieve *more beer*, and I had to accompany them as their sobriety was wavering at best—basically I was to drive the car.

I ended up at the store with my uncle, he being the closest to faked sobriety so there was no other choice for the beer run. I couldn't conceal that I was still in pain from cramming food down my gullet or the fact that I was struggling to not pass the food baby in the middle of the isle. I retreated toward the restroom to trade my baby for an empty stomach, but as I passed the registers I heard someone call, "Penelope!"

I gave serious consideration to just continuing on my way, but they reached me before I could make the final decision. It was Clayton; he was working. I now knew, as if there was ever any doubt, which of the old high school group would never leave our home town.

"Hey, how's it going?" I murmured with the best faked interest I could muster, which between you and me wasn't convincing.

"Not bad. What are you doing here?" he asked politely.

"Just here with my uncle, picking up a few things. What about you? How are you?" I replied, running out of fake niceness.

"Pretty good, just working," he said.

"Riiiiight, well, I need to..." I began to explain my escape.

"Would you want to go out sometime, you know, again?" he interjected.

"Um..." I stammered, stunned by his gall.

"Penelope!" my uncle called from behind me. He was at the door, ready to go.

"I'm sorry. I've got to go," I said, then bolted for the door.

"But..." He blustered, trying to stop me.

"I'll talk to you later," I shouted as I ran from him.

When we were out of the store I full out ran for my car and my uncle clumsily tried to keep up. I climbed into the car without looking back, afraid he would be watching me—all creepy stalker-like—from the windows of the store.

We arrived back at my house to much applause from the rest of the adults. Everyone stayed up far too late, passing around comments about Santa and the like while they drained the beer procured during the beer run. At least my bumping into Clayton hadn't been for naught. *eye roll*

Chapter Eleven

AFTER THE interesting Christmas festivities, I had a little over two weeks until I had to return to Seattle. I intended to spend it entirely with Summer. I figured it might be nice to include her in my plan of the prefect ending to winter break, so I texted her.

Penelope: Hey, how was your Christmas?

Summer: Good. I got some new art supplies and some monies!

Penelope: Sweet! Me too. Well... not the art supplies part but yeah...

Summer: Cool.

Penelope: I thought so. So, I had a couple of ideas about the next couple of weeks, if you're interested in hearing them...

Summer: Sure!

Penelope: Well, I was thinking me, you and 17 days + some nights of awesomeness!

Summer: Lol, well, while that sounds amazing, we're leaving tomorrow for Canada. I thought I told you? My family always goes there after Christmas to see my grandparents. We've got a cabin there.

Penelope: I totally forgot! You go every year. I know this!

My world sank out of the fluffy white clouds it had been floating in since my confidence boost from the elders. This threw a major, unappreciated kink into the next few weeks of my life. I also supposed this meant I would not get a proper response to my confession before I left for school.

Summer: I really am so sorry! I would like to stay here with you, but, you know, grandparents...they only live so long.

Penelope: Yeah, I understand. Just bummed. Will you be back before I leave for school on the 16th?

Summer: Probably not. We drive there, since flying five people is quite expensive. I'm at the mercy of my family. All I can say, is we usually end up staying about a month.

Penelope: Bah! Well then... :P

Summer: Do you want to hang out today, though? I can be ready in a few minutes.

Penelope: Uh, let me think...YES! Omw.

I raced downstairs, grabbed the keys, called to my mom that I would be back at some indeterminate time in the future, and hurled myself out the front door. I made it to Summer's house a mere seven minutes later. She was waiting in the front yard for me, hair down and blowing in the slight breeze. She wore simple jeans and a tee-shirt, a jacket over her arm. My stomach dropping into the floorboards only further proved it didn't matter what she wore because she always looked amazing, and I would love her until the day I died.

She climbed into my car, a little less bouncy than normal. She was smiling though it didn't reach her eyes.

I asked her, "Are you okay?"

"Yeah, I'm fine!" she beamed though her voice was pinched.

"Okay," I said, not believing her but she obviously didn't want to talk about it. "What would you like to do today? I was thinking, the mall."

"Sweet. My Christmas money is already burning a hole in my pocket. Let's go."

We joked and laughed all the way to the mall. I couldn't fool myself into believing I wasn't on edge. I wanted desperately to know if she loved me back, but it wasn't within me to force her to respond before she was ready. I did, however, try my luck at subtle hints. When we climbed out of the car, I offered her my arm.

She took it with a smile on her face, her eyes flitting to mine before looking away again. We walked into the mall arm in arm, my heart soaring. We eventually got hungry, and I grabbed Summer's hand to lead her to the food court. I loosened my grip as we got in line for Chinese food, but she didn't let go. Her fingers wrapped around mine, and it was my turn to smile from ear to ear.

The rest of the mall passed in a blur, her hand in mine the entire time. We climbed into the car as the sun began to set. When we pulled up to her house, I was reluctant to leave her.

"I had a great time today," I said. "Still sucks that you're leaving town."

"I had a good time too," she replied, avoiding my eyes and scratching at something nonexistent on her jeans.

"Is everything okay?" I asked, concern furrowing my brows.

"Well..." She trailed off, no trace of a smile on her face.

"Whatever it is, you can tell me. I love you," I said, the words coming out as they always had but with new meaning.

"Don't, that just makes it worse," she said.

Not wanting to upset her but unsure of how my love made anything worse, I just sat there, waiting for her to speak.

"I don't know how to say this," she started. "And honestly, I've contemplated just not saying anything at all, but I know I can't leave with things open-ended."

Silence.

"Fine, well, you seem to have, I mean, I don't blame you because it's not like I mentioned—but there is the small little fact of me having a boyfriend," she said.

The air was sucked out of the car, my mouth moved as if trying to say something but my lungs just groped for air. I hadn't any intelligent thoughts in my brain and I wouldn't have known what to say even if I had air. So maybe it was best that I couldn't breathe properly. I just stared at a spot on the seat of the car.

"I'm so sorry, I really am. I never thought in a million years you would want to be with me. You had always been so adamant about being heterosexual. I thought we were just hanging out like we always had. I didn't know, or I would have mentioned him more," she said, raising her head.

"Yeah, why didn't you ever mention him? I haven't heard his name out of you in months. You never told me anything about him when we talked during school," I said, looking her full in the face now, my head spinning.

"I know. I blame myself. I never wanted to hurt you. I didn't mention him because he wasn't here. He left to go to Florida for Christmas, staying in a cabin with his ex, who is now dating his brother. I was mad and then I kind of wanted to forget and just have fun with you," she said. "I did have fun." She gave me a small smile as if that fixed it.

"Glad fun is all I am to you. At least that definitively answers my sentiment from the other night!" I said, my rage growing with each word. "Did you have *fun* holding my hand today?"

"Don't be like that. There was no way I could have known you were interested. And I don't know what happened today—I went with the flow," she cried, affronted.

"No, of course not. It's not like I posted my news on a public forum or anything. OH WAIT!" I screamed, my temper reaching a feverish pitch. I wanted to leave, the pain in my heart matching my temper.

"Don't yell at me!" she shouted. "It's not up to me to glean life changes about my best friend from her Facebook page! For all I knew you could have made it up just to spite your mother. It seems like I'm not the only one with poor communication skills!"

My mind reeled from the surge of anger and unwanted information. The bonfire that roared in my chest at the mall diminished and extinguished. In a matter of moments all hope was gone.

"I don't know what to tell you. I didn't have any expectations for us, but today you gave me hope," I tried to explain. "In my head, I had played out the worst—you telling me you just wanted to remain friends. I thought I was prepared for anything. But then you didn't reject me. You seemed to entertain the idea, if not enjoy it. I guess I wasn't prepared, and it hurts like hell to know that you already have someone and I'm just left broken. Please just go. I can't take being next to you right now." I turned away from her and looked out the window.

Summer silently escaped from the car. I didn't turn around to see if she looked back. I didn't watch her as I drove away; I just left. How could I have been so stupid as to not remember she had a boyfriend? I had made such a fool of myself! Why hadn't she talked about him over the past three month? Not even in passing had she mentioned her boyfriend.

A boyfriend she was ready to use as a roadblock to something we could have shared. Though, maybe it was me; maybe she wasn't interested. The thought sent me even deeper into my mounting despair. I pulled over. I couldn't go home in this state. I needed some time to myself, which automatically discounted being anywhere near my mother.

My mind was spinning with an unwillingness to accept the facts. I knew I wasn't thinking logically. I found myself, some odd minutes later, perusing the grocery store. I was innocently meandering through aisles of food, not really looking for anything specific. I wanted something to make me feel better. I may—or may not—have been known to eat my feelings, but that was not the reason I was in that grocery store at such a late hour on that particular night of destruction.

I was inadvertently looking for Clayton. If Summer was going to reject me, then I at least knew one person who wouldn't, the one person who—in the end—had wanted me. I was still contemplating the depths to which I wanted to plunge to exact my revenge when he happened upon me. I was idly poking cans on the shelf to knock them over.

"Hey, what's up?" I asked, forcing enthusiasm, knowing almost instantly that this was not my best idea.

"Not much. My manager just told me to come stop the kid who was making a mess of our inventory."

I abruptly stopped, the last can almost toppling over.

"Oh, sorry," I said, pocketing my hands.

I looked into his face—full on—for the first time in over a year. Toward the end of senior year, I had taken to staring at his shoes. I had forgotten, in the time I had grown to dislike him, how truly attractive he was. His features weren't particularly striking, but there was something about looking into his eyes that could make things okay. I had always loved looking into those eyes, eyes which I once believed truly saw and understood me. I abandoned my misgivings and committed myself to this decision.

"It's okay. I actually do something similar when I get mad at my boss, so I can't be too mad at you for it," he said.

"Yeah, I guess," I said, making a pouty face to win his sympathies.

"I thought after you ran out of here the other night I wouldn't see you in here again," he said, raising his hand to run it down my arm.

"Well, you thought wrong, obviously. That night was just crazy. I had to get back to my family—Christmas eve and all," I lied, stepping away from his touch.

"Yeah, I guess I get it. So did you want to hang out?" he asked, unfazed by my movement.

"Okay," I replied. "What time do you get off?"

"I'm actually going to clock out now, since I'm done 'telling the hooligan to stop messing with things,'" he said, laughing loudly at his own humor.

Wincing slightly, a little less sure of what I was doing, I said, "Cool. Well, I'll meet you outside then."

I waited outside for Clayton, taking in the fresh air to decide if I was being stupid or if maybe this would turn out all right. I was still hurting over Summer, and it felt good to be wanted, to be the pursued instead of the pursuer. He had charisma like you wouldn't believe. Matter of fact—after thinking it through—it was *never* his looks that won a girl over. It was the way he talked, the way he acted like I was the only girl in the world, the only one who mattered to him.

He came outside and asked what I wanted to do. After a few minutes of debate, we ended up deciding on the park. The sun was gone from the sky, the park was free, and I hadn't sat on a swing in a really long time. This seemed like a good way for us to hang out without me doing something dumb like I would if we were to watch a movie alone together.

The park was dark but strategically lit with lamps. There were four swings, two slides, a spring action teeter-totter and a tire swing. I circled around the outside of the gravel-laden section which was the parameters of the playground, delaying the inevitable rock-in-shoe debacle. I climbed onto a swing. Clayton came over and climbed onto one next to me. We swung in silence for a while, each of us seemingly lost in our own heads. Or maybe it was just me.

"So, what happened to us?" he asked, breaking the silence.

I choked and gagged a little as I sucked in air.

"What do you mean, 'what happened to us'?"

"Well, I mean exactly what I said. We were friends, we made out sometimes, but when I told you I couldn't kiss you anymore because I wanted to be with Summer, you stopped talking to me," he said, shrugging with a legitimately confused look on his face.

"Wow, you really must be thicker than I thought was possible. Silly me for thinking you might have grown as a person. This was a poor idea—I'm going to go."

I stopped my swing immediately. Effectually pouring rocks into my own shoes, I jumped off the swing to leave.

"What? Wait! Don't go. I'm just trying to understand. I thought we were on the same page in high school, but then you seemed so hurt." I heard his feet hit the ground as well, gravel sliding.

"I can't believe you are this stupid!" I shouted, turning to him in rage. "I loved you! You were my first love. How could you have been blind enough not to see that? I can't believe I wasted my only first love on you, the only love where I would be able to fall freely and blindly. I threw caution to the wind and plummeted, trusting you to catch me.

"You took that from me and didn't even care. You took it from me and threw it away! I'm so stupid for showing up at the grocery store. You are always the wrong choice, but somehow I keep fooling myself into giving you more chances."

Smacking myself on the forehead, I turned my back on Clayton and walked toward my car.

Maybe that's my problem. Maybe not thinking is why things went so badly with Summer. I should have thought about why she hadn't responded immediately on the night of lights. It was a simple thing wasn't it, to know if you loved someone or not? She was so undecided I should have known there was a reason for it. I lied to myself. "She needs some time," I'd said. "She'll let you know when she's ready," I'd said. She was trying to give me an easy out, give me the option of pretending like I hadn't said anything.

I was so lost in thought, I was only vaguely aware of Clayton calling my name from the vicinity of the swings where I had left him. I didn't care enough about anything he had to say to turn around, thus it was incredibly startling when I heard his voice right next to me, yanking me from my mental berating.

My head snapped to the side. He grabbed my face and he forced his lips onto mine. There was nothing pleasant or wondrous about this kiss. When we had been "friends who made out," I would have killed for this moment, but now I was just disgusted and offended. After a moment of pure shock and confusion, I put my hands flat on his chest and shoved as hard as I could.

His hands, still holding my face, slipped as our lips were pulled apart. I started to move back but he grabbed my arm and pulled me to him again. I put up my hands and shouted "NO!" as he made to kiss me again. He wasn't listening. His lips were on mine in an instant and he had hold of my arm so I couldn't shove him again. I used my free hand to try and push him from me but he was unmoved. I tried to pry his fingers from my arm, scrambling to release myself. My nails bit at his skin and my own.

Clayton seemed to be excited by the fact that I could not get away despite my efforts. His other hand slid around my back and pulled me closer to him. I began thrashing my head from side to side—anything to remove his lips from mine. His hand forced its way under my shirt and to the front of my body. I struggled trying to kick or knee him, but I could not hit him in any effective way.

His hand found my breast, and adrenaline coursed through my blood as unbridled terror struck me anew. Summoning all the strength I had, knowing worse was to come if I could not remove him from me, I raised my free hand, pulled away from him in the same moment, and brought my hand forcefully down on his face. His hand flew to his face from under my shirt. I wrenched my arm free of his grip and ran for my car.

I was only a few steps from it when I heard his feet hitting the pavement. He was yelling at me, but my mind blocked out the words as I ran for safety. I clambered into my car and locked the door as it shut from the force of his body slamming into it. His mouth still screamed words which fell on deaf ears. I turned the key and the car sprang to life. I put it in drive and floored it, wishing desperately that I would run over some part of him. My mind shut down without comprehending the events which had just transpired.

What the hell just happened? What was he thinking? What was I thinking? What do I do? Where do I go? I need Summer. I need help. Oh my god. Oh my god. Oh my god. I thought things like this only happened to slutty girl, girls who wore skanky clothes and showed too much of their bodies. What is wrong with me? No one deserves this, no matter what they wear or what they do with their body.

I instantly felt ashamed. How could I have ever let myself believe the victim could be to blame in a situation like that? I had grown up being taught you didn't wear certain things or act a certain way because if you did, you were "asking for it." but I hadn't been asking for anything! This had been the night of failure, and I was scared and alone. I decided it was time to go home to my mother; regardless of her stance on my life, she loved me. I needed someone who could help me figure out what to do.

It was a conversation I was not looking forward to having. I knew what I had just experienced was nothing compared to the hell some are put through, but I felt violated and unsure of myself. I walked into the dark, silent house. In my panic, I had forgotten everyone would be asleep already. I knew if I put it off and didn't tell my mother now,

I wouldn't tell her at all. I trudged up the stairs and pushed open the door to my mother's bedroom; it groaned in an unpleasant sort of way. I sidled up to my mom's bed and tapped her on the arm. She woke with a start, like always.

"What's going on?" she questioned urgently.

"Mom, I need to talk to you about something," I said.

She sat up to look at me, the moonlight pouring through the window. "What happened?"

I told her the story of the horrible occurrence in the park. She let me speak while a mixture of horror and anger spread over her face. When I was done she pulled me into a tight hug.

"I'm so sorry. He had no right to touch you, especially without your permission. We'll go in the morning to the police and you can talk to them and get a restraining order."

I was exhausted. There were no more words to be said and it seemed like a weight had been removed from me, even if only temporarily. Despite my mother's ill-placed wishes for my life, she at least knew when something was real and when I truly needed her to be my mother. She patted the bed next to her and I climbed in. It took me a long time to fall asleep, and even when I did it was fitful.

Chapter Twelve

In the morning, I didn't want to leave the soft, warm bed. As far as I was concerned, it was the safest place in the world, and nothing short of a backhoe was going to remove me from it. My mom came in around 11 am with breakfast. I pretended to be asleep, and she left the food on the dresser. She made another appearance an hour later, greeted by a completely empty plate of food. I continued to pretend to be asleep. There was no fooling her really, but she let me have my little game and took the empty dishes with her when she went.

The next check was not made by my mother, but she instead sent Cooper. He was not as easily fooled. Cooper was two years younger than me, and shy in his affection, which manifested itself as roughhousing. He came over to the bed and poked my foot a little bit. When I didn't stir, he moved up and poked my stomach. When I still didn't respond with an action he found appropriate, he progressed to my face. There were rules to this sort of game—anywhere but the eye was fair play. He poked my cheek and then my nose, stuck his finger in my mouth and then my ear. His rumbling chuckles were the only sound in the room. I struggled but remained unfazed. I thought I had won out.

I heard his footsteps recede to the door, but out of nowhere he screamed, "Bonsai!" My eyes popped open in time to see him running full-tilt at the bed. I curled into the fetal position as he leaped into the air and landed in a belly flop on top of me. I grunted as the air escaped my lungs and began wrestling with him. This was undoubtedly one of my favorite past times.

In moments like this, I couldn't understand how someone could go their whole lives without having a sibling. Rough housing was more to me than just a little bit of energy expenditure. It was bonding and the kind of play you can only have with a sibling or someone just as close. I knew in whatever relationship I eventually ended up in, it would have to include wrestling.

"Fine!" I shrieked while he pinned me to the bed, and I tried to buck him off onto the floor. "I concede. I'm awake! What more do you want from me?"

"I don't know. Mom just told me to come in here and make you get your lazy butt out of bed."

"Bah! Fine. Tell her I'm up, but I refuse to leave this bed or make myself presentable in any way—forever."

He stood to go but turned back and quickly hugged me. This both surprised and annoyed me. Surprised because he was not a big one for the affection (typical in my family) and annoyed because this undoubtedly meant my mom told him, no matter how vaguely, something about what had transpired the previous eve.

Thinking about their conversation made the slight happiness of our adrenaline-fueled wrestling match drain from me as the memories of the previous night flooded my head again. In one night my life had taken a nose dive. I now wanted—very badly—to return to school.

"There is nothing you can say that will make me let you stay in bed," my mother said from the doorway. "I know it's hard, but you have something you need to do, and I'm going to make sure it happens."

"But, Mom..." I whined. "I feel silly. It wasn't *that* big of a deal. What if the police think I'm lying or exaggerating?"

"And that is exactly why you need to go," she said. "He needs to know that he can't get away with what he did, and you need to know that this is a big deal. It's the police's job to help protect us, and they *will* care about what happened to you."

I huffed from under the sheets until she crossed the room and pulled the blankets off and onto the floor.

"This is not optional," she said, her arms folded and face set. "Get out of bed and get dressed, or I will have Cooper help me drag you to the car, and you'll go in your pajamas."

"Fine," I shouted. "I give up. Leave so I can get dressed."

An hour later, we were driving down the road to the police station. I had taken my sweet time getting ready, but in the end it hadn't mattered. I was on my way. I had never been to a police station before, and I didn't know what to do, but my mother strode in with confidence. Before I knew it, I had paperwork in my hand to fill out. This would be my first act—at least according to the law—as an adult.

Thankfully, I was put into a room with a female officer, and I requested for my mother to come with me. Of all the things I wanted to do alone, this was not one of them. I gave the officer all of the information I had on Clayton. She asked a few questions, and they took pictures of the bruises which had shown up on my arm.

When the officer was done, she left, and a crisis counselor took her place. She was yet another person for me to tell my story to. I was tired of talking about what had happened. I wanted to crawl back into bed and stay there. My spirit was weary.

"So, Penelope, or do you prefer Penny?" the therapist asked, raising her eyebrows.

"Penelope," my mother and I replied in unison.

"Ok, Penelope, tell me honestly. How are you feeling about everything?" she asked.

"I don't know. I mean, I was really scared and confused last night, but now I just don't know," I said, answering as honestly as I could.

"And that's perfectly understandable. It's hard for our minds to process things of this nature—likely you are still in shock. Your mind will process the events when you are ready to handle them and able to take a step back from the situation," she said. "There will be a time when you feel the need to talk about it. I want you to find a support group where you feel comfortable talking with other people. Let them help you come to terms with everything."

I shuffled in my chair, unable to imagine a time when I would be able—much less *want*—to talk about the incident openly.

"Some strong feelings may emerge following what happened to you, such as fear, shame and hatred. Those feelings are really common to many people after this type of situation. They're your mind trying to cope," the counselor said. "Those emotions sometimes cause people to blame themselves and let their attackers get away with the things they have done."

I could not argue with her logic as it had been my mom forcing me which had taken me out of bed and into the police station. I might not have been able to imagine myself sharing my story for my own mental health, but I could share it to help others, even if it was only one person. That would be a good enough reason for me.

As we were driving home, my mom asked, "Do you want me to drop you off at Summer's? She can bring you home later."

"No, she's in Canada, and I don't think she wants to talk to me anymore, anyway," I said. I stared out the window as the houses passed by. *And even if she does want to talk to me, I don't want to talk to her.*

"I doubt that's true. You two are best friends, and I think she would want to know about this, especially given your shared history with Clayton."

"Well, Mom, I don't know what to tell you, other than she doesn't want to be my best friend anymore as I told her I'm in love with her and her response was, 'Well, I have a boyfriend.' Then she left for Canada after I told her I couldn't be around her anymore," I said.

That stunned her into silence, maybe because my confession was a challenge to her "it's just a phase" mentality. We got home, and I retreated to my room. I didn't want to talk either situation out with anyone, and I didn't want to pretend like everything was okay. I wanted to sulk and cry away from everyone until I either felt better or withered up and blew away.

I spent a few days in my bed, only leaving to go to the bathroom, but on the fourth day Cooper came in and sat on the end of the bed. I covered my face with the blankets as the door cracked open.

"Mom says she's not sending anymore food up here to you," he said. "And she says your room is starting to smell."

"Bah. I don't care if she sends food. I'll just starve to death."

"No you won't. You'll sneak downstairs in the middle of the night like you always do."

I mumbled something unintelligible from under the blankets.

"You're letting him win, you know."

"Am not."

"Really? Because this doesn't look like any kind of life to me, and he's done that. He's stupid and a jerk and you're letting it keep you here.

"No."

"Okay, whatever you say. Dinner's ready," he said and pat my leg then left the room.

I don't know when he got so smart, and I wouldn't admit if what he said was true or not, but I did get out of bed and join my family at the table. It would be time for me to return to school soon, and I didn't want to miss the little bit I could spend with Cooper. For the next couple of weeks, I would devote all my time to my brother.

Chapter Thirteen

I was back in Seattle before telling Noah about what happened with Clayton. I wanted to tell him face to face. Selfishly, I wanted hugs, and you can't get those over the phone. We met in my dorm room with Alyssa. I didn't want to have to tell the story more than once.

"I know that night wasn't full of my best choices," I sobbed on Noah's shoulder as I wiped my nose with the back of my hand. "But no matter what, I didn't deserve that."

"Of course you didn't," he cooed. He had one arm around me, hugging me to him and the other was stroking my hair. "No one does. His particular breed of awfulness doesn't deserve to be breathing."

"I can make that happen," threatened Alyssa, her eyes fierce and hands clenched with anger.

"I know," I wailed. It felt good to have them comforting me in a way I could never get at home.

I had cried on my own about the Clayton fiasco, but since my friendship with Summer was out of commission, talking to Noah and Alyssa was the first time I had been able to get the understanding I desired. The emotions the counselor had warned were hiding inside came into full swing when I was back at school.

"I'm nervous on campus now," I told them, still clinging to Noah. "I don't go outside the dorm after dark if I can help it. I haven't been to any of the night time events because I'm just scared of people. I want to be comfortable, but I feel like humanity has betrayed me. I don't know what to do to get back what has been taken from me."

"Well, I don't have any magical answers for you—" he said.

"I do. Let's make him a eunuch," interjected Alyssa.

"*But*," Noah talked over her, "I do know you're not going to find any answers without leaving this room, and you're not going to find them until you want to."

"But then I have to—you know—do things," I whined. "Can't we just take Alyssa's suggestions?" I motioned to her with one arm.

"I mean, I'm happy to hide with you in your room, but eventually you're going to get tired of only seeing my face," he said, petting my back.

"That's not true," I replied. "You're face is like a Van Gogh. One never gets tired of staring at it."

"I am gorgeous, aren't I?" He took a step back from me and posed with mock seductiveness, complete with duck lips. "Why don't we start by going to sit outside today?"

"I suppose." I fiddled with the hem of my shirt. The sun had already set. I was truly nervous of not having a door between me and the rest of the world. "Only if you promise not to leave me alone, and one of you has to be on either side of me."

"We promise," they said in unison.

We sat in the little commons area outside of the door. Not only was the situation completely fine, but the outing was entirely uneventful. No one noticed us. No one said hello. I sat between Noah and Alyssa. He talked to me, trying to get my mind off of things, and she whispered of all the ways we could get revenge on Clayton.

Over the next few days, I roamed from class to class living almost completely inside my head. I sat in the back corners of my classes and often made a hasty retreat before the end of class so I could return to the comfort of my room. Being outside with Noah still hadn't done much to hasten my ability to be around people.

When the weekend rolled around, Noah called to see if I was up for going out.

"Are you *sure* you don't want to come?" he pleaded.

"I want to—I just can't," I said.

"I promise I won't leave your side," he said.

"It's a concert, and I have more than one side. It's the other ones that I'm worried about," I said.

"Fine, Penny, stay home and nurse your wounds. I'll send you video from the crowd," he said then hung up.

"It's not *Penny!*" I screamed at my phone.

As anger-induced adrenaline coursed through my body, I was motivated to get out of bed and do something. I decided I *would* go to the concert. I made it all the way outside the dorm before the emotion wore off and going anywhere seemed like a bad idea once again. I went back to my room to hide in my bed.

Penelope, you can't live your life this way. Cooper's right—you are letting Clayton win. Don't do that. Don't wince because you thought of his face. He is nothing, and you are letting him control you. Get out of bed and go take a shower. You are going to do something, even if it's only baby steps.

I gathered my shower items and darted to the showers. I took a shower in record time, encountering only a few people but proud of myself for leaving my room and my comfort zone.

That wasn't a small step—it was huge. I left my room, I didn't cower in a corner and I exposed my body in front of others. I'm pretty sure that all equates to sky diving.

I smiled to myself, back in the comfort of my room. Alyssa walked in right after I had crawled back into bed.

"Oh, my god, you're still in bed?" she chided me, but her look was a concerned one.

"No, I just got back in it," I said. "I took a shower." I beamed at her like it was the magical feat it felt like.

"Oooh, movin' on up. I told Noah there was no way you would go to that concert."

"You were talking about me?"

"Of course, dear, because we love you. We're worried about you and want you to be okay. I told him it would take more time, but far be it from him to be patient."

"I want to be okay." My eyes fell to look at the bed spread.

"I know you do, and you will be."

"I think I want to do something about it. I think I'm done letting him win."

"Good for you." She hugged me tightly. "Let me know if you need my help." She trotted over to her bed and plopped down with a book.

"You're not going out tonight?" I asked, puzzled.

"No, tonight I wanted to be here with you."

I was touched. My friends were concerned enough about me to turn down plans in order to be with me, but I didn't want things to be this way. I knew I couldn't change Alyssa's mind, but I could change myself and my situation. I wanted to help myself by helping other people. I was ready to get back the feeling of security I had lost. I needed something where I could go at my own pace but also be held accountable if I started to back-slide. I needed responsibility—I needed a group.

"Hey, Alyssa?"

"Hmm?"

"I need you to do something with me."

"Yeah?" She looked up from her book and into my eyes. I could tell she hoped for revenge, but I ignored it.

"I want to start a club and since you are the queen of social activities, you're going to lead it with me."

"I'm in. Just tell me what to do."

"Never thought I'd hear those words out of your mouth," I said, smiling with a hint of sarcasm. She responded in kind, half smiling, half glaring at me.

I stayed up late brain-storming and called Noah fairly early in the morning as payback for him calling me Penny.

"Hey," I said once I heard movement on the other end.

"Why are you calling me before noon?" he mumbled, sleep lacing his voice making it almost unrecognizable.

"Because," I said. "I've had an idea, and I need my gorgeous best friend."

"Flattery will get you everywhere."

"I've decided to start a club based on violence and assault prevention," I said, plunging in. "I want you and Alyssa to be officers with me. I'm going to find an advisor and talk to the police. I need you two to collect members and get more people involved."

"Penelope," he groaned.

"No! Soon we'll have a respectable amount of members, and I'll have a reason to leave my room. I need you to do this with me!" I interrupted his whining, practically shouting in my excitement.

"Uhhh, why do you always get your way?" he asked.

"Because I'm cute and you love me." I batted my eyes despite the fact that he couldn't see me.

"Do I get some kind of perk? Like a title or a costume?"

"What?" I laughed. "I suppose you get a title, but more importantly, you get to help me take my life back."

"Yeah, yeah," he joked.

Chapter Fourteen

THERE WAS a surprisingly large turnout for our first meeting. The sheer number of members gave me hope but also made me nervous. I had signed on for commitment and responsibility, but had I bitten off more than I could chew?

"Hello, everyone, and welcome to the first official meeting of RAVPA, the Rape and Violence Prevention Association. I'm the President, Penelope, and these are my officers. Noah, the Vice President." Noah stood and bowed. "Alyssa, our secretary." She stood and waved at the members. "And this is Terrance, the treasurer."

Alyssa had called in one of her friends to fill our officer's cabinet. The meeting proceeded as one would expect. We talked about recruiting and what we were trying to accomplish as a club. We had the local campus police come and talk about campus safety. By the end of the meeting, I was feeling accomplished and a tiny bit sure of myself. I felt like I could do this, and I knew I had made the right choice.

The second meeting was a presentation from the college counselors and a small demonstration from a local group who had special classes for quick and effective self-defense.

The third meeting was supposed to be with a local women's shelter, but due to a particularly bad bout of the flu, they didn't have enough staff to spare for the appearance. Noah and I had talked about what we could do instead, but I wasn't sure I could pull it off.

"Okay, everyone." I raised my voice and spoke clearly to get everyone's attention. "Welcome to the third general meeting of RAVPA. Today we're going to deviate from the planned activity. I know we were supposed to hear from one of the local women's shelters, but they couldn't make it. So instead we're going to do something a little different. I was assaulted in December, and I want to share my story with all of you. Anyone who needs to leave, please do so now. We will see you in two weeks."

I waited to see if anyone needed to exit. I knew I couldn't rush my recovery, much less anyone else's, and I didn't want to make anyone uncomfortable. After a couple of people had exited and everyone remaining had refocused their attention on me, I began.

"I know some of you here might have a story to tell similar to mine. I started this club because I wanted to empower people to help themselves and to avoid situations like the one I've been through. I also wanted to empower myself to regain trust in my fellow human-beings, which was taken from me by one man.

"Over the winter break, I was attacked by my ex-boyfriend. We were going to hang out in a park, at night, just the two of us. I was having a really rough night and knew somewhere in the back of my mind the choices I made were stupid at best. But poor decisions considered, I never would have thought him capable of what happened.

"He and I broke up in junior year of high school and didn't have much of a friendship afterward. I hadn't even really spoken to him since then until we met again by chance. He wanted to hang out, and I needed to keep my mind off the bad night I was having.

"We ended up in a park swinging side by side. He asked me why we had ever broken up, and I couldn't believe he could be so dumb. I knew I had made the wrong choice in deciding to hang out with him. I told him I had to leave, jumped off my swing and headed for the car. He yelled at me, trying to get me to stop.

"I didn't know he was chasing me until his voice was in my ear. He caught me by the arm and pulled my body to his. He held me forcefully and put his hands on me. I fought back the best I could and eventually got away."

My mouth was dry, and I could no longer look at the club members. I stared at the podium I stood behind, my eyes filling with tears, not sure if I could continue. Out of the corner of my eye I saw Noah move then felt his hand in mine. I turned to look at him and felt love and appreciation flow through me. Clearing my throat and only looking at Noah, I continued.

"I was able to get away before he raped me, and the next day my mother took me to the police, but nothing could return to me what was stolen from me that night. This boy who touched me without my permission took away my sense of security and my ability to be comfortable in a world full of people. It was physical and mental abuse, but I'm ready now to take back my confidence and my life. I will not let *anyone* ruin what my life is supposed to be, least of all him!"

I ended my story with force and determination, sweeping my eyes from Noah back to the rest of the room. After a moment of silence, Noah removed his hand from mine to applaud and the room erupted. I felt a glow inside me grow until it engulfed the horrible feeling of retelling the nightmare. I stepped aside to let Alyssa take over and dismiss the meeting and found myself in the arms of Noah as silent tears rolled off my cheeks and onto his shoulder.

Empowered by my large steps toward recovery, I did research into subjects and topics trying to help everyone that I could. I wanted to be prepared for questions and plan meetings which would be truly informational. I watched a lot of Youtube videos and fell in love with a channel called Sex + by Laci Green and started studying some of the topics that were broached on the channel.

The channel broached something termed as "slut-shamming," which encompassed the awful thoughts I had held prior to my run in with Clayton. It's a mentality that involves blaming the victims of rape for the rape happening. Slut-shaming includes ideas such as, "Well, of course she got raped, look at what she's wearing." or "Oh, she's asking for it." It also encompasses pushing ones morals onto someone else pertaining to their sex life: "She probably enjoyed it—you know she's a slut."

The problem is not confined to women either. Men who come forward about being raped are sometimes told, "Why are you complaining? You got laid." or "You're a guy. You could have stopped it." Sexual violence doesn't have to happen to a woman for it to be unwanted.

I was hell bent on changing this mentality and bringing to light how undoubtedly wrong it was. The next two meetings were spent talking about slut shaming and how to handle people who slut shame.

Chapter Fifteen

"So, you still haven't heard from her?" Noah asked me as he pushed open my door. I had been complaining earlier in the week about Summer.

"No, but thanks for reminding me. It's been over a month now," I said, rolling my eyes.

"If I was going to remind you of anything, it would be that you need to move on," he said.

I glared at him with my best disapproving look.

"I don't want to move on. I'm not ready to date anyone. That night ruined men and women for me. I'm just not interested," I said.

"You'll never know unless you at least look," he said. "I've checked out more ladies lately than you have."

"It doesn't count if you are coveting their clothing," I said.

"Ah. Excuse me, don't be rude," he mocked me while wagging a finger in my face.

"Hahaha. Seriously, though, I don't need anyone except you, of course," I said to appease his offended look. "I just need to get back to myself."

And truly, between LGBTQA, RAVPA and classes, I was kept incredibly busy. I had almost no time to dwell on the Summer situation or to play out the one million scenarios which ran through my head.

Therefore, I was shocked when I received a text from her in February.

Summer: I'm sorry about everything that happened. I'm sorry I opened my big mouth and I would take it all back given the option!

Penelope: I'm sorry too. I was obviously underprepared for the situation. I overreacted and regret it. That night was one of the worst nights of my life.

Summer: Yeah, I ran into your mom today in the grocery store. I asked about you and she told me what happened. I'm so sorry.

Penelope: Is that the only reason you texted me?

Summer: No. It was the catalyst but I miss you, and I've been dying not talking to you. I was just scared you wouldn't respond, and I couldn't handle the possibility.

Penelope: Well, you see, I could never not respond to you. I happen to love you, regardless of our relationship status or how mad I am at you.

Summer: I love you too, but I still have a boyfriend.

Penelope: I know, but even friends can say they love each other, even if one of them wishes it was more.

Summer: Hey, I was wondering if I could have your address there? I want to send you some things.

Penelope: Sure.

I gave her my address, and we chatted via text for most of the day. It was nice just to talk to her, but I knew I would fall back into the same pattern of our relationship if I didn't make a change. I knew if I couldn't have her I would go crazy in the same rut we had been in. It was time for me to find someone new—it was time for me to brave the crazy world of college dating.

I still didn't think I was altogether ready for the world at large, but when I stopped receiving responses from Summer by the end of the week, I was more sure. I was determined not to go down the same path I had already been down so many times.

I was confident with my new-found sexuality and interested in experiencing a new avenue. I started noticing—for the first time really—all the women around me. I had been so caught up in my love for Summer, I hadn't noticed the beauty passing me by. There was one girl in RAVPA who was extremely attractive. There was something about her I couldn't put my finger on, but I found the idea of her tremendously comforting and endearing. I pointed her out to Noah one day, as his gaydar was much better than mine.

"No way!" he said immediately.

"Why not?" I asked, shocked at his instant impulse to shut down someone I wanted to pursue, especially since this had been his idea.

"She's almost an exact replica of Summer. Don't think I didn't Facebook stalk her after all the endless nights you spent talking about her and crying over her. I wanted to see what all the hype was about, and *she*, my friend, is the reason you are drawn to poor little miss redhead over there. I should have made that bet with Alyssa. I knew you were going to choose that girl once you decided to plunge into the dating scene."

"Are you kidding me?" I shrieked indignantly. "You are banning me from redheads? I *love* redheads!"

"I know you're in love with a redhead. That's what we're trying to cure you of!" he said.

As flawed as his logic might be, Noah had obviously put a lot of thought into this, so I just shrugged and told him he had to pick out someone for me then. He snorted and told me I didn't want to give him that kind of control over my life.

It was funny how when I was infatuated with Summer, people just passed under my radar. But when I began to look, I became intensely aware of a person in biology lab who stared at me often. I was now one of the many looking for companionship and not knowing where or how to find it. So I did what every twenty-first century girl does—I went on the internet. Noah picked out a few pictures he thought were best. I made a profile on a couple of dating websites to see if anything would happen.

I kept looking at the people around me, though. I was turning into a veritable people-watcher. I started up a few conversations which never really went anywhere. I never asked for anyone's number, and no one ever asked for mine.

It was mid-February, and teachers were beginning to assign big projects, some due before spring break and some after. I was in my gender studies course and locked eyes with a girl when the teacher told us to split up into partners.

She was tall for a girl, but then again, so was I. Her hair was so black it seemed to have highlights of blue, framing a rounded face with a small, cute nose. She was wonderfully curvy in all the right ways, and she was smart, always speaking up in class. I had noticed her before—as far as attractive females go, she was well fit—but saw she had a ring on her finger, so I hadn't thought on it further.

For the project, I wanted someone who would share the work with me instead of my doing everything and gifting someone an A with no effort. I was not normally a big fan of group projects. After the teacher was done explaining, the girl and I made our way toward each other. A couple of other people made for her, trying to step in front and stop her, but she would not be deterred and breezed past them.

"Hi, I'm Sophia," she said boldly, sticking out her hand.

"Hi! Penelope," I stated, shaking her soft hand.

We pulled two desks together and sat down to discuss topics for our project.

"So, did you have anything in mind?" Sophia asked.

"I had a couple of ideas. What about you? Anything special?" I replied, my misgivings about group work winning. I didn't want to share until she contributed.

"I have a few," she said simply.

We sat there in silence for a minute, neither of us wanting to be the first to share.

After a minute, she cocked an eyebrow at me. "So, you've been down that road before too have you?"

"I'm not sure what you mean," I said, wondering if she was in the same boat as me or if she wanted to sail for free.

"The road where you're the only contributing member in a group project," she said.

"Yes. More times than I care to count." I sighed with relief.

"I understand. I'm not like that, though, so no worries," she said. "I'm not good at coming up with concepts that interest anyone other than me. If I was doing this on my own, I would probably do the whole project on the role of patriarchy in the fall of Rome, and almost no one wants to hear about that."

"Ah, yes. Well, as interesting as that does sound," I said, making a sympathetic face balanced with an "oh, god" face. "I was thinking about gender biases, specifically in reference to transgender people. I think every facility should be required to have a family bathroom, and there should also be more than two check boxes on any form where it is required to specify sex."

"See?" said Sophia. "That's much better than mine, and you know, current..."

"Great." I laughed. "When do you want to get together to work on it?"

"How about this Saturday?" she suggested. "We can work in the library."

"That sounds good. I'll get us a group room."

I showed up at the library around six-thirty in the evening. The campus library was quite large, with many floors of books. Some floors were designated for quiet study, and on others you could make noise, within reason. It was getting a bit dark outside and I hurried inside. Our group room was on the fourth floor, so I got the key and went up. I arrived at the room to find Sophia already waiting. We had to make a power point and a poster, so she had come prepared with her laptop and some cardboard. I opened the room, and we sat down across from each other at the small, round table which took up about half of the room.

"I'm fairly crafty," I told Sophia, pulling out my laptop. "So, if you want, I can do the poster while you work on the presentation."

"Hmm," was all she said.

I showed her some of the pictures I wanted to use then went to print them. When I came back, she was on her laptop. I grabbed the cardboard and a glue stick and sat down on the floor. Almost immediately, she was next to me before I'd gotten far. I didn't mind if she wanted us both to work on both items. We started arranging things on the poster together, passing the time by talking. We chatted about ourselves and what interested us. When I told her about the clubs I was in, she raised a curious eyebrow at me but didn't ask questions. I asked her what it was like managing a marriage and school life, and she broke out in robust laughter.

"What's so funny?" I asked, giggling because of her abrupt, barking laughter.

"I was curious if it actually worked, but now I know it works too well!" she exclaimed between laughs, practically rolling on the floor.

All my mirth gave way to confusion, but I could not stop giggling at the sight of Sophia laughing so hard. I sat chuckling until she could control herself.

"Explain," I said.

This sent her off into laughter again, but she tried to explain herself asides.

"I wear-" Sharp inhale. "-the ring-" Snort. "-to ward off-" Cough. "-guys!"

While I didn't quite find this to be the outrageously hysterical joke Sophia did, now that I was clued in, I joined in her laughter.

"So, you didn't think it actually worked?" I asked.

"That's the thing—it doesn't work. At least, not for its intended purpose," she explained. "I still get hit on by guys, but I thought, 'if I still get hit on with the ring, it might get worse if I stop wearing it.' So, I continued to wear it. I never imagined it was having the opposite effect of what I wanted."

"What do you mean, 'you never imagined?' You just said it wasn't stopping guys from hitting on you," I said, confused.

"Penelope, I'm a lesbian. That's why I don't want guys hitting on me. It's easier to just avoid guys than to tell them because some just take my being a lesbian as a challenge, and things get weird fast," she said.

My mouth dropped open in shock. I didn't have a clue she was a lesbian. Another casualty one could chock up to my awful gaydar. Yet here she was, in front of me, unattached—as far as I knew—and utterly gorgeous.

"So does that mean you are single?" I asked.

"Maybe. Why? Are you interested?" she asked with a bit of mocking in her voice.

My eyes widened, and I blushed, turning my head back to our poster.

"Oh my... You are? I didn't mean to be rude. I thought for sure you were attached, someone as smart and attractive as you. Plus, I see you hanging out with that brunette guy all the time. I guess I just assumed. I'm sorry," she blurted out. "Now I've gone and made a jerk of myself." Her voice trailed off.

I looked up at her, a smile spreading across my face. "You think I'm smart?" I beamed.

This made her laugh; it was obviously not what she expected me to say. She smiled too.

"So, let me get this straight—err, correct," she started. "I'm single, and you're single." I nodded vigorously. "I'm interested in you." My eyebrows raised. "And you're interested in me?" I nodded again but a little less emphatically due to a touch of shyness and looked down at the poster we were supposed to be working on.

I could feel her staring at me. I didn't want to meet her eyes, but I could feel the heat of her gaze. I don't know why I felt so shy. Sophia was beautiful, and I *had* noticed her before tonight. But she was forward, and I wasn't used to someone being so honest with me about their feelings. As I lifted my head, I could feel my face going pink. She smiled at me. She leaned closer to me so her face wasn't far from mine. I could barely breathe. It's not like I hadn't been kissed before. I had kissed plenty of boys, but I had been in relationships with them for a little bit, and they had all been, well, *boys*.

She came toward me slowly enough I could have stopped her if I so desired, but I didn't. I wanted new experiences, and I wanted to move forward with reckless abandon. I wanted to be more like Sophia. I felt a rush of excitement and adrenaline as her lips met mine—they were soft. The rush was amazing, and I was truly sucked into the moment. I didn't think about Summer or the pain this kiss might cause me afterward or even what my eventual plan was with Sophia. I just lived in the moment, and it was awesome.

The kiss was light and sweet. When it was over, she pulled away from me so we could look into each other's eyes. She smiled at me, and I smiled back, a large grin that threatened to split my face. Then she kissed me again, still soft but longer. Her hand came up to cup the side of my face, and I kissed her back with enthusiasm. The gentle kiss became deeper, and next thing I knew, we were making out in the library.

Chapter Sixteen

THE NEXT day, I beat on Noah's door until he answered. Grumpy, disheveled, and in his super hero pajamas—complete with cape—he ushered me inside. I followed him through the formal dining room and into the kitchen. I opened my mouth to speak, but before the air could leave my lungs to make a sound, he looked at me with the most withering look I had ever received from someone other than my mother.

I leaned against the smooth, marble counter as he pulled a mug from the cabinet and placed it under the spout of the coffee machine. I hadn't met anyone who loved coffee quite as much as Noah did—for him, it was close to a religious experience. He jabbed at the buttons on the fancy contraption, and it immediately began producing Noah's *elixir of life*. He pulled the mug from the machine, steam rising in happy little swirls above it. He lowered his head to inhale deeply and then set about adding creamer and sugar. Only after the coffee had cooled and Noah had taken three long drags from the mug did he speak.

"You know, I could charge you with cruel and unusual punishment for waking me before noon this often."

"The world does not always wait for you before it begins turning, Noah. My world is spinning, and I thought you would want to know about it."

"Well, go get your hamsters calibrated and stop waking me at the crack of dawn."

"Ugh! Whatever." I rolled my eyes and chose to ignore him. A goofy smile spread across my face, and I told him, "I kissed someone."

"Shut up and tell me everything." He playfully slapped my arm and refilled his coffee.

I told him everything. Then he made himself presentable to the rest of the world and we went out for lunch.

When I had finally finished over analyzing everything, Noah said, "Make sure she's not your rebound. You know, someone you shove all of the feelings from your old relationship onto. Making the new relationship too intense and too much, too quickly. Rebound relationships are doomed to failure and the consequences of the fall-out are horrible for all parties, including but not limited to friends and family. I don't want to go down like that." He added the last part with a smile and a wink.

"I don't think I am. I'm just excited! I hadn't even thought about Summer until just now, thanks for that," I said, Noah rolling his eyes at me. "How do I know if it's a rebound?"

"Well, I would have told you to take it slow. But as you have already sucked half of her face off from the sound of it, I would start taking her out. I mean, don't just sit in your room and make out all the time. Why don't you bring her to a LGBTQA meeting?"

"I think I will." I smiled at him. "I'm seeing her again tonight." My face spread into a grin at the mention of seeing her.

We ate and chatted about Sophia and kissing then moved on to school and club stuff. After lunch, we went our separate ways, and I went back to my dorm room to get ready to see Sophia again. She was going to come over so we could work on our project some more.

She knocked on the door around four, and I leapt off my bed to yank open the door. She stood on the other side of it beaming at me. I bowed slightly and swept my arm to indicate for her to enter the room. She stepped in the room then pulled me in after her and shut the door. Her mouth was on mine before I had uttered a word. All thoughts of talking to her about anything flew out of my mind. We were lost in each other until Alyssa opened the door. We broke apart like we had been doing something wrong. I began giggling and Sophia followed. When Alyssa caught sight of us around the door, she stopped dead in her tracks. I hadn't been able to share my news with her yet.

"Well, hello," Alyssa said and wiggled her eyebrows at me then looked meaning fully at Sophia.

"Hi," I said. "This is Sophia."

Alyssa rounded the bottom of my bed and came to where Sophia and I were standing. She stuck out her hand and said, "My name's Alyssa."

They shook hands, which seemed oddly formal, and then Alyssa perched on the edge of her bed and stared at us. I looked from her to Sophia and knew that it was now time to actually work on the project. I slid the poster board from under my bed where I had stowed it and tapped on Sophia's shoe so she would move. She climbed onto the bed, and I swept the board into the middle of the room.

"Whatcha doin'?" asked Alyssa. Her eyes had not moved from us since she sat down.

"Working on a project for our gender studies class," replied Sophia while she pulled her laptop from her bag and turned it on.

"Fascinating." Alyssa's tone dripped sarcasm.

"Alyssa," I said, smiling far larger than the situation warranted. "Can I speak with you in the hallway?"

"Why sure," she simpered.

Had Sophia known anything about Alyssa, this would have been a huge tipoff to the storm brewing inside of her, but as it stood—I was to handle the gale force winds alone. We stepped into the hallway, and I closed the door behind me.

"Excuse me, what is your problem?" I demanded.

"I know what you're doing," she said, dropping all pretenses of being happy or nice.

"What? Working on a project? Kissing my classmate? *Moving on!*"

There had been a sneaking suspicion building in the back of my mind for a little while now. One that included Alyssa being "Team Summer," and I had a sharp feeling that it was about to be confirmed.

"I thought you loved Summer?"

"You know I do!" I cried, feeling a little affronted at the accusation and a little upset about having been right in my fears and—of course—guilty for kissing Sophia.

"Then what are you doing? You're in the middle of trying to sort things out, yet you're making out with someone else?"

"There is no 'working things out.' Summer doesn't want me—she has a boyfriend."

"She has a distraction, and you're butt-hurt, which is understandable, but now you're dragging someone else into the mix. Now there is no way that someone won't end up hurt."

"Me, Alyssa! I'm hurt, and I'm trying to move past being rejected by someone I loved for years."

"Does she know she's a rebound?"

"She's not a rebound. I'm keeping my feelings for Summer separate—I'm starting something new."

"This is a rebound, and you're lying to her like you're lying to yourself."

Irritated, Alyssa turned on her heels and stomped down the hallway. I turned to go back into the dorm and realized that Sophia and I would be alone again, only this time I wasn't excited about it. Alyssa's words made me feel bad, but they also made me more thoughtful of what I was doing, which probably wasn't a bad thing.

Sophia was sitting on the bed where I had left her, diligently typing at her computer—assumedly working on the project.

"Is everything alright?" she asked.

"Yeah, she wanted a word. She wants the dorm to herself later, so we should get to work."

Sophia eyed me a little oddly, but must have assumed it was for the best not to comment on the inner-workings of my roommate relationship. We worked semi-diligently after that. Really, the project shouldn't take more than two or three meetings, but we were both dragging our feet, looking for a reason to continue meeting.

We worked in silence for a bit, small questions or one of us sharing something we had found here and there until I remembered about asking her to a club meeting.

"Hey," I said to Sophia, startling her a little. "You want to go with me to the LGBTQA meeting tomorrow?"

"Sure, sounds like fun," she replied. "We're almost done with the project, despite my best efforts, so I need another excuse to follow you around."

"Oh, have my own little stalker do I?" I giggled.

"You have no idea," she said as she put her computer aside and scooted closer to me on the bed.

We kissed for a bit, but—thanks to Alyssa—I couldn't get Summer out of my head. I pulled back and so did Sophia with a sound of reluctance.

I pecked her once more then said, "I think it's time to call it a night. Alyssa will be back soon, and we should save some of the good stuff for later." I smiled a little devilishly to imply my meaning.

"Or we could have more of the good stuff now," she replied, her own look far surpassing my own. "We could go somewhere else. I bet we could find a place in the library again." She reached for me and pulled me to her.

"Uh, I think not," I said, an uneasy feeling seeping into my stomach. I put my hands on her shoulders to keep us apart—I could feel her still pulling on me. "It's time for you to go. I'll see you for the meeting tomorrow."

"But..." she began.

"No buts, time to go. I need to clear out of here and I have other homework to do," I said as I pushed her toward the door.

To my relief, she pecked me on the cheek at the door and left quietly. I crawled back into bed and had a small cry over my hurt feelings about Summer and my almost instant panic when Sophia was pulling on me after I had said no. I knew she didn't mean harm but that didn't mean she hadn't caused any. I was still raw from my ordeal with Clayton, and she had pushed just enough to bring it back.

Chapter Seventeen

I HADN'T left my bed after Sophia left the night before. I cried myself
to sleep after being emotionally exhausted by Alyssa and then Sophia. I
woke the next morning in turmoil. I was angry with Alyssa and annoyed
at her poor timing. Not to mention I was uneasy with Sophia but also
excited to see her. All of these emotions swirled in front of my eyes as I
opened them to see the sun creeping through the window. I had fallen
asleep early, and though I had slept more than my allotted eight hours,
it was still early when I woke.

I rolled on my side and saw Alyssa's lumpy form under the covers of
her bed. My eyes narrowed, and I snatched my pillow out from under
my own head and hurled it at her. It was a direct hit in the shoulder-
head area of the lump. She jerked awake and bolted upright in her bed.
She looked around with crazy eyes, and as mad as I was I couldn't stifle
my laughter.

My giggles gave her somewhere to aim her shock and subsequent
pillow retaliation. She chucked my pillow back at me and it hit me
squarely in the face.

"Hey!" I shouted.

"Ha," she cried back and threw *her* pillow at me too.

"No fair. No retaliation when you deserve it."

"Deserve it? I thought we were playing?"

"No, I'm mad at you." I crossed my arms over my chest in the traditional pouting stance.

"About yesterday?"

"Duh." I rolled my eyes at her. "You care more about Summer, who you haven't even met, then you do about me. You hurt my feelings yesterday and made me feel bad for something that I should be enjoying."

"I just didn't want you to make a mistake I've made several times. You give up on one path because you think the door is closed, but then as you're running down an adjacent hallway toward a different door, you find out the place you were trying to get to before opens up into that hallway too and the door smacks you in the face."

"I..." My face screwed up in confusion. "Have no idea what you just said."

"All I'm saying is, I don't want to watch you go through hell when I could have done something to help. I'm sorry I hurt you."

"Will you at least try to like Sophia? You didn't even talk to her. You just immediately objected and, frankly, were unbelievably rude."

"I know! I'm sorry!" She buried her face in the covers. "I'm a horrible friend."

"Yep," I said and threw her pillow back at her.

She emerged from the covers looking chastised. "Are you giving up on Summer?"

"I'm living my life with the cards I've been dealt. I'm moving on because I need to. If Summer becomes available *and* interested, I will cross that bridge when I get to it."

"Okay. I'll keep quiet unless you ask my advice."

Alyssa seemed really interested in my relationship with Summer, and that made me a little wary. She didn't even know Summer, yet she was fighting in her corner. I chalked it up to things I would never understand and climbed out of my bed. Alyssa had lain back down, and I flung my body on top of hers in an I-accept-your-apology hug then went to the restroom.

The LGBTQA meeting didn't start until two, and I had a morning class. I got ready for my day and set out about campus. It was still a little chilly in Seattle. It was the beginning of the last week of February and the second to last week of school before spring break. I had decided to stay in Seattle for the break since it was only a week long and most of my friends were staying. After class, I returned to my dorm room to wait for Sophia so we could head to the meeting together.

Sophia showed up at my room at the same time that I did. She was hours early. I knew what she had in mind as she pulled me to her before I could get the door open, but I had other ideas. I kissed her back, but not nearly with the enthusiasm she had. I turned to open the door, Sophia still holding my waist, and we went inside. Alyssa was still there, which was both good and bad. I needed to talk to Sophia alone, but at least Alyssa's presence would hold Sophia off for a little bit.

It was obvious to me that Sophia was an exceedingly sexual person, and I was completely inexperienced. Mixed in with my uneasy feelings about her eagerness and slight use of force was something else I couldn't place. It was almost an unwillingness to take the next step. I had felt it before when I had rebuffed Clayton's wishes to go all the way when we were dating in high school. Maybe it was nerves—everyone felt those when entering into uncharted territory, right?

I had thought up a plan to deter Sophia in the event that Alyssa wasn't in the dorm. I had packed up all the stuff for our project the night before. We walked into the room like a four legged creature, and I turned within the circle of Sophia's arms and told her we were going to the library.

She nodded vigorously, and I gave her a stern look saying, "We're going to work so we can turn this project in on Friday."

"Yeah, no problem. We can finish it quickly enough." She winked at me.

We finished the project within thirty minutes. The approximate amount of time the whole project should have taken was two hours. We had again secured a study room, and there were windows in each room that looked out into the library. They had blinds on the inside. I knew it was to lessen the distractions from outside if the group was having a hard time concentrating, but Sophia lowered them with completely different intentions.

I don't know why the library had become our make out spot, but we were lying on the floor losing ourselves in each other before I could gather my thoughts to stop it. A large part of me wanted so badly to be normal, without baggage and without second thoughts about everything. I wanted to lose myself in Sophia like I had when I had fallen for Clayton, so I threw out my misgivings willfully and recklessly, enjoying our time in the library.

Before the meeting, we dropped off the poster at the dorm. I wrenched her from the room, where she would have gladly stayed, especially in Alyssa's absence and we walked to the meeting room across campus.

"Did I upset you last night?" she asked, her fingers brushing mine. "I just wanted to spend more time with you. You intoxicate me."

"No," I lied, scared to tell her about my feelings. "I just don't want to move too fast."

I grabbed her hand and stopped. She turned to face me, her expression curious. I knew there were things I couldn't hide, things Sophia deserved to know.

"I was in love with my best friend, but she didn't return my sentiment. I'm trying to make sure none of those feelings seep into this and mess things up. I don't want you to be my rebound."

"Do you want to talk about her?" she asked.

"I don't want her anywhere near this relationship," I replied.

"Well, when you're ready, I would like to know what I'm up against," Sophia said.

"I was hoping we could just never talk about her, and it would be like she never existed," I said, smiling sweetly and trying to look cute.

"Is that how much she meant to you?" Sophia asked, her expression concerned.

"Ugh, see. This is what I don't want to happen," I whined.

"You can't run from your past. She obviously meant a great deal to you if you're wishing her out of your memory."

I sighed, "I'll tell you, but I'm not ready yet."

"Do you want me to back off until you are?"

Her offering made it seem unnecessary; to know that she was willing to cool things off solely for my benefit was enough.

"No," I whispered.

She tugged my arm to pull me closer; I threw my arms around her neck. I looked into her eyes and pushed my lips to hers, closing my eyes when I felt her lips against mine. I kissed her gently then took her hand, and we continued walking. We were late for the meeting, but no one seemed to notice except for Noah.

We spent every day of the next two weeks together. I slowly shared my story about Summer, not mentioning Clayton and the catastrophe since she hadn't made me feel scared since that night. I wasn't ready to see pity in her eyes when I told her. We made out a lot. I knew she was ready to move things further, but I still had a strange feeling when I thought about it. My feelings were completely unrelated to the incident with Clayton. I wasn't scared or feeling forced. I was happy with the way things were and didn't have the desire she did.

Chapter Eighteen

I OPENED my door on the first weekend of spring break to Summer standing on the other side. I felt like I had just been bludgeoned, the part of me trying so desperately to forget her lay beaten and out cold in the corner.

"Surprise!" she shouted and threw her arms around my neck.

I was confused and sluggish with sleep, yet I was trying to figure out why she was here. I couldn't remember us ever talking about her coming to visit, but then again I guessed it made sense with her yelling *surprise*. I stood there, eyes wide and mouth slightly open, and didn't think to return her hug.

She straightened up and tentatively uttered, "Uh, hi?" She waved her hand in front of my eyes.

"Right, sorry," I said. My mind snapped back to the present, and my mouth closed. "I'm just shocked to see you here. We haven't talked in a while, but here you are on my doorstep. Um, come in."

Summer stepped inside my room and surveyed the small area. She pointed to Alyssa's lumpy bed and raised her eyebrow in question.

"My roommate, Alyssa," I said.

At the sound of her name, she muttered a sleepy, incomprehensible few words and rolled over. I would have been worried about waking her except it was 2 o'clock in the afternoon, and there wasn't a chance I was going out onto campus with Summer. Last thing I needed was someone telling Sophia before I could.

"So, how are you?" I asked Summer.

"I'm good," she said.

I motioned to my bed so she could have a seat. I sat at the other end of the bed and faced her.

"How's school?" I asked.

"Is that really how we're going to do this?" she asked.

"Fine," I said. "What are you doing here?"

"Well, this isn't exactly the welcome I was expecting, but I wanted to surprise you." She frowned. "I've missed you. I had some free time and some frequent flyer miles of my parents' to burn through. You gave me your address, and I thought I would come see you. I've kind of been talking with Alyssa on Facebook, but I made her promise not to tell you. You don't seem happy to see me, though." She cocked her head to the side.

"I'm just flustered and surprised," and would burn Alyssa at the stake later, "So yeah, congrats. You surprised me." I gave her a wry smile. "It's just that a lot of things have changed since we last talked. You haven't returned my texts in over a month. I think we both need to get a little better at this whole communication thing when we're apart. I know we're great together, but it doesn't seem to translate well. Why haven't you talked to me?"

If I sounded hurt it was because I was. Summer's head had snapped up to my face when I had mentioned us going great together, but she looked ashamed at my last question.

She looked me in the eyes and repeated, "We are great together. I'm sorry."

She took my hand and pulled me to her. In a moment of confusion and panic, I pulled her into a hug, scared she would kiss me.

What does this mean? Is she trying to tell me she's finally interested in me only to turn around and leave again at the end of spring break? I'm not prepared for anything like this. This explains why Alyssa is all about Summer. They've been talking. I need to have a serious talk with that girl. I know she means well, but when I began seeing Sophia she should have spilled the beans.

I hadn't known I would need to have the "what are we" conversation with Sophia so soon. While we never agreed to be exclusive, I knew in my heart if I kissed Summer it would all be over for me. I would fall back into the way I had lived in for years. That was a trench I had only recently started digging my way out of, mostly due to Sophia.

I finally knew I was capable of feeling something for someone other than Summer, even if I would never stop loving her. It wasn't fair to Summer or Sophia to kiss Summer right now, but mostly it wasn't fair to me. She was only here for a week. If I didn't take control of this situation, she would leave my life in shambles. I released her from our hug after holding her maybe a bit too long while I thought up a plan.

"Want to go get some breakfast?" I asked as stood up from the bed.

"Breakfast? It's like 2:30 in the afternoon!"

"Don't leave on my account," grouched Alyssa, who was rising from her nest. "You've already woken me, and now you might as well stay."

She got up and went to our small bathroom.

"Give me just a second," I told Summer.

I followed Alyssa and saw she was gathering her things to take a shower.

"I'm sorry we woke you," I told her, even though I wasn't. "Do you want to come with us to get food?"

"And interrupt your date? I would never be so rude," Alyssa said.

"It's not a date," I said firmly. "And this is your fault."

"Maybe it is," she said. "But that girl is like a whirlwind, and you knowing in advance wouldn't have made it any easier."

"I-" I began.

"Don't worry, I won't say anything to anyone," she said as she walked past me toward the door. "Except maybe Noah."

She was out the door, and I wouldn't chase her.

"So, breakfast? There's an all breakfast diner not too far from here called 10AM Somewhere," I said while holding the door open for her.

Now that the room was empty, we definitely needed to leave before something stupid happened, like I really needed anymore temptation in my life right now.

Since Summer and I had such poor long distance communication, we had plenty to share with each other. I told her about the club I had started in the aftermath of the Clayton incident and how it had helped me move forward. She told me she had gone to see him in the grocery store where he worked and kicked him in the gonads before running away. This made me splutter and launch orange juice out of my nose, which in turn had forced Summer to spit pancake halfway across the table.

It was so easy to be with Summer. I had known her for so long. We both knew how to make the other laugh. On the other hand, everything with Sophia was so new and exciting. I was learning more and more about her every day and she was taking an interest in my interests. How was I supposed to compare two relationships that were so different?

"So," Summer began. "I wanted to surprise you because I wanted to tell you, in person, that me and 'the boyfriend,' as you so lovingly call him, broke up. And don't be mad, but I happened across your dating profile online, and my hopes were confirmed about you still being single. I want to give us a try—that is, if you still want me," she said.

Oh, shit. Why did I think being in a public place would stop this sort of disaster from happening! How could I forget about my dating profile?

My mind reeled. There was no way to get out of this without making a few hard decisions.

"Uhh"—I cleared my throat—"It's not that I don't want you, but why now? I can't handle being your rebound. If we try being together, I want it to be an honest try at a real, lasting relationship. I also need to know if a romantic relationship doesn't work out between us, our friendship can survive it. I'm not sure I'm capable of that. You know how poorly I responded before I even had you." I cleared my throat a second time. "I, also, uh..." *How could I tell her this?* "I'm kind of seeing someone."

Summer's face went from smiling at the end of her announcement to furrowed brows to frowning slightly to frowning a lot to jaw clenched, lips pursed and eyes fierce. She turned to look across the restaurant as her eyes filled with tears. The waitress came by, and I asked for the check. I knew, no matter where this conversation went, at least part of it was going to make a scene. I needed to take Summer somewhere we could talk where we wouldn't be interrupted. Somewhere she couldn't unnerve everyone around us.

She got up and went to the restroom while I waited for the check. After paying, I followed her to the restroom. She still had not emerged. I opened the door and walked in. Sitting on the sink, dabbing her eyes, was a blotchy-faced Summer. My heart sank, awful decision number one was made, and here were the consequences.

"Come on, let's get out of here. We can go someplace and talk," I stated matter-of-factly.

"Why? You've already said everything, obviously. I might as well go back to the airport!" she cried.

Belligerent Summer had arrived.

"I'm not going to do this here. I will be waiting outside for you when you are ready to come with me. There's a park not far from here—we can talk and walk," I said.

Chapter Nineteen

It took nearly ten minutes for Summer to join me outside. I loved her, but when her emotions ran high, it always left me walking on the edge of a cliff. One way you could run forever, but the other direction was a long fall to your death. We were alike in that fact, but my emotions were usually less volatile. We walked in silence in the direction of the park. I knew the choice to speak could make things worse, so I just waited for her. She would either ask me what I was thinking—when she was ready—or she would come at me with whatever she was mulling over in her head.

"So, do you love the guy you're seeing?" she asked.

"It's only been three weeks, so I don't know if it's love or not," I said.

"Well, you would know if you love him like you love me. If you don't love him, which I'm going to assume you don't since you couldn't answer that simple of a question, why can't you just be with me?"

"First of all, you know I don't qualify love for every person in the same way," I said. "Second of all, you didn't immediately leave your boyfriend for me, and you didn't even mention him for an entire month and a half! Tell me, why did you two break up?"

"Don't change the subject."

"I'm not changing the subject. I'm having a conversation, and you're being unreasonable."

This was like putting water on a grease fire. I regretted it immediately and started looking around for something to smother her with—I mean it, not her, it—the fire—yes. She exploded. I knew better than to tell someone who was upset that they were being unreasonable, but I had done it anyhow, and now she was in a tirade. I tuned in and out to her wailing, waiting for the wrath to subside. When she finally calmed down we were on our way back to the dorm room.

Then I made obnoxious decision number two. I texted Sophia, because we had plans the next day, and told her Summer had surprised me. I told her I wouldn't be able to make it and would contact her later. Her response was understanding, if a bit terse. This was unprecedented for me—not even I would have been okay with this situation if I were Sophia. I had started to wonder what it could mean when I felt someone jab me in the side. I turned to Summer, her eyes expectant, a small fire still burning in them.

"Did you hear me?" she asked, starting to rise back up into a rage.

"I'm sorry, no, but if you would like to repeat yourself, I would be more than happy to answer you," I said.

She glared at me, apparently trying to decide if I was mocking her or not.

With a roll of her eyes, she asked, "Do you want me to go home? I'm flying on miles, so I think I can change my flight. If need be, I can call my dad—he flies so often they'll do it."

"No, I don't think you need to go home. I would love to show you Seattle, but you're going to have to calm your business. I will not have every day of our vacation turning into a large fight. And there is a chance you might also have to play nice with Sophia," I said.

"Who's Sophia?" Her eyebrows furrowed.

"She's the one you've been yelling about for the better part of two hours."

"*You're dating a girl!*" she cried and threw her hands in the air.

We were outside my dorm in the small courtyard. There was a moderate amount of traffic, and they were all looking at Summer. I pulled her off to one side, refusing to take her inside until we fixed this.

"Well, yes. Why does it make any difference?"

"It makes all of the difference!"

"*How?*" I said, exasperated.

"I don't know, it just *does*. I thought it was just some guy, and I might have to wait for you to be done with him like you were supposed to do for me, but it's a girl. I thought I was the only girl in your life. What am I supposed to do now?" She buried her face in her hands.

"You wanted me to just wait for you?" I asked, confused and stunned, while my voice came out disgusted.

Summer pulled her head up, her eyes moist at the corners. "Well, obviously not logically, but yes—somewhere deep inside—I wanted you to wait for me," she said.

"Why didn't you give me any inclination that you intended to break up with the boyfriend?"

"I hadn't intended to. I don't know. I'm just selfish, I guess. I took for granted that you would always be there, loving me. We broke up because he started hitting on my sister."

"So you didn't even chose me over him? You just came here because he wasn't an option anymore?" I crossed my arms over my chest. The story was only getting better and better.

"It's not like that. I love you, and that scares me. I didn't feel anything like that for him, but it was easier to use him as a shield than to face you."

I couldn't think straight, and I couldn't process this information.

"That was really shitty of you," I blurted out, turning away from her to look at the sun going down.

"I know. I'm sorry," she whined. "It looks like I'm going to pay for my mistakes, though. Can you forgive me? I'm stupid and sorry it took me a month after you left to figure it out."

"I forgive you, but I'm still hurt. You're right, I'm with someone now and you've missed your chance," I said with an air of superiority and then turned to sit on one of the benches lining the courtyard.

She came to sit next to me, carefully not touching me. I felt lost. She was so close and finally wanted what I had wanted, but now I wasn't sure what I wanted. If she were going to stay in Seattle, would it make a difference? I knew it would. Despite the pain in my heart, I loved her, and if she were going to stay here I would try to make it work.

We sat in the courtyard for a long time, both of us looking sad and confused. Most of the time I looked at the ground, but when our eyes met she would look away. I could see the tears glistening in them. I knew this couldn't last all week, so I swallowed my pain. I reached for her hand resting on the bench between us. She finally looked at me, and I pulled her into my arms. She fit so naturally that it hurt more.

"I really am so sorry," she sobbed.

"I know."

After her tears subsided, I stood up and pulled her to her feet.

"Okay, once we go inside, there will be no more of this. No more arguing, no more fighting. Therefore, if you have anything else to say to me about this, you should say it now," I said quietly.

"I don't want to meet Sophia. I can't handle meeting the person who's worth not being with me for."

"I understand, but then you'll have to entertain yourself while I'm with her."

"My flight is on Thursday. Will you go with me to the airport?"

"Yes, I will," I told her then paused. "I still love you."

I brushed a strand of hair from her face, and she turned away from me.

"Don't do that. It makes me want kiss you," she said.

So I made possibly dumb decision number three.

I brushed her hair back again. She turned to me, hurt in her eyes, but mine were soft and understanding. I had wanted nothing more for so long that it just seemed inevitable for my lips to end up on hers. I took half a step forward to close the small space between us, and gently placed my lips on hers.

Kissing Summer was nothing like kissing Sophia. Where Sophia's kisses held passion and fervor, kissing Summer was tender and sweet. Her arms stretched up around my neck and mine wrapped around her waist. I felt my eyes well with tears. I broke the kiss and pulled her to me so she wouldn't see. I loved her so much, but I knew she would leave again soon. I would be ripped open, having no one else to blame but myself.

I pulled my head back, after I could control my face and looked in her eyes. I kept Summer close to my body. We breathed in rhythm together. I inhaled deeply, and she sighed. I led her inside and up to my room. I opened the door and looked for Alyssa, but Summer told me she was spending the break with her family. I was going to have to have a serious discussion with Alyssa about her tactics. Exhausted, Summer and I laid down together as we had so many times before, and I fell asleep.

Chapter Twenty

Even though it was unexpected, I was happy to have Summer with me. I wasn't naive enough to believe everything would magically work itself out, but I was delusional enough to push everything aside to be dealt with later. She had never visited Seattle before, so I took her on a true tourist excursion. We collected shells on the coast of the Sound in the morning. I showed her the lay of the city from the Space Needle in the evening.

The best part for me was, even after everything that had happened, we were best friends again. Hanging out and having fun like nothing had happened to touch or change our relationship. This is what I wouldn't be able to live without, and it was what made me want to be with her all the time. On the other hand, the part of her that reared its head the first day was the part that made me scared. What if we tried a relationship and it didn't work? Would I lose her forever?

I knew it was the perfect time for me to introduce her to Noah. There were few things more important than the guy best friend's approval. He had already met Sophia, and they got along nicely enough. I called Noah to set up a diner date for the three of us. He was hesitant to agree but eventually relented, and we met at a restaurant on the water front.

Summer and I arrived at the restaurant to find Noah already waiting in a booth for us. We walked up to the table. From the first look Noah gave me, I knew he was going to be difficult.

"Noah, this is Summer," I stated as we arrived at the table. "And Summer, this is Noah." She was standing closest to him and stuck out her hand.

"Sup?" Noah queried half-heartedly, not even meeting her eyes.

"Noah," I scolded with one word.

"It's okay," Summer said to me and dropped her hand. "It's nice to meet you, Noah. I heard a lot about you. I'm glad you've been here for Penelope when I couldn't be."

At this, he looked her full in the face and narrowed his eyes. I pulled her to the other side of the booth and gestured for her to slide in first. After she sat down, I glared at Noah as I took my seat. He sat back and pouted.

I turned to Summer and smiled, and she shined right back at me. I was going to ignore Noah until he decided to behave better. I grabbed my menu and opened it in front of me and Summer. She beamed at me again and asked if I wanted to split something with her. I shook my head. I was hungry from walking around again during the day.

As Noah watched us interact, I sensed his attitude change. I don't know what he thought she was going to be like, but apparently she had surprised him. Summer noticed Noah's relaxation, and she took my hand under the table and squeezed it. She began to let go, but I laced my fingers in hers.

"So, Summer, why don't you tell Noah about your love of *The Last Unicorn?*"

This movie, though barely passable in my opinion, had been Summer's favorite movie since she was a child, and Noah was also a die-hard fan of the animated story. With the shared love of a bad movie they were off and flying, and Noah reverted to the man I had come to know as Summer's personality won him over.

I left Summer to explore on her own on Wednesday. I had a date with Sophia, and we were going to spend the day together. Despite how much I loved Summer and how confused my head was, I was ecstatic to see Sophia. I wanted to confirm that things really were okay between us. I had plans for us to just hang out in my room, doing the things we normally did, like talking and making out.

Summer left in the morning to go explore downtown, and I began to get ready. I took a shower and put on a comfortable but flattering outfit. There was a knock at my door around two, and I flung it open all smiles and eagerness. I was met by an unpleasant looking Sophia and generalized bristliness.

"I want to go out," she stated as soon as she saw my face through the open door.

"Okay... hi." The smile faded from my face. "Let me just get my stuff," I said. I grabbed my purse from the bed, and then we headed out.

I made a tentative reach for her hand, brushing it slightly, but she didn't make any move to take mine. I just let my hand fall back to my side. Her attitude was not looking promising. I followed Sophia, as she obviously had a plan all laid out. We ended up at 10AM Somewhere. This was not too shocking as it was fairly common knowledge that I loved breakfast above every other meal.

We sat opposite each other in a booth only a tad bit sticky with the remains of syrupy child fingers. I made to wipe the sticky from the table but felt Sophia's gaze boring into my head. I turned slowly to look at her and sure enough she was shooting eye darts at my forehead.

"I thought you would have called or texted me if you had changed your mind on wanting to go out with me tonight," I said, exasperated. "You didn't have to come just because we set this up before Summer got here."

"Okay, just know that I tried. I really did. I didn't want to add more burden to you than you already had with Summer being in town, but it has come to my attention that you go out with Summer a lot, and you two, from what I have heard, look very much the cute couple. I would like to know, before I'm made a fool of, if you intend to continue a romantic relationship with her."

My eyes narrowed. "How do you know we go out all the time, and who told you we're a couple?"

"Penelope, I grew up around here. I know it's a big place, but I still know a lot of people. After we started dating, I told everyone. I was quite proud. Now I'm answering a lot of questions which, frankly, aren't anyone else's business, but it has made me a bit crazy!" Her tone grew in desperation and annoyance as she went.

"You told people about me?" I asked, batting my eye lashes, quick to avoid another public scene in this all-too-familiar venue.

She laughed in spite of herself. "How do you always do that? Pick out the oddest thing from what I say, and cling to it for dear life. Of course I told people about you, you're quite hot and fun to be with."

I giggled. "I'm sorry you were worried. I don't intend on having a romantic relationship with Summer. I do still love her, and I think I always will, but she's only here for a week. I like being with you. Things with Summer will always be complicated for me. I think it's only fair for you know that right off, and I won't stop being her friend."

"You like me?" she said, playfully mocking me in tone and expression. "But seriously, I can accept your relationship with her as long as you're always honest with me. I *cannot* handle being lied to."

I was saved from responding by the waiter who came to take our order. Sophia ordered what I ordered; she liked to try my favorites, and today was no exception.

After receiving our drinks she looked at me and said, "I'm still waiting for you to agree to my terms. I need you to be honest with me always and about everything. I'm not normally a jealous person, but the thought of you with her, hiding things from me, is enough to make me want to be proficient with a sword."

"I'll be honest with you, if that is what you want," I said.

"It is," Sophia said.

"I kissed her," I said, waiting, with squinted eyes, for the grease fire to erupt but it didn't.

After a few seconds, I opened my eyes fully to look at her. She was watching me most curiously.

"Is she the reason you shy away from conversations that are truthful but hard?" she asked.

I had never thought about it, but it was mostly family members who got all but riotous when the truth was uttered. I was instinctively protective of Summer and insulted that Sophia assumed she was responsible for my fear.

"No, Summer has nothing to do with it. Please don't talk about her, you don't know her. I've never had a truthful relationship that didn't involve explosions, or an untruthful one for that matter. Summer can sometimes be hard to handle but my family has done more damage than she ever will. When it comes right down to it, I have also been known to explode from time to time when the truth is something I don't want to hear."

"Then I have one further request: please don't explode at me. I can handle a lot of things, but explosions are not something I'm rated for. I'm sorry all of your relationships have been volatile ones. Hopefully we can change that," she said, sincerity evident in her voice. "Now, I won't say I don't care that you kissed her, as I do, but we haven't talked about being exclusive. As much as I would like to, I cannot stake claim to your lips." She reached her hands across the table and held them out for me to put mine in them, and I did. "Thank you for being honest with me."

I nodded at her but didn't know what else to say. I knew we hadn't talked about being exclusive, and I wouldn't have kissed Summer if we were exclusive, but I expected her to be less practical. The silence stretched between us. She rubbed the back of my hand with her thumb.

"I want to ask you something," she said, breaking the silence with ease. I met her eyes. "And I don't expect you to answer until after Summer is gone. I understand things are going to be different as long as she's here, but I *would* like to make our relationship exclusive. This is not solely because of Summer, though the last few days have made me realize exactly how deeply I care for you. It's something I was thinking about before she got here. I want you to be with me and only me."

I was glad she didn't expect an answer right away. I wasn't sure I had the ability to properly analyze what I truly wanted until Summer was gone. I needed time to sort through things on my own. And what I meant by "on my own" was I needed Noah and at least one pint of ice cream. I felt like I was stuck in limbo. Sophia was understanding and passionate, while with Summer there was so much history and things were so easy when she wasn't being unreasonable. However, Summer had hurt me, and we had poor communication at best.

I didn't have much to say after Sophia's question. I was trying to sort my thoughts into piles, but really I was just making more of a mess. Sophia had cleared her mind and was much more at ease now. The tension in Sophia's body, which had been present since she showed up at my dorm, had melted away. We separated our hands when the food arrived, and I pulled myself from my mind so I could be at least partially good company.

Chapter Twenty-One

THE SUN was setting by the time we left 10AM Somewhere, and it was drizzling from the gathering clouds. We walked down the street to a frozen yogurt shop. It really wasn't warm enough to eat anything frozen, but if I waited for it to be hot, I might miss my chance entirely when I went home for the summer.

Oh, my god. I have to go home for the summer break. Wait, it might not be so bad. If Summer and I can make things work, we could be together for three months. But then what do I do about Sophia? I really like her, and it could be love. I don't know. Is a quasi-long distance relationship with the woman I for sure love worth giving up a shot with someone who hasn't been given a proper chance? I could love Sophia.

I was being dragged along in Sophia's wake and only resurfaced from my thoughts when she tugged on my arm. She was standing in front of me, holding open the door to the yogurt parlor. I smiled at her, hoping she wouldn't ask too many questions, and kissed her cheek on the way in.

We got a medium cup of birthday cake flavor to share, both of us fans of strawberries and brownie bits on top. We walked back to Sophia's car and climbed in. The drizzle had stopped, but it was still a bit cold. She turned on the heater to keep us warm, though we both had jackets on.

"You want to go somewhere?" she asked and wiggled her eyebrows at me.

Yes! Back to the way things were. "Sure. What did you have in mind?"

She looked at me significantly but didn't say anything else. Turning on the car, she began to drive us toward the campus. I assumed we were headed for the dorms. Hopefully, Summer would still be out exploring or things would get awkward fast. But Sophia turned the car, and we ended up at the library.

It was spring break so no one was there when we got out of the elevator on the fourth floor. I dumped our trash and grabbed Sophia's hand in mine. She turned to me and stuck her finger to her lips. I remained silent as she led me to the group room in the back corner of the library. She turned the handle and swung the door open, pulling me inside the room behind her.

I made to turn on the light, but her hand stopped mine from reaching the switch. Sophia crossed the room and closed the blinds overlooking the study area. As quietly as she could, she pushed the table to the edge of the room against the wall. I was looking at her quizzically when Sophia grabbed me and pulled me to her.

I wrapped my arms under hers and clasped them behind her. She brushed back my hair with her hands as she looked into my eyes. She stared at me for a moment, her eyes greedy and wanting. I leaned in to kiss her. She tasted like strawberries and chocolate.

It became clear to me that Sophia had more on her mind than just making out. I felt uneasy, but I didn't know why. With every kiss, she seemed to get further and further from the place where I was. She was impassioned, bordering on desperation for something I couldn't grasp, and I was simply happy and content to just be with her as we were. I couldn't quieten my brain enough to fall into the moment like she had.

Why am I not feeling like she's feeling? I love kissing her but I don't feel a sense of urgency like she seems to. I know I like her, and I want what she wants. Maybe there's just something wrong with me. Maybe I'm just nervous. That's it. I just need a second to calm my nerves.

"Hey," I said into her lips.

"Hmm?" she responded, not stopping.

"I think I need a drink of water." I pulled away from her.

"What?" she replied.

"I just need a drink. I'll be right back."

I slipped out of the room in search of a water fountain before she could say anything else. Sophia's face hadn't been the most pleased one I had ever seen, but I couldn't be concerned. I needed to think. I needed to calm my rising panic.

Why can't I do this? It's not that I don't find Sophia attractive. On the contrary, I find her stunning actually. Maybe it's because we're in a public place. Or maybe it's because I hoped this would happen with Summer.

I hit myself on the forehead. It was time to stop that train of thought in its tracks. I was not going to sit here and begin comparing the two of them when I still couldn't be with Summer. Sophia was my option for a long-lasting, fairly uncomplicated relationship.

Besides, the only reason Summer is here is because her boyfriend was a jerk, not because she chose me. I'm just the next in line to her. Well, I'm not going to stop my life on her whim. And yet here I am, standing in front of a water fountain instead of back in the room with Sophia.

I should have quit while I was ahead. I had become incensed with myself. I had been standing at the water fountain for at least five minutes, but I turned around and marched back to Sophia without so much as a sip.

I was tired of waiting. I was tired of putting my life on hold or changing my plans because of Summer. If she was more reliable or caring, she would be going to school here with me.

It's her fault I even met Sophia in the first place. I'm moving on tonight. I will find that part inside of me that feels the passion Sophia does. I will do this for me and for us.

I entered the study room and ignored Sophia's look of concern and generalized disgruntlement. I pulled her to me and picked up where we had left off before my trip to the water fountain. I would either feel what she felt or pretend. Either way I wasn't going to stop this from happening. If Sophia wanted this then so did I.

We left the library two hours after we arrived. In that moment, I would have taken Sophia's offer of a monogamous relationship. She was so happy. I loved being around her in general, but after our time in the library, she seemed different—or maybe I was different. Either way, our relationship was changed, and I knew I had to return to my dorm room and my best friend, whom I loved despite some obvious issues. Things would change again for me when I saw her again. I knew myself well enough to know that.

Sophia drove me back to my dorm room and got out of the car. I didn't know if Summer was in my room or not, so I told Sophia it was for the best we not risk the fight that might break out if they did meet face to face.

She nodded, her jaw tightening. "Please think about what I asked you at dinner. I want to be with you and only you. I would like it if you chose me even though she's here, but I understand if you can't."

Sophia pulled me to her and crushed me in a tight hug. I wrapped my arms around her and squeezed back. We stayed that way for a little while. When she released me, I met her with a kiss. A sweet goodbye kiss turned into more. Sophia's need bordered on desperation as she held me to her. I pulled back to look at her. Sophia placed her hand on my cheek and rubbed with her thumb.

"No matter what happens in the next few days, you will remember me," she said then climbed into her car without looking back.
I walked up toward the dorms and turned to wave at her, but she didn't look as she drove off. When she turned the corner, I trudged back up to my dorm room with a great mix of emotions flowing inside of me.

Chapter Twenty-Two

I REACHED my dorm room and flung open the door. Summer was sitting on Alyssa's bed, surrounded by shopping bags and wares.

"Did you know you could spend an entire day in Pike Market and not notice the time until they start closing the shops?" she mused as I walked through the door.

"I did know that," I replied, only barely glancing at her. "I've done such a thing on several occasions. Did you see the gum wall while you were there?"

"I glanced at it, yes, quite disgusting as it were." She feigned a proper air and made a face. "But I took this one for you."

She thrust her phone toward me, holding it so that I could see a picture of her with her tongue dangerously close to the wall—all of the gum far from the spot she had chosen.

"Aw, how sweet. You were going to lick bricks for me?" I joked.

"Well, I wasn't going to put my tongue close to anyone's chewed up gum, so that's what you get!"

I laughed, and she smiled at me. She scooted over on the bed, pushing her purchases aside, but I chose to sit on mine.

She eyed me then said, "Sorry, just thought you might be cold and want some extra body warmth."

I returned her gaze. "Why?"

"Why would you want my warmth, or why would you be cold?"

"Why would you assume I would be cold enough to need special heating?"

She halfway turned and motioned to the window with a nod of her head.

"You were spying on me?" I asked, feeling incredulous and a tad embarrassed, though I didn't know why.

"No, I was looking for you since you left me alone all day."

"Did you enjoy what you saw?" I asked nastily, turning to anger to stamp out my other emotions.

"Trust me, I regretted it when I had to watch you two tongue each other down like it was your last day on Earth," she said.

"Had to watch, my ass, you could have looked away."

My emotions fizzled away. I would not have this fight, unable as I was to sustain my anger. My emotional capacity already spent elsewhere and far too depleted to deal with her jealousy. I was still trying to sort through how I felt about what happened in the library. Summer knew I was with someone. She knew what was likely to happen if she chose to watch us.

"I couldn't look away and still imagine she was me. I needed the visual. I just held my hand in front of my face and blocked her from my view. I would have held up my phone with the picture of me at the wall, but I was facing the wrong way in it," she said, sticking her tongue out.

I laughed in spite of everything and flung myself onto my back, staring at the ceiling. It was only a moment before I felt her hands on the bed. When I didn't say anything, she climbed in next to me. Why did everything have to come at once? I was okay with not having options.

She snuggled up to me, and I felt her head on my chest. I looked down to kiss the top of her head but she was already looking up at me. Our lips were so close together.

"Kiss me like you kissed her, and *then* tell me you don't want to be with me," she pleaded, frown lines creasing her forehead. "Don't peck me like I'm your sister or only a friend. You said you loved me just a few months ago. Are things so different now?"

"I'm not going to kiss you," I said. "You're jealous because you saw me with Sophia. I will not kiss you because you're going to leave and go back home tomorrow, and then God only knows what will happen."

"Kiss me because you love me and I love you." She propped herself up on her elbow. "We're supposed to be together. I see that now. I was stupid when I let you go in December, and I won't let you go now." Her face hovered just above mine. "Kiss me," she whispered.

I stared into her green eyes, the depths of her staring back at me. I knew her so well in some ways, but there was still so much to learn. I thought about how badly I would have taken hearing about "the boyfriend" every day, or worse, seeing them together. I felt sympathy for her. My heart ached for the pain I had caused her. The pain we had caused each other.

"I still can't be with you," I choked.

"I know."

My mouth found hers as tears trickled down my face. My arms encircled her, clinging to someone who meant more to me than I could fathom. I loved her so much it hurt, but the thought of passing on a chance to show her hurt even more. Even if it was only for one night, I wanted to hold her and kiss her. I was confused even further as Sophia entered my mind, but I pushed everything out and focused on Summer. I kissed her like I had always wanted to.

Her hand caressed my face, and when she felt the tears, she wiped them away with her thumb. She pulled away and said she was sorry as she pulled me to her chest. I didn't know what to do. I was exhausted and clung to her as tears escaped my eyes. She ran her fingers through my hair, and I fell into deep asleep.

In the morning, I woke with Summer next to me. I brushed her hair out of her face and watched her sleep for a minute. I didn't want to be too creepy, so I nudged her. She stirred slightly then her head snapped to me, her eyes mostly closed. She cuddled up to me and buried her face between my arm and the bed.

"I don't want to go home," she said into the sheets, her voice muffled.

Turning, I wrapped my arms around her but did not say anything. I wanted her to stay with me, but I knew she couldn't. I wanted to be with her, but knew we couldn't do long distance. I would have room to think without her around to intoxicate me. Holding her in my arms, we stayed wrapped together until we had to start getting ready to go to the airport.

We climbed out of bed, and she changed in the restroom. Searching the room for the remains of her scattered clothing, I found two shirts and a sock and stuffed them in her bag. She emerged dressed for the trip, and I grabbed my clothes and went in next.

"So, are you still determined not to be with me?" I heard her ask through the door.

"Are you still going to be living so far away?"

Silence. I opened the door and walked out into the room. Summer was sitting on the edge of the bed looking at her hands, folded in her lap.

"Summer, listen. We can't do long distance and you know it. We're not even good long distance friends. That's what got us into this mess."

"I know but I want you. I want to be the one to make you happy."

"Then talk to me. Keep talking to me until summer break, and we'll see what happens."

She still didn't say anything.

"Well?"

"I recluse without you there. I'm actually really unhappy at school, and it makes me quite depressed."

"And don't you think it would make even more sense to talk to me then?"

"Logically? Yes, but unfortunately I'm not a purely logical beast. But I will try."

I wasn't going to push her into more. It *was* news to me that she felt depressed. She hadn't told me anything in the last few months to indicate anything. I assumed she was having the time of her life and didn't have time for me.

Noah had borrowed his parent's car and came by to take us to the airport. He hugged her goodbye, and they exchanged numbers. Maybe she really would try. She collected her boarding pass, and I kissed her goodbye at security.

Chapter Twenty-Three

NOAH AND I rode back to my dorm in silence. My head was running a million miles a minute trying to sort through the last week. Noah made a detour at a grocery store, and I waited in the cold car for him. I was beginning to feel numb on the inside; I might as well be that way outside as well.

He came back out with a few bags and climbed into the car. I looked at him with the most desolate face I could muster.

"I know, I know," he said. "I'm working on it."

I looked back out the window as we drove. He pulled into a parking spot at my dorm and climbed out of the car. I crawled out and began to trudge toward my room.

How am I going to fix this? What if she keeps her word this time? If she does, what do I do about Sophia? I still like her and want to see where things might go. Is that worth not being with Summer? Should I hold out from a real relationship for a long distance whatever-my-relationship-with-Summer was? What the hell am I going to do?

I unlocked the door and pushed it open. Alyssa was sitting on her bed, and that added even more emotions to the pot. We still hadn't resolved what I had begun to refer to as her treachery and betrayal. Noah nudged me from behind because I was still blocking the doorway; I had stopped dead. I slithered onto my bed from the foot of it and laid face down, smothering myself with my pillow. I heard Noah move into the room and sit with Alyssa on the bed opposite mine.

"Are you going to start this, or are we?" Noah's voice was clear but gentle.

I knew I had no choice, but I wasn't going to give in that easily. I was in full sulk mode.

After a bit of silence, he said, "Fine. Alyssa, you're up."

She inhaled sharply and exhaled slowly. "Okay, then. Penelope, I want to talk about my involvement in the Summer situation. I was out of line with the way I acted when I met Sophia. I was so focused on trying to make your happy ending happen that I didn't realize it was changing right before my eyes. I hope you can forgive me. I promise to butt out, and I won't talk to Summer anymore."

I listened intently, and while this didn't make her behavior okay, I could at least tell she was truly sorry for her actions. I heard some shuffling, the rustle of paper bags and something else entirely and then Alyssa moaned. My head flew up from my pillow to see what was happening. Alyssa was happily nomming Vegan Honey Apple Cinnamon Raisin Walnut Low Fat No Sugar Added Ice Cream, also known as the most pretentious ice cream ever.

"Why does she get ice cream?" I cried, incredulous.

"She shared. Do you have something to share?" replied Noah.

"You want me to share? Fine." I turned and fixed Alyssa with my gaze. If this was how it was going to be, I would systematically work through all of my emotions until I was empty, starting with anger. "You know, you could have at least tried a little with Sophia." Irritation radiated through my words. "It's not like your being obnoxious was going to change anything except for our relationship. I don't need you adding your baggage to this train ride through hell. She hasn't done a thing to you, and sympathy hate isn't flattering, especially since I don't hate her. And what in your head snapped and made you think you could talk to Summer behind my back and try to arrange my life for me? What kind of messed up—"

Noah held out his hand to stop me, and I glared at him. He reached into his bag of goodies and pulled out a pint of Sassy Elvis ice cream. My anger ebbed, and I thrust out my hand for it.

He laughed a little and said, "This isn't your favorite, it's mine. I just wanted you to move to the next emotion. You've worn out that one, and I would like Alyssa to still have a butt at the end of this. She doesn't deserve all of your anger, so we'll come back to it after we've headed down the right road."

"But you didn't share! Why do you get to have ice cream?" I crossed my arms and huffed.

"Oh, you want me to share?" He batted his eyes and gestured to himself dramatically. "Okay then."

He put the lid back on his ice cream and stood up. Alyssa sniggered between bites, and I instantly felt apprehensive.

"I like Summer," Noah began and started to pace the small space between the beds. "But I also very much enjoy Sophia. They are different in many ways, but that in no way diminishes their personalities in comparison to each other. If anything, it makes it even harder to compare the two. Luckily for me, neither are packing what I'm interested in, so I don't have to choose and can simply be friends with both of them."

He took a bow to wild applause by Alyssa, and all I could do was sneer. He sat back down with Alyssa.

"How am I supposed to share if you just said it all?" I whined, playing for my ice cream.

"Oh, I by no means said it all. I just blanketed the entire topic—you are the one who needs to dissect it."

"Don't you think I've been *trying* to dissect them? My feelings, I mean. During every spare moment, between every breath, I've been trying to figure this all out. She was so perfect, but then the other one came along, and now I just don't know."

"That last sentence was as clear as mud. When you're talking about two women you can't only use pronouns." Alyssa pointed her spoon at me, and I pointed my eye daggers at her. She held up her spoon and made a sweeping motion, indicating that I should continue.

"I want Summer. I've wanted her for what seems like forever, even if I only just realized it. It tore me apart for her to brush me aside for a boyfriend even she admits was only a distraction. She's so selfish sometimes, but so perfect much more of the time. She knows me, and she understands me." I stood up and began to pace, my hands gesturing without my being aware of it.

"But with Sophia, everything is new. She's strong when I don't expect her to be, and she's calm when most people wouldn't be. She's like a rock in the ocean, and I'm clinging to her for survival. I don't know if that's fair or not, but sometimes I feel like she's keeping me from downing, and I don't want to let her go. And I could love her. I don't know yet, but she seems to want things that I don't or at least not like she does. We had sex yesterday, and I still don't know how to feel about it, especially since I had to come back to my dorm room with Summer."

Both Alyssa and Noah exploded at my disclosure of Sophia and I's sexual escapade, but I held up my hand trying to stifle the noise so I could finish.

I plopped back down on the bed and looked at my two friends. "And I'm mad Summer came here, and I'm mad she left. I'm hurt because she abandoned me to come here by myself and none of this would have happened if she hadn't. But I love her, and I will see if she hangs onto her promise to keep in touch this one last time. If she doesn't, I will commit myself to Sophia, and I won't look back. I can't play this tug-of-war, using myself as the rope, for the rest of forever."

Without another word I stuck out my hand for my ice cream, and Noah obliged by putting a pint of Milk and Cookies ice cream into it. I held out the other hand and was granted a spoon. But my hands simply fell to my side before I could take a bite and I began to cry. The weight of the last week finally fell in on me and I collapsed with it. Noah abandoned his ice cream and flew to my side. He set my ice cream on the small desk and took me into his arms.

I slumped against him and sobbed. I felt Alyssa tentatively rub my leg and my back. I couldn't be angry with her anymore—I didn't have the strength. I turned to her and threw my arms around her neck. Yes, she was wrong to try and arrange my life, but I could forgive her easily enough once I knew she had meant well and promised not to do it again.

She petted my hair and made odd cooing noises at me, which sounded like a sick and dying bird. After a couple of times, I couldn't stop myself from laughing. I turned to Noah, and he was looking at her with unadulterated bewilderment. His look sent me into hysterics, and Noah followed suit. Alyssa tried being offended, but soon she fell into a pile with us, fits of laughter consuming us all.

After the laughter had died down but we were all still piled together, Noah cried, "Hey, wait! What the hell were you saying about Sophia?" I was unable to answer because I was laughing again.

Chapter Twenty-Four

THINGS STARTED really well with Summer. We would text every day or every other day, and on the weekends we had lengthy skype calls. I began to see a way we could work things out despite the distance. Sophia was understanding at first but grew tired of waiting for an answer. She wanted me to herself and made her sentiments known quite often.

I should have known better than to hope, but one thing was different this time than other times—Summer kept up a pretty constant dialogue with Noah. I would begin to tell him about something I had talked about with her, and he would respond with, "Yeah, I know." At first it was a little maddening, but then I figured it had to be a good sign.

But all of the effort in the world didn't keep her attached—our text conversations went first. I remembered her talk about depression, so I would ask her if everything was okay, but I would get either no response or "yeah, everything's great" with no elaboration. During our skype calls, she would act like everything *was* fine, but they too began shortening.

By mid-April we were in communication black-out. I felt the all-too-familiar twinge of heartache as I listened to her voicemail tell me she was unavailable yet again. On the second Saturday she didn't answer my skype attempt, her Facebook relationship status changed to "It's complicated." I felt torn apart again and vowed to myself this would be the last time. If she was done, then so was I.

I knew what I needed to do—I had vowed it in front of Alyssa and Noah. I was going to commit to Sophia, and that would be that. I called her immediately after reading Summer's status change.

"Hello?" Sophia answered on the second ring.

"Hey, where are you?" I sat up straighter in my chair.

"I'm finishing a paper at my house."

I pursed my lips. "How much more do you have to do?"

"Not much, and I have all day tomorrow too. Why, what's up?"

"I want to see you. You want to meet me somewhere?" Something in me began crying that I was moving too fast, but I ignored it—probably butterflies, anyway.

"I can come get you. It's pretty cold outside today. Are you hungry?" I heard the smile in her voice.

I supposed the abruptness of my phone call gave her an impression of what was happening, or it could have been all in my head.

"Sure, I could eat." Although I wasn't totally sure that was true, my stomach was starting to tie itself into knots.

"Okay, give me half an hour, and I'll be there."

"Sounds great."

"Okay, bye."

"Bye."

I flung the phone down on the bed as tumultuous emotions washed over me. *I know what I'm doing,* I chided myself. *I know I was hoping this would end differently, but I knew it wouldn't. She always does this to me. Sophia has been more than patient, and it's time she was rewarded. It's decided.*

I changed into something more appropriate for cooler weather but was too fidgety to sit still. Tidying the room while I waited for Sophia to arrive, I almost jumped out of my skin when she knocked. Plastering on a smile, I threw open the door. She smiled back and I drew her into a hug before she could notice anything was amiss. After inviting her in, we sat on the bed together.

"So," she said, cutting straight to the point and opening her hands in an invitation to speak.

"So," I replied, feeling the beginnings of cold feet. "I've made a decision."

"Really?" Her voice was skeptical, and her eyebrows shot up.

"Yes," I said firmly and clasped my hands together as I clamped down on my emotions. "I'm not going to wait for Summer." *Anymore.* "I want to be with you and only you." I was staring at my lap, afraid of her reaction. If she rejected me, I would lose them both.

Yet when she spoke, she sounded happy. "Finally!" she cried.

My head popped up to look at her and I barely caught a glimpse of her face before her arms encircled me and squished me to her. I smiled into her neck, and soon we were kissing with a renewed vigor familiar to me from months before.

I called Noah that night and told him my news. He seemed happy for me but also reserved. He asked a lot of questions about Summer and why she had stopped talking to me that I simply couldn't answer. After about a dozen irritated sighs, he dropped the subject and chatted with me about Sophia.

After we were committed, things moved quickly. Sophia wanted me to meet her parents and spend the first two weeks of summer here in Seattle with her. I was happy at the thought, but wary of her parents and staying in their home. She talked to them about me staying with them and they had agreed but insisted on meeting me soon.

Sophia's parents were a special breed not often encountered where I was from. Where I grew up, I knew a few who had come out but usually not to their parents. Of the few who did tell their parents, many changed schools, got sent to live with relatives or—worst of the all—were sent to "pray-the-gay-away" camps. Sophia's parents not only knew she was gay but were also really proud of her in general—no stipulations.

I met Sophia's parents in the first week of May. At first, I couldn't comprehend what Sophia was playing at when she suggested I meet her parents. She didn't want me to pretend we were just friends and she had already told them I was her girlfriend. I was prepared for them to reject our relationship before they even knew me. She couldn't comprehend that this was my experience with parents of homosexual children; it was what I knew.

Sophia's parents were some of the nicest people I had ever met. They invited me over for a cook out on the grill. After dinner we played card games together. When it was time for me to leave, Sophia had to drive me back to the dorms. Her parents walked us to the front door, and her mom gave me a hug. She told me she was glad she got to meet me, and her father gave me a smile and a pat on the shoulder.

Sophia and I walked out holding hands. I was in shock. I heard

Sophia's mom coo to her dad about how cute we were as we reached the car. I was at a loss to process the past several hours. We drove in silence for a few miles, Sophia's hand resting on my knee.

"You were really quiet tonight. Is something wrong?" she asked, squeezing my knee.

"You have the nicest parents ever," I said, staring at my hands in my lap. "I know you told me that they knew you were gay, but where I come from, the way your parents act is not a thing. Some parents say they are ok with their child being gay and they love them anyway, but you don't see any of them acting the way your parents do. Letting the children hold hands or kiss or anything like that."

"I'm sorry your experience with acceptance of gay people has been so poor. What are your parents like? How did they respond when you told them you were bisexual?" She moved her hand from my knee to the steering wheel.

"Well, remember, it's only my mom, and I didn't exactly tell her. I knew any kind of coming out would be treated with such distaste that it would be pointless, anyway," I said, my fingers intertwining with each other. "So, I changed my status on Facebook." I threw hands up a little then let them thud back down into my lap and smiled at her broadly. She glanced from the road to me, frowning. "Which I guess was not the best way to broach the subject." I sighed. "But when she found out, she told me 'it was just a phase' and I would get over it—which is the main reason I haven't invited you to my home for the latter part of the summer."

"What are the other reasons?" she asked, glancing at me again as we turned into the parking lot for my dorm.

"I'm sorry?" I replied, confused.

"You said your mother's intolerance is the main reason you haven't invited me." Her tone was like that of a parent explaining something to a child. "What is the rest?"

Do I have another reason I don't want Sophia to come home with me for the summer? Of course I do—her name is Summer and I can't give Sophia that reason, matter of fact, it's the only reason I can't give her even though it's the truth.

"I just said it. I don't think there is another reason," I said.

She pulled into a parking spot and turned the engine off. She turned in her seat to look at me. "Even if said subconsciously, there was still truth in it. If you won't say it, I will. Summer is the obvious problem. I know it won't be easy. I know there is an excruciatingly real possibility that I will actually have to meet her, but I'm prepared for it. As long as you're still sure you want to be with me, I will help you wade through the slog of going home. I will pretend we're friends if that is what it takes with your family, but I feel in my heart I'll regret sending you home by yourself. I don't want you to miss out on seeing your family this summer, so we can't stay here the whole time."

"You would pretend we weren't together so I could take you home with me?" I asked.

"Yes," she said.

"Does that mean you don't trust me?" My voice was dubious.

"It's not that I don't trust—"

"It's okay," I cut her off. "I don't trust me with Summer, either. Something about her makes me weak, and I don't want to be anymore."

"I wasn't going to say I don't trust you." She eyed me, and her voice was more forceful. "I don't trust her. And don't roll your eyes at me—it's not cliché! She is one of the most conniving people I have ever not met. I don't even have to know her to know she would try to manipulate you over the summer and leave you heartbroken again when school started back. You've always been there for her, and she thinks she can just pick you up and drop you at her convenience."

I remained silent. There was a part of me that wanted to scream at Sophia and tell her she was wrong, but another part knew why she thought those things. Summer could be selfish, but she was much more than that. Sophia would never know her like I did. But after the last time communication had ended, I couldn't bring myself to defend her whole heartedly.

"You don't know her," I growled.

"I'm sorry. You're right, I don't," she replied matter-of-factly, putting her hands up between me and her to stop me. "I just hate the thought of someone hurting you. I couldn't stand losing you, especially to someone like her. She will never be as good as you deserve."

This was the reason I could not fight with Sophia. Even if I felt indignant and maybe a little combative, she was caring and seemed to only want to see me happy. I turned to get out of the car, and she did the same to kiss me goodbye. I cuddled up to her and we shared a long hug.

"I'm sorry if I over stepped my boundaries. I didn't mean to upset you," she said after a bit. "I forget sometimes you can't see Summer the way I do."

"I understand where you are coming from, but you don't see all of her. You only see from a limited perspective." The sound of my voice was muffled with my face against her neck. "But I appreciate that you want to look out for me. I want to take you to meet my family and have you save me from myself."

Sophia sucked in a great breath of air and released it slowly.

"That is, if you still want to go," I said, worried.

"I want to go with you everywhere you go. I'm concerned about your family situation, but I'll follow your lead."

"I'll have to call my mom and work out the details, but I want you to go with me. I don't want you to think you're in competition with Summer."

"I am, though maybe not directly but with your idea of her, which is turning out to be a much more formidable foe."

Chapter Twenty-Five

SOPHIA HAD gone home after Alyssa had shown up the night before. I had crawled into bed exhausted and thinking about what to do. It would be true that I wanted Sophia to meet my family if I had a nice, accepting family, but as it stood, I wondered if taking her with me wouldn't just make matters worse. I had asked her already, though, and I couldn't back out. Plus, I knew if I went home without her, the Summer-Penelope tragedy saga would continue.

By the end of the week, Sophia had booked a ticket on the plane with me. I hadn't had the heart to tell her I hadn't spoken to my family yet. I didn't want her to think I didn't want her to go with me. She also brought up the idea of us living together the following semester. We applied for a dorm room in the middle of the second week of May after Alyssa had walked in on us at a particularly inopportune moment. I won't even go into how awkward the subsequent conversation was.

I was excited and a little scared. This was my first relationship to reach the living-together level, so a little apprehension was to be expected, right? Things were still more or less the same on the physical front of our relationship. I still felt a little panicky in the moment but I was getting better at pushing it aside. She had wants that I didn't understand, but I wanted a normal relationship. I had grown up with sex pushed into my brain from every direction for so long that I had expectations for myself, not to mention the ones Sophia seemed to have of me.

By the end of the second week of May, I knew I was running out of time. The crunch for finals was already starting, and I needed to make sure the way was clear for Sophia and me. On Saturday morning, I called my mother to arrange for Sophia to come with me on summer break. I was still unsure of how to broach the subject, so I figured direct was best. She already knew Sophia was my girlfriend, anyway—we had made it "Facebook official"—and she was already none too happy about my staying in Seattle for a couple of weeks after school.

"Hello?" My mother answered the phone.

"Hey, Mom. How are things down there?"

"Good. How is school going?"

"It's going well. Finals are coming up soon."

"Oh? Well, study hard."

This was usually the extent of the conversations between my mother and me, but with the niceties covered, it was time to plunge straight in.

"Mom, I want to bring Sophia with me for the second part of summer break," I said.

"And how is that supposed to work?" she asked, her voice sickeningly sweet and dripping with false curiosity. I knew whatever she was about to say was going to be simply to irritate or anger me.

"We both pack up our things and board a plane," I said, already annoyed with her.

"Hahaha. No, I mean how are you going to keep your two girlfriends separate if you bring them together in the same state?" Her voice was full of humor and goading.

"Seriously, Mom? Summer and I are just friends." I rolled my eyes and packed in as much annoyance as I could manage.

She scoffed. "Right."

"You know what? This is why I told Sophia her coming with me would be a bad idea. You can't handle the way I live my life like an adult so just forget it. I'll stay here the whole summer."

"There is no need to be hurtful. I try to keep up with you the best I can, but when all I get are updates on the Facebooks—"

"You wonder why you have to get updates from my Facebook? Maybe it's because conversations with you are so pleasant."

She had the audacity to sigh, like the conversation was driving her crazy. "I want you to come home, so if Sophia has to come with you, then so be it. You can't sleep in the same bed, though, and there will be *no* couple stuff in public."

"I respect your desire for us to sleep separately since it's your house, but we will do as we please in public."

The game was on. I knew PDA was a bigger deal to her than us sleeping in the same room, so I started to stack my deck. She pretended to consider this for a moment—the bargaining had begun. What was one willing to put up with or sacrifice so they could get what they wanted? In some cases, the amount of compromising that was involved made what you wanted unrecognizable once you actually got it, if you actually got it.

We finally settled after thirty minutes of back and forth. The ability to show affection in public was traded for being able to share my room. It helped to mention that Sophia could not sleep on the couch for a month and a half. We also agreed upon the fact that Sophia and I would not make out in any of the shared areas of the house in exchange for the right to make out in the backyard. Also, I was not supposed to tell Grandma and Grandpa, which I alone knew was a moot point. I hung up the phone after saying goodbye and went back to my room with the still-sleeping Alyssa. The reality of my decision hit me like a ton of bricks. I had mostly been avoiding thinking about it.

Am I really going to take Sophia home with me? Is this really a good idea? Does it even matter because I'm not sure if I'm going to see or speak to Summer? Maybe the smarter thing to do would have been to wait and see how the first part of the break went. Was this even my idea?

I buried my face in my hands to stifle a moan. Summer break was going to be the longest two and a half months of my life.

"Why can't you have meltdowns at a reasonable hour for once?" croaked Alyssa from her bed.

"Why can't you get out of bed before noon, like, ever?"

"Number one, it's the weekend. Number two, I plan my classes so I don't have to." She stuck her tongue out at me.

"Bah."

"Trouble in paradise?" she mused.

"I'm taking Sophia home with me for the break."

I have never seen Alyssa move so fast. She bolted upright in the bed and stared at me, wide-eyed.

"You're what?" She bit off the words and spit them out.

"I know, I know. Don't worry, I have my own inner monologue

telling me I'm crazy."

"Have you told Noah?" She reached for her phone instinctively.

"No," I said, launching myself from my bed onto hers. "And I don't want you to do it for me."

I grappled for the phone, and she shoved it in her lap while sitting cross-legged. I pushed her shoulder, trying to get her to fall to the side so I could grab it, but she snatched it up and scrambled away.

"I'm not going to tell him, okay? I was just wondering if you had talked this over with anyone before plowing ahead."

I chased after her regardless. I loved to wrestle, and she had responded appropriately to start a match.

"No, I didn't. I probably should have but it's too late for that now. I've already called my mom, and she's bought the ticket."

Alyssa froze and I yanked the phone from her. "Ha!" I held it up victoriously, but my amusement faded when I saw the look of utter horror on her face. "What?"

"You're going to stay with your mom?" Her face distorted with disgust at the word "mom."

"I don't have anywhere else to stay." I plopped down on the bed next to her and handed her phone back. "It'll be all right. I bargained with my mom. She'll be cool even if only to save face. She's one of those 'happy family' kind of crazies—wants everything to appear perfect, even if it isn't."

"And what about Summer? Are you going to see her while you're there?"

"I don't know. I mean, I want to mend my friendship with her if I can, but I need her to know how much she hurt me."

"I do not envy you the next few months, my friend." She patted me on the back then slid off the bed. She picked my phone up off the desk and handed it to me. "You should probably tell Noah. Better he finds out from you."

I wasn't sure why Noah would care as much as Alyssa seemed to think he would. She had me concerned. "Why?"

"Because he's your best friend, isn't he?" She was gathering her things to go take a shower.

"One of them, yeah," I said, as I pulled a "so?" face.

"Just call him." She walked out of the room to take a shower, and I stared after her.

Why was she so cryptic sometimes? She's acting like she had when she was talking with Summer on Facebook before spring break. My eyes grew wide, and I stopped, my hand on the knob. Noah had been talking to Summer when I had. He had known all of the news about her. Did he continue to talk to her after she had shut me out?

I hit his speed dial number and smashed my phone to my ear.

"Hel—"

"Do you still talk to Summer?"

"Uh—not as much as I used to."

"But you do?"

"She said she's tried calling you, but you haven't picked up. She wanted me to get involved, and I told her no. I don't want to be in the middle of this sick triangle of crazy."

Summer had called me the night I had applied for a dorm room with Sophia. Mad and upset, I hadn't answered, and she hadn't left a voicemail. Unsure if I was ready to be friends, I hadn't wanted to hear her excuses. I would forgive her with time, but I needed space. Immensely thankful all over again for the first two weeks of break, I looked forward to spending time with Sophia and her parents.

"Did she tell you about her new boyfriend?" I spat, feeling upset to the point of being sick.

"See, this is what I don't want to do. I have a friendship with her now, apart from my friendship with you. You knew I had her number, and you were happy we were getting along. Do you want me to stop talking to her because you're the one that said sympathy hate is bad, by the way."

I sighed loudly and with excess exaggeration. I wasn't mad at Noah; I was jealous. He could be friends with her if he wanted to.

"I appreciate you trying not to meddle. You can keep talking to her if you want, but please don't tell her what I'm about to tell you."

"Okay."

"I'm taking Sophia home with me for summer break."

"What!" I heard his voice fade and then a loud clatter; I was sure he had dropped the phone. There was a bit of scuffling then he said, "You're going to take her back to meet your family? But they're awful."

"I know they are, but I can't do this alone."

"Are you sure that's the best reason to do this?"

"No, but I'm doing it, anyway."

Noah breathed in like he was going to say something, but he kept silent.

"You won't tell her?"

"I wouldn't drop this bomb on her if you paid me. I'm not going to do your dirty work. You should warn her, though, if you have any hope of being her friend at all."

"I don't know."

"Do you want to go out today?"

"I can't. I need to study. My first final is in a week."

"At least let's go to lunch."

"Okay. I'll meet you at 10AM Somewhere in thirty."

"Okay, bye."

"Bye."

I wasn't sure I needed to analyze this further, but I knew I needed to unload more than this one decision on someone. We hashed out many things over deliciously fluffy pancakes. I was going to fix things in my friendship with Summer, talk through the physical side of my relationship with Sophia, and try not to let my mother ruin my summer vacation. After two hours, I hugged Noah goodbye and returned to my room to study. I certainly didn't want to end the semester on a bad note, grades-wise.

That night, I had a dream about Summer. We were together, and things were simple. I was unsure if feeling emotions during dreams was normal, but it had always happened for me. The dream pushed my love for Summer to the front of my mind and therefore the front of my heart. I woke up aching for her, missing our closeness. I would have sworn I could smell her perfume. I huddled on my bed for a while but pushed myself out eventually, needing to start my day. I analyzed everything about a million times. After my morning tea, I was angry with my subconscious. I had an amazing thing with Sophia, and all I needed to do was get over Summer once and for all.

Chapter Twenty-Six

I SLEPT in until two o'clock in the afternoon the day after my last final. It was Friday, and I didn't have anything to do all day. Sophia was preparing for her last final, which was at six o'clock in the evening, and I promised to not bother her until then. We had spent a majority of the last two weeks apart, both of us studying. I had gotten over my anxiety about the momentum of our relationship, and I missed her. It was all I could do to keep myself from calling. Luckily, I could keep myself busy by packing up my things. I had to have my dorm room packed and ready to vacate by the end of the weekend.

Sophia was coming over on Saturday morning to take me and my meager belongings to her parents' for the first two weeks of the summer. Then we were headed to my mother's home to spend the rest of the summer. Sophia was concerned, especially when I told her about the compromises I had made to keep things running smoothly with my mom. She seemed to accept them, though, determined to make everything work. We would see how execution went once we got there.

Friday was the last day I would spend as Alyssa's roommate. When I woke, I was surprised to find her bed empty. She was usually the one who slept in, and she didn't have any more finals to take, either. I was hoping she'd at least be around for me to say goodbye. I reached for my phone to text her. As I groggily jabbed at the letters on my phone, the door to our room opened.

"Good morning sleepy head," Alyssa said as she walked into the room.

She was carrying several bags, and a delicious smell wafted from them.

"Good morning," I mumbled, pleased she hadn't left for good . "What's all that?"

She crossed the room and set the bags on her desk. "Well, since it's our last day as roomies, I thought we could have breakfast together, but seeing as how it is now way past breakfast time, I had to go pick it up from 10AM Somewhere instead of the cafeteria. I was going to throw things at you if you weren't awake when I got back."

"Good thing I'm already awake, then," I said, smiling broadly, my head the only thing visible from the mass of blankets.

She threw the pillow from her bed at my face.

"Hey," I fussed.

"I was just checking. You could have been talking in your sleep." She giggled.

"Indeed," I replied, throwing back the covers and climbing out of bed. "So, what did you get me?"

"Your favorite." She pulled several Styrofoam containers from the paper bag and placed them on the desk.

"No wonder my mouth started watering." I walked over to the desk, staring at the containers longingly.

"Ok, but first I just want to say, I have loved having you as a roommate," she said, holding out my food ceremoniously. "I'm sad we won't be living together next year, and I will miss your parade of women through my front door."

I laughed, looking up at her face. "I wouldn't exactly call it a parade."

"Maybe you're right." She handed me my meal. "More of a side show then?"

I lightly slapped her arm after taking the food from her. We sat at the desk to eat.

"When do you leave?" I asked, my mouth full of food.

"Tomorrow night. What about you?"

"Either tomorrow morning or afternoon, whenever Sophia is ready." I shrugged, gesturing with my fork.

"You'll have to keep in touch this summer. I would hate to have to hunt you down," she said. "I want to know how this trip of yours goes."

"We'll it's not truly goodbye. You still have to help me with RAVPA next year." I batted my eyes at her and ignored the comment about my summer break.

"Yeah, I know. It's just change. It always makes me sad and excited at the same time."

"I know what you mean."

Saturday morning was one of the first clear mornings in a while. Seattle's usually overcast weather was said to clear for a period of time in the summer—I was excited to be able to see it. I was getting my first glimpse of what a beautiful summer I could have in Seattle when Sophia arrived.

"Hey," said Sophia as I opened the door. Her eyes darted around the room, assumedly looking for Alyssa.

"Hi," I said, smiling.

"Hello," said Alyssa from the bathroom.

"Hi, Alyssa," said Sophia, her smile a chagrinned one. "What are you going to do for the summer?"

"I'm just going home. Nothing awesome, nothing fun," Alyssa called.

"Don't let her fool you. She's got a boy at home," I said, louder than strictly necessary. "They've been together since Christmas break."

I wiggled my eye brows at Alyssa as she emerged from the bathroom.

"You have no room to mock my love life. At least mine isn't terribly complicated."

"Mine isn't complicated," I protested, making a face.

Both Alyssa and Sophia laughed, Sophia's a little less happy and a little more scornful.

"Well, anyway, I was just gathering the last of my things, so I'm going to go get some food before I hit the road. Give you two love birds some time to yourselves," said Alyssa as she sauntered out the door.

Sophia pushed it closed behind her and turned to me like a lioness on the hunt.

"Hmmm. Alone time—what ever will we do with that?"

I realized this was what she wanted when she had looked around for Alyssa. "Arts and crafts?" I joked.

"I didn't bring any glitter," she said, pulling me to her.

"Oh darn," I said as I kissed her.

Sophia tried to hold me to her. She obviously had something specific in mind for us to do, but I danced away from her. I feigned looking around the room for things of mine which had not been packed yet. Sophia came up behind me, grabbed my waist and pulled me back to her.

She kissed my neck, and I knew I wasn't going to be able to deter her. I liked Sophia so much. I loved being in a relationship with her—simply being around her made me happy, yet I couldn't get into the mood to do what she wanted to do.

I would throw myself into the moment as much as I could only to find myself at best only interested in making her happy and at worst being confused and upset, close to a panic attack. American society had shown me from a young age what it meant to be a woman. Sex was in the media every time I turned around, so how could I be so bad at it?

Confusion and doubt would enter in.

If everyone else wants this but I don't then there must be something wrong with me. I'm not normal. No one is going to want a relationship with someone who is so broken.

Then I would get upset.

I mean, it's not like I pride myself on being completely normal, but having sex isn't one of those things people just give you a free pass on. Everyone expects sex in a relationship regardless of if I'm with a guy or a girl.

If the wheels in my head were turning too much, Sophia could tell, which she did right then.

"Where are you right now?" Sophia asked as the last thought crossed my mind.

"I'm here with you," I replied, blinking to make sure my eyes weren't glazed over.

"No, you're not. I'm here. You are somewhere else entirely." She held me with one arm around my back and brushed my hair from my face.

"Oh," I said, my face scrunching at being caught. "I might have been contemplating how the media is largely to blame for unreachable societal standards."

"Oh, is that all," she said, rolling her eyes and releasing me.

Sophia went over and sat on my bed, staring at me.

"Yes?" I asked smiling and feigning innocence.

"Come here," she said. When I didn't move she held out her hand and added, "Please."

I thought we were in for a conversation about my lack of focus, but instead she smiled at me ruefully, and pulled me onto the bed with her. Apparently she wasn't going to be dissuaded so easily today.

Chapter Twenty-Seven

"I'm going to miss being able to do that all summer," Sophia said as we cuddled.

"But at least we'll be able to do this all night," I murmured into her neck.

"Yeah, but it's not quite the same, is it? I rather enjoy the fun that precedes the cuddling."

I just sighed and nuzzled her neck. Her hand stroked my back.

"I have a little confession to make," she said, her other hand holding mine and intertwining our fingers. "When Summer was here, I took you to the library on purpose." I turned to look up at her, but she kept her eyes from mine. "It's not that I hadn't been wanting to already, but I had been waiting for an inclination that you wanted to also, but you never tried to move us in that direction. I got a bit jealous and was convinced you were getting all you needed from Summer." I pulled my hand from hers and used it to halfway pull myself up to look at her fully; her eyes met mine. "So I planned out our first time, and it was amazing. At least, I thought so. But after she left, you still didn't commit to me, so I was afraid you regretted it—that is, until you called."

I sat up fully and gave her the dirtiest look I could manage. "Are you kidding me?"

She sat up too. "Why does it matter? Do you regret having sex with me?"

"That was my first time! Not only *our* first, but *my* first, period."

Her eyes grew wide. "Seriously?"

"And Summer and I have never done anything beyond kissing—even when she was angry after seeing us say goodbye that same night."

Her eyes narrowed; the change would have been comical in any other situation. "She saw us together?"

"Yeah." I gestured with both hands to display my indignation at the irrelevant question.

"You should have told me," she said, her face solemn.

"Excuse me? You basically just told me you had sex with me as some sort of ploy, and you're the one getting upset? I don't think so," I replied.

"Are you upset that we had sex?" she asked again.

"I didn't say—"

"Ok then. It's in the past now, so let's move on." She waved her hands to indicate clearing the air and smiled at me.

Sophia was displaying a side of herself I hadn't seen before. She was incredibly sensible and sometimes emotionally detached, but her calm reveal and disregard for my emotions was too much. I felt betrayed and tricked. She was right—it was in the past, and I couldn't go back and reclaim my first time, but I could be pissed as hell. It was the first day of us spending the next two and a half months together, and she had started it with that.

"I think you need to leave now."

Well, that wiped the floor with her pragmatism *and* her smile. "Seriously?"

"Do I look like I'm joking?"

"But you're supposed to come back to my parent's house with me."

"You should have thought about that beforehand. Get out." I stood and walked to the door to hold it open for her.

She quickly pulled herself together and strode toward me.

"I don't want to leave without you. I didn't think you'd take it like this." She reached up to touch my face, but I turned away from her.

"Then I guess we both learned some things today." I gestured to the open door. She walked through it, and I snapped it closed behind her without a second glance.

I needed to reconcile this with myself. The next two months were going to happen regardless of my astonishment and hurt. For someone who was supposedly so big on honesty, she certainly had thrown me for a loop. I sat on my bed and stared out the window at the beautiful day going to waste. I could have been having a blissful day with my girlfriend, but no. I forced myself to evaluate the conversation which had led to her dismissal.

It's true—I didn't put the moves on her. I didn't feel a desire to have sex with her. I still don't. It's not like I don't find her attractive. Maybe my libido is just messed up. How would I know? I have no basis for comparison. Before Sophia, I thought everyone was as "take it or leave it" about sex as me, but she obviously was not. Is her having an ulterior motive for sleeping with me any worse than me pretending when we do?

I flung myself face first into my pillow and cried out in frustration. The stories I had heard all my life were about how your first time was supposed to be unforgettable. It was supposed to form some mysterious link between you and the one you had sex with. The truth was, I felt no such link, and as mad as I was about the whole situation, when I boiled it down my anger was at her attitude and high-handedness more than it was about the actual act.

Sophia, Noah, Alyssa and I were all supposed to be going to the pride parade in the afternoon. It wound through several streets ending near the Space Needle. After waffling between going and not, I decided I would go regardless of our argument and called Noah to have him pick me up. I filled him in on the argument as we drove to the meeting place for members of LGBTQA, the site of our float and he was appropriately appalled. We agreed not to talk about it after we exited the car. I didn't want to ruin the experience for myself or him.

I pushed Sophia from my mind as I opened the door and the sounds of so much joy filled my ears. The excitement was palpable. We found our club's float and helped with last minute prep, including but not limited to glitter body paint.

"Are you ready for this?" Noah asked me, positively radiating with anticipation and glitter.

"Oh, yeah! Is it your first too?" I asked, looking around and marveling at how many people were there.

"Aw, how cute," he chided me with a reproachful look. "No."

"Bah! Don't give your looks," I said, waving my hand at him and jumping up and down to get a better look.

From behind me, I heard a squeal and turned just in time to be tackled my Alyssa. Like being knocked down by a boney puff of pink, she slammed into me and I smashed into Noah. We all tumbled to the ground, the only one giggling was Alyssa.

"Hi!" she cried. "I'm so excited."

I tried to push copious amounts of tulle out of my face but it seemed to come from all angles. Alyssa climbed off of me and I was able to get to my feet and see her fully. She was dressed completely in pink, complete with a tutu and wings. It sent me into fits of giggles.

We were waiting for the pride parade to start. Our LGBTQA club had a float in the parade, and we were going to walk along with it. I held up a flag, displaying my pride in a community where I finally felt I fit. I had never seen so many people come together to support being different.

When I saw all the people who belonged in such a wonderful group, I started to wonder to myself if we should really be considered different at all. Who got to make the rules and the social norms? Plenty of animals in the wild have engaged in homosexual acts; some could even change sexes depending on what the community needed.

The crowd was amazing. Everywhere you looked there were people dancing and having fun, yelling and enjoying themselves. I walked along with the LGBTQA float while Noah ran around, high-fiving people in the crowd lining the street we were marching down. Toward the end, Noah marched with me, in all his topless glory. There was a block party at the end of the parade. I hoped to see Sophia but she didn't show. Under exploding fireworks, Noah and I promised each other we would march together in the pride parade every year.

I called Sophia after we left. Though I was still plenty angry, I was in a much better place to have the conversation we needed to have. She answered cautiously. I told her we needed to talk and Noah would drop me off. Noah and I had loaded my things into his car after he had agreed to drive me to her place. I showed up a few short minutes later, and I waved goodbye to Noah. Her parents were in her house, so we sat on her porch to talk everything out.

In the end, I made sure she knew I was still plenty angry, and she apologized many times, though I'm sure it was only because I was so angry. I told her we were going to make the best of it, and I was going to work at forgiving her.

Once things were settled, she carried my belongings inside and up to the guest room. We hadn't really discussed sleeping arrangements at her house, but putting me in a separate room was probably for the best, especially now. I had argued sleeping arrangements with my mom for the sake of not conceding everything to her and the fact that there was no guest room there. We would see how the situation played out once we were there.

Her mom was in the kitchen preparing dinner. She smiled at me over her shoulder and called her hello. Sophia sat at the table, and I followed suit. I didn't really have anything to say to Sophia, so it didn't bother me to sit there. Her mother chatted with us about school and finals, asking me about my degree and future plans. I wasn't feeling like chatty Cathy, but I answered her politely—no sense in being rude. Sophia pulled a deck of cards from the hall closet, and we played games until dinner was ready.

I lay awake that night trying to acclimate to the new surroundings. The first night in a new place was always a sleepless one for me. Around 3AM, the door to my room opened silently. Wide-eyed and more than a little terrified, I pulled the blanket up under my chin and stared at the doorway. The ambient glow from the hallway's night light was the only illumination. After what seemed like forever, Sophia's shape was framed in the doorway.

"Oh, my god," I rasped, my lungs filling. I hadn't even known I was holding my breath. "You scared the hell out of me."

She giggled and crossed the room to sit on the edge of the bed. "I'm sorry. I didn't mean to. I was trying not to wake you if you were asleep."

"And what were you going to do if I was asleep?" My voice was accusatory.

"Go back to my room." Her voice challenged me to call her a liar.

"What do you want, Sophia? I'm trying to make the best of this, but I'm still not happy with you, and I don't feel like messing around."

"Wow, I was coming to see if you wanted to talk more. I want to fix this. I don't want to fight anymore. I feel like a jerk for hurting you."

I sighed and reached my hand out to hers. "I forgive you for your plotting. I don't regret being with you, and I don't regret my first time being with you. I wish the circumstances had been different, but I guess it doesn't matter now."

She tentatively reached for me. I allowed myself to be wrapped up in her arms, and truthfully, it was relaxing to be back on more familiar ground with her. After we reconciled, the first two weeks of summer passed amicably. She snuck into the guest room in the middle of the night almost every night, sometimes just to sleep, but sometimes she wanted more.

All too soon it was time for Sophia and me to journey to my home. I knew there was a huge possibility for this all to go very wrong, very quickly, but there wasn't much I could do about it. We were already trying to make the best of a bad situation.

Chapter Twenty-Eight

Sophia and I arrived at the airport to my mother's idea of a "funny joke." She had invited Summer to come to the airport with her. Summer didn't seem surprised by Sophia accompanying me, which was going to require me to slap my mother later. As I walked past the security check point, Sophia close behind me, Summer ran from the crowd of people and threw herself onto me. Her arms encircled my neck in a hug. She squeed and gushed at how happy she was that I was home.

I knew her enthusiasm was only for show. Even if she was happy to see me, she was really seething on the inside. Thankfully, I was saved from the decision of hugging her back or pushing her off since my arms were full of luggage. Sophia had gotten sick on the flight, so I was the bag handler. Summer eventually let go and turned to retreat without so much as a glance at Sophia. I was not going to let Summer get away with her little display of rudeness and jealousy.

As she was turning from me, I said, "Summer, this is Sophia, my girlfriend."

Summer turned around, looking incredulous, but quickly hid it under a plastered-on smile.

"Hi, Sophia," Summer said while sticking out her hand. "I'm Summer, Penelope's best friend."

I have to give large props to Sophia. Although she was feeling sick, she didn't miss a beat. In two steps she had covered the distance which separated her from me and by proxy Summer. She stuck out her hand to shake Summer's while putting the other one around me, pulling me to her side. Summer's eyebrow rose, and she dropped Sophia's hand after one shake.

From the background strolled my mother, who enveloped me in a hug. Sophia released me and took a half step away.

With false sweetness, my mother whispered into my ear, "No public affection."

To which I replied, in a voice like a whisper only in volume, "You brought this on yourself."

She recoiled from my venomous rage, obviously only beginning to comprehend the gravity of the situation she had forced on everyone. I dropped my carry-on at Summer's feet and just looked from her to it and walked away. Pulling my luggage from the carousel, I fumed at the audacity of my mother. Turning to my mother, I thrust the bag into her hands along with one of Sophia's carry-ons.

I took Sophia's hand under the frosty gaze of Summer, who had indeed picked up my luggage, and marched out of the airport to the many glances of on lookers. I no longer cared about the bargaining my mother and I had done on the phone. My mother knew the relationships between Summer, Sophia and I were tenuous at best. She had made certain to test the limits by bringing Summer to the airport.

I had to slow my angry march to the car so I would not drag Sophia along behind me. Though she did not complain, I knew she still felt horrible. I let my mother pass us because she knew where the car was parked, but I did not see Summer, and I refused to look around for her. Once we arrived at the car, I opened the back door for Sophia. She climbed in, and I shut the door behind her. I walked to the trunk. My mother was loading the luggage into it and waiting for a word before she closed the lid. I stopped to look at her, my eyebrow raised, before shoving in the luggage I carried.

"I'm not your chauffer," she stated.

"Well, I guess you are today because if you think there is any way I'm going to put Sophia and Summer in the back seat together you have seriously lost your mind!" I roared.

I was enraged. I felt my face turning red. My mother opened her mouth to say more, but by that time Summer had made it to the car, so she plastered on her fake "happy family" smile and loaded the last of the luggage into the trunk. I climbed in beside Sophia and pulled her into my arms. She rested her head on my shoulder and fell asleep on the way to my mother's house.

I was still angry when we dropped Summer off. I was not going to wake Sophia to say goodbye. This situation was just as much her fault as it was my mother's. I simply grunted when Summer told me to text her later. When we arrived at the house, I woke Sophia gently. Her eyes opened groggily. I felt my mother's eyes on us through the rear view mirror, so I bent and kissed her. She kissed me back and then smiled. My mother huffed and then exited the car.

Sophia was horror struck. "I'm so sorry! I wasn't thinking!"

"No, it's fine. Her actions have nullified the agreement," I explained. "I cannot believe her! I really wonder what she thought she was going to accomplish. Enough, I'm done. How are you feeling?"

Sophia looked into my eyes, clearly trying to gauge where my emotions were erupting from.

"I'm feeling better," she said. "I could use some food, though."

"No problem. Let's get you inside, and I'll make you something." I smiled at her.

She gazed at me bemused.

"You're going to cook for me?" she asked.

"Well, yes. Why not?" I replied.

"It's wonderful." She smiled. "I've never had your cooking before."

This was true. You can't cook in dorm rooms, and Sophia's mom always had food ready for us when we were hungry. I smiled at her and pulled her close for a moment.

"Well, let me take care of you, then," I said as I kissed her on the top of her head.

I cooked Sophia a simple meal of grilled cheese and tomato soup (from a can with added spices). She ate heartily then asked if I would mind if she went to bed early, so I took her upstairs to my room. I opened the door for her, and as she looked in, her mouth fell open. I had completely forgotten to mention to her that my room was like a scrapbook.

She immediately started taking in every detail. There were pictures all over the wall not obscured by furniture. Some were of me ranging in age from infancy to current, but many more were of my friends. In hindsight, I would have removed or at least lessened the number of pictures with Summer and me. It was probably a little disheartening for her to see picture after picture of Summer and me laughing, posing, making faces and hugging, plastered all over my bedroom wall.

Instead of climbing into bed to nap, we spent the next 3 hours going over the photos on the wall. She was fascinated by the stories that went with them. We ended up both lying on my bed and laughing while I shared parts of my past. She really seemed to love hearing about my life. It was different for me to be with someone who needed or wanted to hear all of those stories instead of someone who had lived them with me.

Chapter Twenty-Nine

WHEN WE went down for dinner, Cooper had returned from wherever he had been, and I introduced them. He looked her up and down while her back was turned and gave me the thumbs up. I shook my head at him, giggling. My mother had made a brisket in the crockpot, and I stirred together mashed potatoes while Sophia perused the lower floor of the house. I avoided my mother's gaze. I was still fuming about her poor choices surrounding the airport debacle, and I didn't want to start another argument. I set Sophia between myself and my brother. At least I knew he wouldn't make the situation awkward.

After a quiet dinner, I pulled Sophia in the back yard with me. In the midst of the situation at the airport earlier, Sophia had not realized exactly how hot it was compared to Seattle. When we stepped outside, she let out a low whistle and began fanning herself immediately. I took her hand and walked with her among my mother's garden, which was doing surprisingly well in spite of the awful heat.

We walked until we were shielded by the house and couldn't be glimpsed from the back door. I pulled her to a bench sitting in the corner, but she resisted. She protested against the extra body heat, which would have compounded in the sweltering heat. I sat and patted the bench next to me, promising not to touch her.

"I'm so glad you came home with me," I said, and she turned to smile at me. "And I'm so sorry about the trash at the airport."

"Well, I can't really blame you, now can I? Though I thought you handled it really well. We work great as a team."

"I loved when you bridged the space between us to all but accost Summer with thinly veiled anger," I laughed.

This made her roar with laughter. It infected me, and soon we were both close to rolling on the ground. Despite the heat of being close, we ended up in each other's arms, tears rolling down our faces. After we calmed down and wiped away our tears, we stared at the flowers, illuminated by the last rays of light as the sun disappeared over the surrounding house tops. We stayed outside only a little after the sun had gone, as the mosquitoes came after us with vengeance.

We were exhausted from the plane ride. I went inside and gathered my things for a shower. When I emerged Sophia told me I had a text before escaping to shower as well. I crossed the room to my phone, curious but pretty sure of who had texted me. I opened the phone, only to have my thoughts confirmed. It was Summer, and she wanted to talk...alone. I texted back to tell her we were going to bed. I would let her know when I had time.

Sophia emerged from the bathroom dressed in pajamas which were not suitable for the heat of southern summer nights. I laughed at her long sleeved and pants ensemble while she looked at me dubiously. I closed the door and pulled her night clothes off then crossed to my closet and began to rummage for different clothes for her.

Luckily, she and I were close to the same size, so I threw her a pair of draw string shorts and stepped out with a tank top in hand. I crossed the room and helped her into the shirt. She sucked in air as the back of my hand brushed her side. When her head appeared from the top of the shirt, she looked at me with fire in her eyes. I stepped forward to kiss her, and things got heated.

Mid-make out session, my mother knocked on the door, and without waiting for a response, she opened the door. I had broken apart from Sophia quickly at the sound of the knock. By sheer force of will and lighting quick reflexes, when the door opened, we were no longer locked together. However, when my mother saw us both sitting on the bed together, her eyes narrowed.

"I brought some extra blankets so you could make a pallet on the floor," my mother said, smiling sweetly, though her eyes were still narrowed—the juxtaposition was truly creepy.

Her gaze swept from me to Sophia. I rolled my eyes at her.

"Can I show you something out in the hallway, dear? She'll only be a moment, Sophie. Why don't you start making your pallet?" she continued and handed the pile of blankets to her.

I stepped into the hallway after my mother and shut the door to the bedroom behind me.

"Her name is Sophia, Mom," I said.

"What do you think you are doing?" she seethed through gritted teeth.

"Get a grip, Mother. There is no way she is sleeping on the floor." I glared at her.

"You are crazy if you think I'm going accept this sin under my roof!" she hissed.

"It's not like I'm going to get pregnant!" I exclaimed.

We were arguing at the same time, most words lost in the jumble, but her last words slapped me.

"What?" I spat.

"You heard me. She will sleep on the floor, or she can go home."

"If she leaves then I leave."

"So be it!" she cried.

"Fine!" I shouted.

I opened the bedroom door and slammed it in her face, locking it behind me. Sophia was still holding the bundle, standing in the middle of the room. My mother began to bang on the door immediately. Crossing the room in only a few steps, I pulled Sophia into my arms, and the blankets fell at our feet. I turned my rage into passion to spite my mother. We kissed until the pounding on the door died away and the only noises were ours. I pulled back from her, and she reached for me with her eyes closed then groaned when I didn't return to kissing her. We had landed on the bed somewhere in the mist of our kissing.

"I'm sorry," I said.

"Sorry for what?" she replied.

"Using you to get back at my mother. I mean, I know she couldn't see us but whatever," I said.

"It's fine. You can use me like that any time." She smiled and winked at me.

"Ha, ha, ha." I looked up at her to see the fire still burning in her eyes, but there was no way I could do anything more than kiss in this room, especially with about fifty Summers staring at us. "And for getting your hopes up when nothing is going to happen in this house."

"We could pretend this isn't your house," Sophia said, tracing her finger up and down my arm.

I pecked her on the lips and decided an abrupt change of topic should do the trick.

"Summer wants to talk to me, just the two of us. I suppose if we're going to be leaving early then I should get that out of the way."

"We're leaving early?" she asked, shock lacing her voice.

"Sorry, I just assumed you heard our shouting match in the hallway."

"I did, but I figured it was all hot air. I never thought she might actually expect us to leave."

"Well, she probably won't, but that doesn't mean she never would. It depends on what wild hair is up her rear when she's making decisions. I'm sure I will have to deal with the backlash of the argument tomorrow, but until then I'm going take it at face value."

"So, you want to go talk to Summer tomorrow?"

"I wouldn't go straight to 'want,' but obviously the atrocity from earlier needs to be discussed, along with her appalling behavior, and there is no way it's going to happen in your presence."

"Okay. Can you take me somewhere where I can kill some time or something on your way?" she pleaded. "I don't want to be left here with your mom."

"Sure." I smirked at her. "I know I will say this to you many more times before we leave, but thank you for doing this for me."

She hugged me. "I couldn't imagine you doing this on your own. Growing up here must have been awful."

I shrugged. I was sure there were worse childhoods than mine, but I wanted to soak in the sympathies of my girlfriend instead of expounding on them. The one person who had saved me the most from the horrors of an adolescence spent with my mother was the same person I couldn't mention.

"Come on, we're both tired and could use lots of sleep," I said through a huge yawn.

Chapter Thirty

IN THE morning, we were the first up. Sophia was ready to finish what I started the night before, but I staved her off. We went downstairs to have breakfast. Biting the bullet, I texted Summer to tell her I would meet with her.

Penelope: I will give you exactly one hour for you to explain yourself.

Summer: Hello to you too.

Penelope: You don't get a hello after the nonsense you pulled yesterday.

Summer: Whatever. I did what I had to do. All's fair in love and war.

Penelope: If that's how you feel about it then why do we need to talk?

Summer: What time and where?

Penelope: God, I wish they made an eyeroll emoticon. Around two, outside your house.

My mother came down the stairs when we were almost done eating.

"Mom, I need to borrow the car today," I said drearily.

All she did was scoff at me on her way out to the garage.

"If you have something to say to me, then just say it!" I shouted after her.

A few seconds later, the garage door opened, and we heard her leave in the car. I was obviously not borrowing it—shocking. The only option left to me was to have Summer come and get me. Sophia wasn't too fond of this idea, but with my mother gone, she could hide in my room until I returned.

Penelope: So as you could have probably guessed things with my mother aren't great either. She won't give me the car.
Summer: Are you asking me to come get you?
Penelope: No, I was just going to cancel.
Summer: Don't be this way. You know we need to talk about this.
Penelope: 2 o'clock, don't be late.

Around mid-afternoon, Sophia was standing outside the house waving goodbye to me as I drove away with Summer. Summer took me to her parents' house, but we sat outside in the shade of her garage instead of going inside. The car ride had been silent with me refusing to look at her.

With no preamble, I began, "So, what the hell was yesterday?"

"I don't know what to tell you. You with her makes me crazy!"

"You don't have a right to be crazy over me anymore!" I geared up for the argument. "You are with someone! You think I don't know exactly when and why you stopped texting me? You knew if you kept in contact with me, I would have known what you were doing. It's so stupid because I know you think you are doing me a favor by protecting my feelings, but really you are just being selfish."

"I don't know what you're talking about," she said, genuine surprise on her face.

"Do you not know that we're Facebook friends?" I asked, insulted.

"*Oh.* I only changed my status so people would stop hitting on me at school and randomly on the Internet, not that it stops the ones on the Internet," she said, words rushing from her mouth as she comprehended my meaning.

"What? Why do people do that?!"

"Yeah, it was just a pretense. I didn't mean to stop talking to you, but every day that passed made the possibility of reconnection even weirder. I mean, how long do you have to wait before you can use the phrase, 'long time no talk' and it be applicable?" she rambled.

"You really should have kept talking to me," I said, shaking my head and putting my hand to my forehead. "How many times have I told you, I need communication? I need to know what you are thinking and how you are feeling, especially if you post something like a relationship change on Facebook. "

"I'm sorry. I didn't mean to worry you, but what would it have changed, really?" She tossed up her hands in defeat, but her eyes were pleading.

"I didn't tell Sophia I wanted to be exclusive until I saw your status change after we stopped talking."

"You and Sophia weren't exclusive before?" she asked.

"No! She wasn't my girlfriend when you were there on spring break. You know I would never cheat, even if it was only kissing."

"What? Then why wouldn't you be with me then and there?" Summer replied, her temper rising.

"Because you were going to leave me again when the week was over. I can't deal with this kind of break down every time we are apart. I need to be close, as in proximity, to the one I'm with. I can't handle long distance relationships, especially if this is how they work. At the rate things were going, we couldn't even maintain a long distance friendship." I motioned to myself and her several times.

"You're still my best friend." She looked at the ground, her expression sad.

"And you're mine," I said, placing my hand on her knee.

"Can you separate the two?"

I looked at her questioningly, not understanding what I was supposed to be separating.

"Can you keep being my friend even though you love me? Can you separate the emotions you feel for me?"

"I don't know." I sighed and removed my hand from her knee where my thumb had been running in small circles. I thought about the question and knew that even as I sat there, my anger at her was ebbing, and I could feel my love for her pushing through. "But I'm trying to."

She looked at me with pain and anger in her eyes then looked away. I knew what I said wasn't nice, but I needed to make a wall between us if I was going to make things work with Sophia. A wall that could block out my romantic love for her but still let me be her friend. Would such editing to a relationship be possible? I didn't know.

"What if things were different?" Her voice was strained and she still didn't look at me. "What if we weren't so far apart?"

"I don't want to play the what if game, and by next semester, it won't matter anyway."

"What are you going to do next semester?" She looked at me then, her eyes narrowed, her voice still laced with sadness.

"I plan on moving in with my girlfriend," I said matter-of-factly.

"Oh, yeah? So how is Sarah after yesterday?" She put way too much emphasis on "Sarah."

"Her name is Sophia."

"Yeah, whatever." She waved her hand at my words.

"Don't do that. Don't hide your emotions with petty insults and poor manners." I rolled my eyes at her and pushed up off the pavement.

I turned and walked away from her, leaving her sitting outside of her house. Going home may have been the perfect plan but for the slight hitch of her having picked me up. I wasn't too far from home, and I refused to turn around and walk back to her. I needed to get a grip on all the emotions rolling around inside of me. Yes, her childishness had been enough to make my walking away feasible, but I had simply needed a moment.

Am I really going to hurt her so I can make my life easier? If I have to try so hard to block her out, am I really in it with Sophia? Can you carry a torch for two people at the same time? There is still the problem of Summer and me being so far apart for most of the year now. She seemed different for a minute, but then I said what I said and she was back to being—whatever she was. I knew we wouldn't have the easiest time since we haven't talked in months. She's hurt, so of course she's going to lash out, and I only made it worse. I'm not the one who started the silence of doom, though.

I made it out of the subdivision and down the adjoining street before Summer pulled up in her car. I would deal with whatever side of Summer came out at me—this couldn't go on forever. She pulled next to me and let the car creep along as I continued walking.

"I'm sorry," she said loudly as the window rolled down. "Please get in the car."

"I'm not going to get in the car unless you give me your ironclad promise that we can discuss things like adults, without you acting like I'm personally accosting you every time I mention Sophia's name."

"Only if you promise to go with me somewhere. I need to show you something." She was driving on the wrong side of the road and waved as a car honked but went around her.

"You are going to get yourself killed." I motioned to the passing car.

"If you're concerned," she said, looking quite unconcerned herself, "then you should get in the car."

"I promise I will go with you."

"I promise I will try my hardest not to let my insane jealousy cause me to act like less than I am," she recited.

I stopped walking and the car stopped beside me. I looked into her eyes, and she looked back at me pleadingly. We stood there for a long moment. I wanted some type of relationship with Summer, even after all the pain—even if we continued to hurt each other. I crossed the front of the car and got into the passenger side.

Summer drove off in the opposite direction of her house. We were driving for about ten minutes before I asked where we were going. She told me it was a surprise and I would ruin it by asking questions. I frowned at her, hating surprises. She looked happier, and in the spirit of hopefully repairing our relationship, I sat quietly.

Twenty minutes later, we pulled up to a subdivision with high walls and a huge gate. It looked similar to many we had passed, marked only by Summer slowing the vehicle. She turned toward the gate and stopped to put a code into the keypad. The gates swung open, and I was transported back to the night of lights, remembering how hopeful I had been. Everything looked completely different not decked out in lights, but I would recognize it in any season. I turned to Summer, who was now driving at a snail's pace down the row of houses.

"I found a guy who goes to my school who lives in this subdivision. I convinced him to give me his keypad number," she murmured as I stared at her, mouth agape. "I come here all the time when I need to think or when my emotions are getting the better of me. The night of lights was the best night I have ever had, bar none. I just wish I would have kissed you then, instead of thinking you would be waiting when I was ready. I drive through these houses and imagine us living together. I know it's silly and kind of creepy, but I can't help it."

I continued to stare at her in disbelief. "I—"

"No," she cut me off before I could say anything, glancing at me only for a moment. "Please, I've got more to say, and if you talk, I may never say it."

I closed my mouth and continued to stare at her.

"In February, when I became single, I started the process of transferring to the Art Institute of Seattle. By the time I got home from spring break with you, the transfer was already accepted. I have been working on myself, trying to prove I deserve you once I got there. I was going to fight for you because I thought I had already lost you, but I need to know what you want me to do," she said.

"I can't make that choice for you," I blurted out, bewildered.

She glanced at me again.

"You have to. The only reason I would go is to be with you. I was stupid not to go with you in the first place. Again, I selfishly thought you would always just sort of be there. If you don't want me around, then you need to tell me. If there is no hope of making you love me and be with me, then there is no point."

How am I supposed to make this kind of decision? On one hand I have my nice and fairly successful relationship with Sophia. A relationship that won't survive the continual effects of Summer's presence. On the other hand I have my best friend–turned would-be lover–and no matter what kind of hope is coursing through Summer's veins right now to tell her I don't want her in Seattle will be a fatal blow to any relationship we might have, friend or otherwise.

"I won't make this decision for you. I will tell you, I have no intention of leaving Sophia. We work really well together, and to answer your question from spring break, yes, I think I might love her," I said. I wasn't sure I felt the conviction my words indicated, but they were strong even if I was weak.

"I'm not stupid. I know you brought Sophia with you so you would have protection from me. You brought her so she would be there waiting for you whenever you were out with me. I know, and I don't care. I still want to be with you. I have been and will continue to wait for you as long as there is hope, and you bringing her here is the biggest sign of hope you could have given me."

Summer was staring at the road. I could see tears in her eyes, and it killed me. We drove in silence through the subdivision one row of houses at a time. She stopped in front of one particularly nice house made of gray brick. She pulled to the side of the road and stopped the car.

"I love this house. This is the one I imagine us in. We would have a pool and a hot pool girl to clean it for us," she said, chuckling—never looking at me. "I want you to be with me. I don't want you to love Sophia. You loved me first, and I claim dibs."

I looked at my lap, not knowing what to say.

"I'm going to move to Seattle. If you don't tell me no, then I'm going to go and fight for you. I will not go quietly into this dark night. I'm going kiss you in front of this house like I should have months ago."

My eyes widened with alarm, not knowing if she meant right then or not. I looked at her while simultaneously pulling my head back toward the window, away from Summer. She was looking at me but hadn't made a move in my direction. I supposed she wanted to gage my reaction.

"Well, at least I know now what I'm dealing with," she said, folding her arms across her chest. "I should have known if you were committed to Sophia then you wouldn't have kissed me when I was staying with you. I just fooled myself into thinking you were more in love with me than your relationship was important to you."

She pulled the car back out onto the road.

"I will never cheat. A virtue instilled in me the day Clayton left me for you," I said.

"Such a gem, that one," she said. "I found him at work and accidentally kicked him in his balls." She made air quotes around "accidentally."

I smirked but didn't say anything. We had reached the end of the houses, and she turned to take us home. The ride home was quiet, but it wasn't uncomfortable. My mind was playing the same sentence over and over as I tried to process everything.

Summer's moving to Seattle. Summer's moving...to Seattle. Summer. Seattle.

At some point, the words stopped making sense and became just words that were repeating over and over again like a marquee sign in my mind. She took me back to my house and let me out at the curb.

"I'll text you later," she said as I opened the door.

"Okay," I said, minutely aware we hadn't actually resolved much.

I stepped out of the car and whipped back around to face her.

"You know you are going to have to meet her and play nice if we're going to hang out this summer."

"Well, I will let you know when I'm ready. Don't expect it to be in the next few days, but I will make an effort since I'm going to be moving and will want to spend time with you in Seattle too."

"Yeah," I said as I closed the car door behind me.

Chapter Thirty-One

THE FULL reality of the words became clear when the car door shut. It hit me like a ton of bricks as I was walking up the path to my house. Summer was going to be living in Seattle. *Summer was going to be LIVING in Seattle.* I dreaded telling this to Sophia. It was going to cause a fight for sure.

I was almost at the front door when it opened to Sophia silhouetted in the frame of the door. She pushed open the screen door to let me through. I was still running "Summer is moving to Seattle" over and over in my head, emphasizing different words of the sentence each time. I walked past Sophia without so much as a glance and headed upstairs to my room. I opened the door, expecting, in my obliviousness, to find Sophia there so I could talk to her.

When I found she wasn't, I turned on my heels, realizing she was the one to open the door, and found her behind me at the top of the stairs. I went over to her and put my arms around her. No matter how the rest of the summer went, it's not like it was going to get any easier once we got back to Seattle. Sophia hugged me back tightly.

Sophia asked, "Is everything all right?"

"Define all right," I mumbled as I let my head sag and rest on her shoulder.

"Are you hurt? Did she do something to you?" she replied.

"Well…" I began.

I took her hand and pulled her into my room, knowing that sitting down would be in short order.

"She didn't so much do something to me as she is going to do something to us," I said.

"Did she kiss you again? Because I'll…" she said.

Sophia started to turn like she was going to run downstairs and chase after Summer's car. I grabbed her hand again and pulled her to sit with me on the bed.

"No, she didn't kiss me. I wouldn't let her," I said, trying the ease her worry even though I was about to drop a bomb.

"But she tried!" Sophia raged. "I knew this was a bad idea!"

"Sophia," I said, my free hand reaching up to cup her cheek and gently turn her face to me. "Please listen to me and stop jumping to conclusions. I'm not trying to play the guessing game with you—I'm trying to tell you something important."

The weariness in my voice pulled her back to me. She looked into my face silently.

"Summer has just informed me she's transferring to Seattle next semester."

"What? Why is she so *evil?*" Sophia cried.

"She's not evil! She wants what she wants. Are you telling me you wouldn't fight for something you wanted as much as she fights for me?"

"I do. I fight every day. I fight for you against everything that she is—a memory, a friend and a lover."

"I know, and I've made my choice. We are not to blame for her choices, and more specifically, you are not to blame for any of this. You waited for me during a time when even I didn't know what was going to happen, and she failed me. I want to be with someone I can rely on, and that someone is you. I love you."

Sophia was still so caught up in the thought of Summer being near us on a fairly permanent basis, she did not respond straight away. She grumbled to herself a couple of times, and I began to worry that I had chosen the wrong time to tell her. Or worse, she didn't feel the same way about me. My feelings were not dependent on hers, even though it kind of stung. I continued to hold her as she fought internally with what I could only assume was her version of Summer.

It took nearly five minutes for her to calm down and process the whole conversation. Once she had, her head snapped up, looking into my eyes.

"Wait a minute. Did you say you loved me?" she asked.

My cheeks heated and I turned my head away under her intense gaze. "Yes. I *do* love you"

Her fingers reached to turn my face back to hers. She stared at me, emotions playing rapidly across her face.

"I love you too," she whispered, far different from the pragmatic voice she had used when talking about the situation a few moments ago.

She wrapped her arms around me and pulled me to her. Her mouth was on mine with unexpected passion, and things progressed before I could think about it. Sophia informed me there was no one home at my house, and there was no way I could deny the passion that reared within her. I didn't regret it, since our being together always made her so happy. How could I take that away from her in a moment which was so important to both of us?

We lay next to each other, our breathing slowing back to a normal canter. I was glad the house was empty. I loved seeing Sophia so satisfied and pleased.

"So much for 'never in this house.'" Sophia giggled and kissed me again.

"You got lucky," I teased and pulled back from her.

"Well, maybe I'll get lucky again." She winked at me.

I made a face of concern at her, only partially joking. "And what if you don't?"

She frowned but shrugged. "Okay."

I waited for her to say something—anything—else, but she didn't. I wasn't sure how to take her reaction, so I moved past it. We could cross that bridge when we came to it. When we both had gathered ourselves together, I pulled her downstairs for food. My mother was still not home, but Cooper came home while I was cooking, so I added some more eggs to the pan and we had breakfast for dinner.

I was cleaning the last dish when my mother strolled through the garage door. I motioned to Sophia to go upstairs, and once she was out of sight, I rounded on my mother.

"Are you ready to be an adult yet?" I asked her.

"That's a fine way to start a conversation," she said, her voice patronizing.

"You know what? I have nothing to say to you," I said, ready to argue. "It's you that seems to be the one with a problem around here."

She huffed and made to walk away from me, but I moved to block her way.

"I will not do this all summer," I told her. "You will talk to me and get the giant chip off your shoulder, or Sophia and I will leave by the end of the week."

"You don't have anywhere to go," she replied, her face a sneer.

"Contrary to your belief, not everyone is as hateful as you are. This is why I didn't want to bring her here, and this is why when I move away, you will never be allowed to come visit me. I'm sorry my personal life is such a *huge* challenge for you, but did you ever stop to think maybe I didn't *choose* to be this way?! Why would I *choose* to be at odds with most of my family if I was happy just being the way you wanted me to be?"

My mother was taken aback. It was fairly obvious she had not considered that I might actually have thought out the situations that would follow my life changes. She was also forced to consider my sexuality as possibly more than the "phase" she believed it to be. I had nothing more to say to her, so when she turned to leave a second time, I let her.

Sophia was in my bedroom, watching videos on my computer. She looked up as I came in.

"How did it go?" she asked.

I just rolled my eyes at her and flopped down on the bed. She came over and sat next to my sprawled body, brushing my hair from my face.

"I'm sorry things with your mom aren't easier. I know you want the support of your family. It's why you fight with her so much. If it didn't matter, then you wouldn't care enough to fight about it," she said.

I huffed at her. "Don't you logic me. I'm immune."

We went downstairs to cuddle on the couch and watch a movie, both of us falling asleep halfway through. I woke in the middle of the night, cold in the air conditioned house and from the absence of Sophia. The television was already shut off. I got up and blindly made my way to the bedroom, figuring Sophia would be there, but she wasn't.

My mind made more of an effort to emerge from its sleepy haze, trying to figure out where Sophia was as I walked back down the stairs. The whole house was dark, and I searched inside for her to no avail. I opened the back door to a rush of hot air. I walked to the end of the back porch and looked around the garden. Around the side of the house, in the corner where we had sat on the bench, was Sophia.

I walked over and sat next to her. Her face was set in a hard line, and she hadn't even so much as glanced at me. I took her hand in mine, but she continued to stare out into the garden, so I stared out too. I didn't ask her any questions; I just waited for her to need me. If she didn't, then that was okay, but I was there for her anyway.

"I don't know why she can't just leave us alone. She should admit defeat and bow out gracefully. This is going to turn into an all-out bloody war, and the worst part is, you're going to be the most affected by it," she said, squeezing my fingers. Her voice was harsh and came out like a growl. "I've even considered bowing out myself to save you the trouble of what I know is coming. I mean, you love her after all, but then you said you loved me.

"It began something in me which made me hate her. I resent her for having had your love first. She might have made the first mark on your heart, but she also hurt it first. I don't intend to ever hurt you. I know she's going to fight dirty, but I will fight back because you are mine now. Just know if you cheat on me, I won't be able to take you back because I know if she wins even once, then she will always win."

Once she was done, the noises of the hot summer night rose back up to engulf the silence. I took in everything she said slowly, trying not to misunderstand anything.

"I have no intention of doing anything with Summer, but if she kisses me then I have no control over it. I can only control how I react to her actions. I will keep our lines of communication open and honest, but you have to talk to me too, and not well after the fact. It wasn't okay that you had an agenda and didn't tell me about it until months later. I don't want this to be the end of us. I want to be with you, and I want us to be happy."

The night turned to dawn as we sat on the bench, occasionally looking at each other but mostly staring into the garden lost in our own thoughts. As the light of the sun touched the flowers in the backyard, I rose from the bench and pulled Sophia after me into the house and up to bed.

Chapter Thirty-Two

MY MOTHER was moody the rest of the week, but she came into my room on Saturday, and we talked while Sophia was in the shower. She agreed to try and be more pleasant but still denied that she did anything wrong at the airport. I took what I could get. She calmed down after our talk but still wasn't nice or friendly toward Sophia.

Sophia and I explored my home town for the next two weeks. I showed her where I had gone to grade school and the different places I liked to eat. It was nice showing her my past, especially since I got to choose what she saw. For instance, I didn't take her to the park where Clayton attacked me, but I did take her to my favorite donut shop. I liked mixing the past and my future. It was different. Where Summer already knew everything first hand, Sophia got a different view—my view.

By the time the end of June was upon us, I missed my friends. I was ready to see someone other than Sophia, even if things were going really well. I called Noah, but Sophia was always around. It's not like I was hiding things from her, but I couldn't have a true Penelope-Noah conversation with her right beside me. I needed to pour out my feelings so he could slap me with love and tell me to stop being dramatic. I needed to talk to him about the sex life Sophia kept trying to make happen, and I needed to talk about Summer. We texted occasionally, but it wasn't enough; I wanted to hear his voice.

One night I snuck out of Sophia's arms and out into the backyard to call him. It was 1 a.m. his time but he answered promptly enough.

"Hey!" he cried into the phone.

"Hi!" I squeed back.

"How are you? You're calling late."

"I desperately needed to talk to you, but I haven't been able to get away long enough to."

"Get away from who?"

"Uh—Sophia," I murmered.

"Should you be trying to get away from the girl you're in love with?"

"Oh, Noah. I just needed a moment. She's been right behind me every time I turn around for a month and a half now. It's not that I don't want her here but I need to breathe."

"I understand."

"I miss you."

"I miss you too. Why don't you come back early? We can go out all night," he said, his voice enticing.

"I wish I could, but I think I'm stuck here. I haven't even really been able to see Summer."

"Well, she'll come to you when she's ready. She's working on it."

"You still talk to her, don't you? What do you guys talk about?"

"No, no, no, Penelope. I told you, I'm not going to do this."

"I just want to know if you talk about me." I felt my stomach flutter at the thought of Summer and Noah discussing me.

"Quite the little narcissist, aren't we?"

"Noah." His name coming out as an anguished cry after which I clapped my hand over my mouth, remembering the hour.

"No. No pleading. She's my friend too. We bonded over unicorns and ice cream—at your behest, might I add."

"Fine, just tell her to call me. I want to hang out with her."

"She's hurting, Penelope. She'll call when she's able. I'm not here to make you feel bad, but you're not the only one with feelings caught up in this mess."

"I just want my friend back," I whined.

"Do you?" he asked, sounding genuinely curious.

"Of course I do. I'm happy with Sophia."

"Okay, honey. I'm glad." There was a long pause and I was sure he was going to say something else but changed his mind and instead said,

"Just give her time."

"I'm trying to, but all this time spent solely with Sophia is sometimes uncomfortable."

"How?"

"She wants to have sex, like all the time."

"And you don't?" he scoffed, like sex was what everyone wanted.

"Don't say it like that! I don't know, should I? She's my first, so I have no basis for comparison. Am I broken, Noah?" I tried not to let the last question come out as desperate as I felt. I needed an answer.

"Penelope, you're not broken."

"You promise?" I hated myself for sounding like a child.

"I promise. Have you talk to Sophia about this?"

"No. I'm worried because she's so full-throttle in the bedroom. I don't want this to be what ends us."

"If it is, then she doesn't deserve you anyway. You have to talk to her about this, or you could end the relationship with the silence."

"What will she say?"

"If she's smart, she'll listen and figure out a way for both of you to be happy."

"Okay."

We sat on the phone in silence for a while until I said, "Okay, I'm going to go to bed. It's so late here."

"Okay, I miss your face."

"Thank you, Noah. I love you, goodnight."

"Love you too, goodnight."

It wasn't quite the conversation I had wished for, but I guessed there wasn't a quick fix to the situation I had gotten myself into. I went to bed thinking about Summer and Noah, what their conversations could be filled with and how to talk to Sophia about our sex life.

When I finally received a text from Summer, Sophia was in a much better mood to handle meeting her. We had spent about five weeks just us, and there were only about five left in the summer. We planned to meet up and grab some dinner before going midnight bowling. This was all Summer's plan, so I had suspicions the midnight bowling was part of a plot more than it was part of a nicer plan to get to know Sophia.

I told Sophia of the times Summer and I had gone bowling together before. I didn't want anything coming out to make her doubt me. She didn't seem disheartened, though. On the contrary, she seemed to take the information I had for her and log it away. She acted like she was preparing for battle. I watched the gears turn in her head. I supposed our night out together would be the first true test of how Seattle was going to play out.

When I thought about it, this was kind of how things were going to be from now on. I hoped they would both just chill and let things happen naturally, but I knew it was only a pipe dream. Especially when I saw the determination on Sophia's face as we were leaving the house.

My mother had relinquished use of the car to me. She was pretty much back to her normal self. She had never made a real effort to be kind to the significant others I brought home. Sometimes, though, she would say things leading me to believe it had less to do with Sophia as a person and more to do with her being "Team Summer."

She would walk by Sophia and me watching a movie and say, "Have you heard from Summer lately?" or "How is Summer doing?" or, my least favorite, "Poor Summer, she was so happy over winter break." My mother was ridiculously conniving, even if she wasn't subtle. She had obviously gotten it into her head that if I was going to be with a girl, then I should be with Summer.

Chapter Thirty-Three

We arrived at the restaurant early, so I texted Summer to see if she was there yet. We walked inside, and I saw her coming toward us from the table. She definitely hadn't sat at home doing nothing for the last four weeks. She looked amazing. She had dressed up for the occasion, whereas Sophia and I were in simple jeans and a tee-shirt. She walked up to Sophia and stuck out her hand. I could tell Sophia was taken aback, but she held out her hand to shake Summer's. When their hands dropped, Summer turned and hugged me. I felt Sophia's hand slip into mine, holding my hand down. Even with the momentary irritation at Sophia, I hugged Summer happily.

Her smell overwhelmed my senses. She was wearing the perfume so closely associated with so many good memories. I was thrown into euphoria in her arms. I released her reluctantly, and reality was thrust upon me as the scent was ripped from me. I glanced at Sophia, her face tense. I squeezed her hand, which was still clenching mine.

Summer led us to the table, and we sat down, Sophia and me opposite her. The night had begun, and only time would tell if it was a single battle in the war or a peace conference to end the fighting.

"So, Sophia," Summer began. "What are you going to school for?"

Sophia had been sipping her drink, and she kind of spluttered at being addressed.

"I'm going into architecture. I want to build things that are beautiful and will last forever," she said, glancing from Summer to me then smiling.

"That's interesting. Maybe you can design me a house. I would like to see what you come up with," she said, the enthusiasm in her voice a mix of forced and genuine. "Something in gray brick, maybe."

I shot her an angry glance, not wanting the night to go badly so quickly. Summer wasn't looking at me, though; she was looking at Sophia. Their eyes had met, and it almost seemed like they were communicating telepathically. I squeezed Sophia's hand under the table, and she broke her gaze as the waiter approached to take our order.

"What can I get for you folks?" the waiter asked politely.

We all ordered, and, probably not by coincidence, everyone ended up with the same thing. I ordered first, and Sophia had followed me as she often did, particularly because we were in a place where they did not serve the food she was used to. Then Summer ordered, but I knew for a fact she had not copied my order to try it. I couldn't tell why exactly, but I knew a cheeseburger with ranch and mashed potatoes instead of fries did not even normally rank on her list. I looked at her, but she was again not looking at me. This time she was taking an interest in her silverware.

I was already resigned to the fact the night would be long. It had been decided by every party but me that their covert battle would start then. They hid snide remarks and insinuations under politeness and mock niceness. The up side was that in order for Sophia and Summer to try to one-up the other constantly, they had to talk. Without realizing it, they were inadvertently getting to know each other, and during the conversation, I would see one of them have a true reaction.

After a dessert shared by all and a bit of a scuffle over who was going to pay the bill—both Sophia and Summer had tried to claim the whole thing—we were on our way to midnight bowling. Summer had been dropped off by her parents, devious woman that she was, so she requested to ride with us. This seemed to enrage Sophia more than anything else had. She crushed my hand in hers, so I had to wrench my fingers from her grip or risk losing them. When we got to the car, Sophia kissed me before climbing into her side. We had discussed this before leaving the house; kissing could only make the situation worse. I rolled my eyes at her and went to the driver's side of the car.

We drove to the bowling alley. I made to go rent shoes while Summer grabbed my ball—the regular happenings for our outings to the bowling alley—but Sophia was ahead of me and paid for the lane. I was left with an odd feeling of being displaced but recovered quickly and went to get my own ball. I walked over to the rack and started to pick them up and test them when Summer came over.

"That's not the weight you use," she said.

"What?" I replied.

"You haven't used that weight in a long time. Your arms are stronger than you think, and you tend to hurl the ball into other people's lanes when you use a lighter one." The corners of her mouth twitched up, the only thing hinting at amusement on her nearly blank face.

"Oh," I said, grinning sheepishly.

It was true. I hadn't picked out my own ball in quite some time. Bowling was something I had reserved for Summer and me, which I could only assume was the reason she had picked this particular outing.

"Here, I've already gotten you one," she said as she held out a bowling ball with both hands.

I reached out to take it from her. My hands held hers as I took the ball. When our skin touched, a tingle shot up my arms and down my spine. My eyes went from the bowling ball to Summer's face. She was smiling openly now, and I couldn't help but smile back. This was going to be an unmitigated disaster. Sophia appeared next to us. Her excited smile faded from her face as she glimpsed Summer and me. I took the ball and turned to Sophia.

"Did you get our shoes?" I asked, my smile forced.

"I didn't know everyone's sizes, so you guys will need to go get yours," she said, perturbed.

I let Summer go get her shoes while Sophia picked out a bowling ball. I went over to our lane to get things started. We began bowling, and it took me two rounds to realize Summer was not doing her usual bowling ritual. I had never been bowling with her on an occasion in which she hadn't done it. She took her turn like the rest of us, but she bowled like a serious competitor.

"Why are you bowling all serious-like?" I whispered to Summer during Sophia's turn.

She shrugged at me, smiled slyly, and got up to take her turn again. She did bowl much better than she had before, but I didn't know if it was because she cut out her ritual or if she had been practicing in preparation. I wouldn't be surprised if she had even taken lessons because as the night wore on, it became increasingly obvious that Sophia and Summer were truly fighting to see who could win.

After they had each won a game apiece, I called it.

"Ok, ladies, I'm done. We should get going." I waved my hands above my head.

"But we're tied!" they protested in unison.

"Guys, seriously, I want to go home. It's past midnight, and I'm tired. I'm not having fun anymore because you two are taking this to a whole new level, and you're ignoring me in the process."

I pulled my ball from the ball return and marched off without a backward glance. I was returning my shoes when the girls walked up behind me. They returned their shoes, and we walked toward the door, passing the arcade room on the way.

Summer said, "Hey! Don't you want to DDR before we go?!"

I had no intention of playing in front of Sophia—I sucked at DDR—so I just shook my head.

"I'll play you," Sophia chimed in.

"Great," Summer stated, her eyes blazing.

They retreated to the arcade room, and I was left with two choices: Go outside and wait or play witness to their pissing contest. I chose the former. At least without an audience maybe they would get tired more quickly. I couldn't have been more wrong.

I went to my car and locked myself in. I entertained myself by listening to the radio for a little while but soon found myself dozing off in the driver's seat. I turned off the electronics and laid the seat down. They didn't come out until the bowling alley closed around 3 am. I was passed out in the car. Startled awake by a rapping on the window, I bolted upright and saw Sophia at the window. I unlocked the door to let them in. They were both shiny with sweat but didn't seem to be getting along any better.

"You could have told us where you were going." Sophia huffed.

"Excuse me for not wanting to watch the two of you go at each other," I said, shooting her a dirty look.

I also glanced back at Summer in the back seat, but she kept her mouth shut and her eyes down. This was understandably not an argument she wanted any part of.

Sophia had gotten the clue the car ride should happen in silence, and even after we dropped Summer off, she still didn't say anything else to me. I was sore from having slept in a car for a few hours and angry about them not caring about my being gone the whole time. If Sophia was worried about where I was, she should have tried to find out before the bowling alley closed.

I went straight to bed when we got home. Sophia followed silently but veered off to the shower at the top of the stairs. I didn't wake again until the morning. I rolled over to find I had much more room than I was supposed to. The bed was a full-sized, and I was supposed to be sharing it with my girlfriend. I groggily looked around and began to roll out of bed to find her. When I put my foot down, it didn't touch the floor. I saw her curled up, my foot on top of hers. She was snoring lightly. I snuck down onto the floor and cuddled with her, falling back asleep easily.

We both woke up a few hours later, and she stretched, smiling at me while I simply blinked several times. She turned over and pulled me to her, kissing me.

"Good morning," she said, her eyes scanning mine.

"Good morning," I replied and lay down on her chest.

I could feel her head swiveling as she took in the situation.

"Why are you on the floor with me?"

"Why were you on the floor in the first place?"

"I didn't want to wake you again, and the floor was preferable to the couch. You know, where your mother would have found me before you did."

"You're right; the floor is preferable." I chuckled.

I didn't offer an answer to her question. I just snuggled her tighter then got up to shower.

Chapter Thirty-Four

I CONSIDERED Noah's advice seriously and frequently, but I couldn't bring myself to broach the subject with Sophia. I didn't know how one would even begin a you-want-to-have-sex-with-me-too-often conversation. Every time I thought things were going well enough to bring up the topic, I would keep quiet about it because I didn't want to spoil the mood. When things were tense or she was irritated, I knew it would only have made things worse. All the while, it was harder and harder to fend her off.

I knew I was making up excuses when she was trying to coax me into the bedroom, in spite of my continued resistance, and she asked me flat out why I didn't want to. I had dismissed other such comments by saying "we're in my mother's house" or "they could be home at any minute" even if I knew it wasn't true. I knew it was time to bite the bullet, so I did.

"No, Sophia. I don't want to." I smiled, trying to soften the blow of my words, which was a bad idea because then she thought I was playing.

"There's no use in playing coy," she said, wrapping herself around me and pressing her lips to mine. "I already know what an unbearable tease you are."

She smiled like a wolf and lifted me off the ground. I pushed on her, and the act brought a surge of panic when she didn't let go. Her words were terribly offensive, since I would never consider myself a tease, and I wanted my declarations of "no" taken seriously.

I stopped fighting back and let her take me into the bedroom. When we landed on the bed, I tried to sit up, but she was already on me. I felt claustrophobic, and there was a tightness in my chest, one I couldn't breathe deep enough to release.

I grabbed Sophia's shoulders and worked to get her at arm's length. She looked at me, actually looked at me, and I saw unease seep into her face.

"You really aren't interested, are you?" she asked.

"It's not that I'm *not*, but maybe not right *now*."

"What about all the other times? We haven't done anything in weeks, and I thought now was perfect. You've run out of excuses so what's the real reason?"

"I just don't want to have sex as often as you do." I splayed my hands face up as my shoulders pulled up.

"I see." Sophia sat up and stared at the wall with all of the pictures on it. "Why?" Her voice was harsh.

It was the one question I was sure she would ask but wished she wouldn't.

"I don't know." I sat up also and reached for her arm.

She twisted away from my touch and turned on me. "What kind of answer is that?"

"It's the only one I have."

I knew she wouldn't be happy, but I hadn't expected hostile. Maybe sullen and disagreeable, but never angry.

"Fine." With that she left the room.

I avoided her for the rest of the day, which wasn't hard, as she seemed to be doing the same. I found myself wanting to see Summer again. It had been a week since our communal outing, and I hadn't really heard from her since.

With something more akin to reckless abandon than sane maturity, I messaged Summer.

Penelope: Hey, you know I'm totally over the night at the bowling alley, right?

The response was almost immediate which made me smile then scold myself.

Summer: I didn't figure you would stay mad. You just needed a

nap. :P

Penelope: Maybe.

Summer: lol

Penelope: So...

Summer: Yes?

I couldn't respond; I couldn't bring myself to force her deeper into my mess than she already was. Noah and his words rose up to haunt me. I couldn't hurt her more than I already was.

Penelope: Nothing. Nvm

Summer: Really?

Penelope: No, not really but yes.

Summer: Okay, well I'll be here when you figure it out.

"Uuuuugh," I cried at the empty living room.

Sophia came down the stairs then, pointedly not asking what my issue was. I couldn't take it anymore. There were only three weeks left of summer, and I couldn't wait for them to be over. Then, I slapped myself on the forehead so hard I cried out.

How can I be so stupid? Every time we fight, I imagine us going back to Seattle and we'll get a break from each other and I'll get to see Noah. He'll come over to Alyssa's and my dorm, and we'll sort out my feelings with ice cream and hugs. But NO! I'll go back to Seattle, and everything will be the same. We are going to LIVE together now. What the hell was I thinking?

I needed a moment. Stepping out the front door with the intention of getting some fresh air, I didn't stop walking. I found myself at the park. It was late afternoon, but with the summer hours, there was still plenty of light. Swinging was always a happy thing for me, the closest activity to flying readily available (and free). It also enabled me to think more clearly.

I decided texting Summer had been stupid. How did I expect my relationship to work after we were all back in Seattle if I ran to Summer every time I fought with Sophia? There was a time when I turned to her more than I turned to Noah, but that time was long gone. It wasn't so simple anymore, and I had to be careful in rebuilding a friendship with her. The relationship couldn't be based on unhappy times with my girlfriend.

I also decided to grin and bear it when it came to Sophia. Was it really so bad that the worst problem we had was that she was so taken with me that she wanted me all the time? I told myself I was being silly even though I felt a sinking feeling inside.

Jumping from the swing at a particularly high point, I landed on my feet, a tingle shooting through my feet to past my knees. I headed home to patch things up with Sophia. She was sitting at the table when I got back, looking at her phone.

I opened my mouth to start the conversation, but I hadn't thought through how it would actually go. What was I going to say? "Okay, you win. I'll just grin a bear it" or "Ha ha ha, I was only kidding. Come on, let's go do it"? I shut my mouth as soon as I opened it, but it was too late—she noticed my pause.

She turned to me expectantly with a brusque look. "Yes?"

I made a face of disgust and walked passed her. She was making this such a horrible conversation to have. I was simply trying to be truthful with my girlfriend, but to see the way she was acting one would have thought I was attacking her.

I turned back around, anger and resentment swirling inside. "You know, I was trying to be honest like you asked me, to and this is the thanks I get? How am I supposed to be completely honest with you when you act this way?"

"You aren't being *completely* honest with me. All you've told me is that you don't want to sleep with me anymore. You haven't told me why, which is the really honest part."

"I *have* been truthful. I just don't feel like you do." I gestured at her emphatically, trying to make her understand by sheer force of will.

"So you don't love me?" She crossed her arms across her chest and looked at me like I was pure evil.

"Are love and sex synonymous for you?" My eyes narrowed, and I crossed my arms too.

"Sex is indicative of love. It's how I show you how much I love you."

"It might be for you, but it's not for me."

We stared at each other. I wasn't going to give in and tell her something untrue, like "You're right, I don't love you." I could tell she was going to be stubborn also.

"What do you want from me?" I asked after ten minutes of silence.

"I want you to want me, and I don't feel like you do, especially since we've been here."

It was my tragic idea to combine our being home with my trying to stop her libido from steam rolling me. I thought being in my mother's house would have made it easier to come up with excuses to waylay her, but the excuses had run out in the end. Sophia would forever think that my being disinterested in sleeping with her every time we were alone was inexorably tied to—to what? My proximity to Summer, my being with my family, the heat? There was no telling what she thought since she wouldn't come out and say it.

"I can't create something that's not there, but I do love you. I'm sorry I can't desire you like you need me to." I spun on my heel and walked out of the room and up the stairs.

Screw it, I'm not going to sit here and make myself miserable so she can have what she needs, especially if she's not even going to meet me halfway. From now on, my body is closed for business.

That night Sophia apologized, but it seemed half-hearted. I accepted because I didn't want to fight anymore. I knew this would be the end of us if we couldn't figure out a way around it.

Chapter Thirty-Five

Summer messaged me in the middle of the following week to see if we all wanted to hang out again. I almost fell out of the chair at the mention of all of us getting together for another horrendous night of "fun." I told Summer I wanted it to be only her and me, knowing full well it would probably only make the situation worse between Sophia and me.

I found Sophia playing on my computer. "Hey, I'm going to go out for a bit."

"Okay, where are we going to go?" She clicked the mouse a few times but didn't look at me.

"Actually, I was going to go see Summer."

I could only see her profile from where I stood, but there was no mistaking her displeasure at the idea. Her lips pursed, and the clicks of the mouse became more like stabbing it to death.

"I can take you somewhere if you want," I offered.

"No, please, don't worry about me. I wanted to spend all summer trapped in this house with you," she said harshly.

"I'm sorry being *trapped* with me is so awful for you. It's not like I'm not trying, but you don't seem to have any interest in making things any better. You seem content to sit there and blame me for the failing of our relationship and passively watch it go down the toilet. I don't have

Noah or Alyssa or any of my other friends here to talk to, so I'm going to see the only one I *do* have."

I didn't wait for her response—I simply left. Given my emotional state, going to see Summer was sure to be disastrous at best. When I pulled up to her house, she was already waiting outside for me, a glass of sweet tea for each of us. I plopped down next to her and sighed in disgruntlement.

Summer eyed me but I didn't offer any explanation for my mood. Leaning against the brick wall behind her, she handed me a sweating glass but didn't turn to look at me. We sat there in silence until I felt it pressing in on me.

"So what have you been up to?" I asked, urging her to fill the silence.

"Not much. Working on stuff, myself—us."

"Oh," I murmured.

This wasn't exactly the conversation I expected, but it gave me fuel to add to the Sophia fire. How was it the girl I wasn't with was working on a relationship we had both helped destroy, but the same couldn't be said for my girlfriend? The paradox was staggering. I took a moment to remove myself from my head and *really* see Summer for the first time since spring break.

"And how's that going?" I smiled wryly.

"It'd be going better if we could be like we used to be. Or if you'd just be with me." She laughed, but it was uneasy.

"I'd like for us to be able to talk again. I've missed our friendship."

It was her turn to hide her feelings with a smile, but I saw her heart aching anyway.

"I will never stop wanting you." She wasn't trying to persuade me like she had so many times before, she was simply stating a fact. "I can't go on without our friendship. I will give you up if that's what it takes to keep you, but you have to tell me I don't stand a chance."

Any reply I would have uttered was stuck in my throat. Had I tried to speak, I would have choked on it.

How can I tell her I don't want her when I very clearly do? Will Sophia and I even make it back to Seattle in one piece?

Unaware of my mental torment, she said, "Or maybe once we're in Seattle, I'll find someone too."

The small laugh following her statement was lost in the roaring in my ears. My heart skipped a beat, and my mind exploded with jealousy.

The forcefulness of my reaction was entirely involuntary but completely consuming. I didn't want Summer to find someone else, but I didn't have the right to stop her from moving on, unless I was going to claim her. I might not have had the right but it didn't stop me from wanting to lunge myself at her and pin her to the ground, forcing her to swear she would never touch anyone else ever again.

"What are you thinking?" Summer asked.

I snapped back to reality—the one where I was sitting next to Summer and not acting crazed.

"Nothing?" I replied, my throat tight with things unsaid.

"You look like you wanted to murder someone."

I made my face a blank slate. "Maybe you *should* try to find someone once we're in Seattle. Between school and Sophia, I'll probably be pretty busy."

"They'll never be you, but if that's what you want, I'll..." Summer's voice trailed off and she began playing with the condensation on her glass.

Is she playing me for a fool, or have I acted out my part too well? Does she really believe I've buried my feelings so deep I don't want her? Or does she believe they don't exist anymore?

My heart twisted painfully, and I winced and turned so she couldn't see my face.

This is all my fault. I'm the one who can't sort my feelings enough to definitively choose one of them, and now I'm going to lose both.

I stood up, unable to sit still and keep my mouth shut. I needed to leave before I created more problems.

"I have to go," I told her shortly, berating myself for letting my emotions get out of control.

"Don't." She looked up at me, her eyes holding my gaze even though I wanted to flee.

When I didn't move further away, she said, "Don't go. I need to talk to you."

She patted the pavement next to her, and I sat down despite my better judgment. I let her take my hand, not wanting to pull away but knowing I should all the same.

"Did Sophia ever talk to you about the night at the bowling alley after you left?"

"Not really, I didn't think there was anything to tell."

"Well, we were in the arcade playing DDR. It was around one am, and we were in the middle of a song. I was winning—*again*. You know how much I love DDR and how well I play," she added while smiling to herself. "Sophia turned to me, gave up all pretenses of trying to win, and told me she knew you loved me but there wasn't a chance she would let you be with me. I asked her why, expecting the response to be something like she loved you or whatever. And while she did say that, she told me even if she didn't love you, she would keep you on pretense—to make sure I never got a chance to be with you. She said it was her mission to ruin you for me forever."

I sat there with my mouth opening and closing like a fish, my mind reeling, trying to catch up. I had cycled through too many emotions in the past twenty-four hours. Part of me wanted to kiss Summer, and the other part of me wanted to slap her. I wanted to rewind time and never leave Summer to go to Seattle. I wanted to shake Sophia until she told me the truth and then shake her more until she saw reason. The mess of the three of us was finally too much for me.

I clamped down on my emotions with an icy, iron grip of determination. I screamed through gritted teeth as I rose from the pavement. Summer didn't make a move to stop me as I stomped to my car. She always knew when to stay out of my way. I sped home and surged up the stairs to find Sophia. I knew I couldn't simply take Summer's word on the situation, so I would give Sophia a chance to explain herself, even though I doubted Summer would lie to my face. I found Sophia sitting at my computer watching videos. She spun to face me as I slammed the door open then closed again. Her eyes were wide with surprise.

"Tell me the truth!" I yelled at her.

Her eyes narrowed instantly as she said, "I will tell you whatever you want to know as soon as you calm down."

"I will *not* calm down. Did you only tell me you loved me so I wouldn't leave you for Summer? Have you been playing me this whole time so you could 'win'?" I shouted.

"I did no such thing. Who told you that, your little lover on the side?" she accused.

"What?" I spat.

"You heard me. I know you sneak over there to be with her. That's why you never want me. You get everything from her, and I get the crumbs when you return home! If you desire her so much, why are we even together? Why don't you *ever* want me?" screamed Sophia.

"What are you talking about? I have never cheated on you," I said, floored.

"Then why don't you want to have sex with me?" she accused, still shouting.

"I already told you I don't know. I thought we had plenty."

"Ha!" she scoffed. "Even when we do you're not the one who wants it. It's always me. Always!"

"I'm sorry, I..." I had no answer for her. I didn't know why I didn't want her like she wanted me or as often. I just didn't.

"Why don't you want me?" she said, her voice trailing off as her anger deflated into confusion and sadness. "I didn't mean the things I said to Summer. She was just being so smug. I wanted to hurt her. I would never keep you from her if I didn't want you for myself so badly. Loving you just makes me crazy."

"I believe you," I said as I crossed the room and took her into my arms.

I couldn't stand to see her hurt even if she had said hurtful things to me. I truly loved her, even if it got muddled in with everything else when we fought.

I couldn't figure out why I didn't feel the way she clearly wanted me to, but I would at least make an effort to be what she so obviously needed. I sat in her lap and soothed her crying. When she calmed down, I kissed her. I kissed her cheeks where the tears had fallen, down to her lips where she kissed me back without passion. I looked into her eyes; they held only defeat. If this was what she needed for our relationship to be, I could fake it.

I laid awake long after Sophia had fallen asleep. I had too many things going on in my head. I knew why Sophia had said those things to Summer, but I couldn't figure out if that was a good enough excuse for her behavior. Was it really necessary to incite Summer when she was the one who was alone? Sophia had me, but she chose to slam Summer's face into it.

I also didn't know how to get a grasp on my lack of desire to have sex with Sophia. Did it mean I didn't really love her, or was I simply too hung up on Summer? Was my wanting to please her and fix the rift between us enough reason for me to try and change myself? If I brought

Summer into the equation, I couldn't remember ever having a sexual fantasy about her, either.

Then I remembered Sophia saying I made her crazy, and while some people might consider this to be a compliment, I knew crazy love didn't last. Crazy love was like burning a candle at both ends. Everything went twice as fast, and in the end, someone always got burned.

Chapter Thirty-Six

"Wake up, sleepy," Sophia said as she woke me with a kiss.

"Mmmmmmmm," I grumbled, trying to keep my mouth as closed as possible.

I got up almost immediately to brush my teeth. Sophia stepped into the bathroom behind me and put her hands around my waist. She was being more affectionate than I had seen her since we first got together. She apparently had taken last night as me forfeiting to her desires. I wasn't sure I liked it.

"What's gotten into you?" I asked.

"Nothing. Do I need an excuse to touch you?"

"No," I said. "It's just seems a bit of a coincidence."

"What do you mean?" she purred.

"Well, I finally gave you what you've been complaining about, and now you're acting like nothing is wrong," I said. "We still need to finish our conversation from last night. Many conversations, in fact."

She rolled her eyes at me and walked back into the bedroom. I finished brushing my teeth and followed her. She was sitting in the office chair, so I sat on the bed. I wasn't satisfied with Sophia's excuses for some of the awful things she had said to Summer, especially since it wasn't even Summer's fault that things were happening this way. I was the one who couldn't cut her out. I was the one who couldn't pretend

I didn't love her anymore just to make things easier.

"So, what now?" Sophia asked, seemingly uninterested.

"Now we go over the horrible things you said to Summer and how your saying things like that, no matter who they're to, is not acceptable," I said. "And the fact that you were once again not honest and up front with me, which I would like to remind you is *your* rule."

"I didn't lie to you," she said, immediately defensive.

"Not telling me is the same. Were you hoping Summer would keep her mouth shut or that I wouldn't believe her?"

"I don't know," she said, throwing her hands up in the air. "I wanted to shut her up, and I was angry that you left us there."

"Are you kidding me? You knew I wasn't going to hang around and watch the two of you constantly trying to one up each other, just like you had while we were bowling," I said. "And no matter the reason, you can't say things like that, or I will start to believe them."

"We can't keep doing this."

"You don't think I'm tired of arguing too?"

"No, I mean we can't keep hanging out with Summer."

"Well, you don't have to, but I already told you, I'm not going to stop being her friend or spending time with her."

"You mean you won't stop having sex with her," Sophia accused.

"Really? Are we on this again?" I cried. "Why are you so sure I'm sleeping with Summer?"

"Then tell me you're not." She folded her arms across her chest.

"I'm *not*."

"Ha."

"Mature, that's really mature. Why are you being like this? We're supposed to move in together in a couple of weeks, but you're accusing me of cheating on you."

"Well, you still haven't answered me. If you're not having sex with me, then who are you having it with?"

"Did it ever occur to you that I just don't want to?"

"Don't feed me that!"

"Seriously?"

"Yeah, seriously. I don't believe it for a minute."

"Well, you should because it's true. I've gone so far as to think there might be something wrong with me, like a chemical imbalance or something, but the truth is, I don't want sex as often as you do."

Sophia was clearly not taking in what I was saying. She was arguing with me before I finished my sentence, and she was rolling her eyes when she wasn't arguing.

"I need you to hear me," I beseeched her. "I need you to listen to what I'm saying and know I'm being as honest with you as I can be."

"You're being totally honest? I find that hard to believe."

"Are you kidding me?" I replied. "I think the real problem here is you're confusing me with you, so maybe I should be worried about you cheating on me when we get back to Seattle!"

"Who?" she cried. "Who would I be cheating on you with? I'm here because of you, remember? I followed you, remember? It seems pointless now because you're seeing Summer anyway. I should have stayed home and at least spared myself the agony of knowing when you're over there cheating on me. I would still just be assuming."

"Maybe you should go home early."

"Yeah, you'd like that, wouldn't you?" she spat.

"Not really, but I don't think I like having you here right now either."

"Well, I'm not going to pay for another ticket so you can have unlimited sex with her for a week."

"Say it one more time," I dared her. "Accuse me one more time, and you will find yourself with nowhere to stay for a week. I will not take this from you. You 're just taking assumptions and running with them."

"Fine," she said as she got up from the chair and walked out of the room.

I called Noah immediately. He picked up on the third ring.

"Do you know what time it is?" he croaked into the phone.

"Yeah, it's like 11," I said.

"Which means?" he asked.

"It means it's, like, 9 your time but I'm in full-swing, crazy-girlfriend mode, and I'm playing the best-friend-crisis-hotline card," I said.

"Fine," he moaned. "Let me make some coffee."

I listened to him shuffle around, banging various things together while making many disgruntled noises.

"Ok," he grunted. "What happened?"

The story of the argument tumbled out of my mouth.

"And now she's walked out, and I don't really care to go after her," I finished.

"Wow. Well, that deteriorated quickly," he said.

"Yeah it did," I said. "I just don't know how to fix this short of never seeing Summer again. She thinks I'm doing something I'm not and won't listen to reason."

"I think she's really stressed out, and remember, when you go and spend all day with Summer, she's stuck at your house with your less than stellar mother and with nothing to do but contemplate what you're doing without her."

"It's was only a couple times! I gave her five weeks of undivided attention."

"Really?"

"Yeah, and when we were all together, it was even worse." I then proceeded to tell him about the night of bowling in full detail, including the part I had found out the day before.

"I'm not saying there is a perfect solution. I only know the sadistic love triangle you're trapped in is likely to implode at some point, and you will have to choose. I say that with all the love I can manage, but you know you can't keep both of them forever. Eventually, something will have to give."

"And which one would be your choice?"

"My choice is to see you happy, and you will never be that while you're caught in the middle. Decide your course of action and stick to it before it's too late."

I found Sophia at the park down the street from my house. She was sitting on a bench by the pond. I walked up beside her and sat next to her.

"How do we fix this?" I asked.

"I don't know," she said.

"Well, let's start with you have to stop accusing me of cheating on you," I said. "I have not cheated on you nor will I. I'm sorry you doubt my commitment to you, and I will do everything within my power to help you trust me. But I need you to talk to me and tell me what you need."

"I need you to stop seeing Summer. I know it's not fair, and I don't expect it to happen, but that's what I truly need," she said, grabbing my hands. "I need you to be mine and only mine, which means cutting her out of our lives completely. Every time you go to be with her, my mind just goes wild with the possibilities of what's happening."

"Then you will have to concede to going out with us every time we hang out," I said. "We have a week left before we return, so maybe you can work on your jealousy between now and then. Maybe another group outing, and you can try to get along instead of trying to compete with her?"

"I will try anything to keep you."

I set up a play date with Summer, who was less than excited but agreed. I desperately wanted for things to work themselves out, but all I could see in front of me was a long, hard road to a future I couldn't make out. Sophia made efforts, but I couldn't forget the sting of her words.

The weekend came, and we all went out Saturday night. It was disastrous, to put it nicely. If the first time we went out was a game of chess, then the second time was World War III with live nukes.

The climax of the evening was the moment I had to physically separate Sophia and Summer after Sophia accused her of being a home wrecker. Needless to say, I wouldn't be instigating any more hangouts between the three of us. Noah was right—I was going to have to choose.

Things between Sophia and me were patched up at best. I held my tongue and went along with what she wanted. She was a dark cloud of foul temperaments. I fell into a bad mood right alongside her in the absence of someone to show me another way. I wanted to go back to Seattle, to my friends and the last place of sanity I could remember.

At first, I had always seen Sophia as kind of like a unicorn. She was perfect and patient. She seemed to always have the truth for me whether I liked it or not. She was the rock I clung to in the aftermath of everything that had happened over the winter break. She had never shown me anything to make me doubt her perfection—until now. I was admittedly a little disenchanted. She was no longer a unicorn but instead just a woman, flawed as we all were. I didn't appreciate being accused of cheating, but she had said she would work on it. The only thing left was for me to decide if I still wanted to be with her.

Chaper Thirty-Seven

We arrived in Seattle in the afternoon. Summer took the same flight but had sat apart from Sophia and me. Sophia had slept a good portion of the way after I had fed her medicine for her motion sickness. I looked forward at the back of Summer's seat, her arm only barely visible.

We had a shuttle to take us to campus and Summer to her new apartment. I hugged Summer goodbye, Sophia's eyes boring into my back the whole time, then Sophia and I headed to check into our dorm room. There was nothing special about the room itself, but it was supposed to be magical, living with my girlfriend out from under the hawk eyes of parents. This was particularly true in the case of my mother, who would shoot us dirty looks when we were sitting too close together on the couch.

I sheltered the flame of my love for her against the gale she had been all summer. I wanted things to go back to how they were, but I was different from the experience—we were different. Summer kept radio silent, which was okay even though it hurt. I didn't need more added to my plate.

I thought things would be better once we were back on Sophia's home ground, but since she had voiced her accusations, they seemed to consume her. Two weeks after we got back, when it was clear I wasn't seeing Summer anymore, Sophia began to come up with other reasons to explain why I didn't desire her. They all seemed to have something to do with one of two categories: One, some self-deprecating reason about her not being good enough or two, Summer.

How the latter still factored in was beyond me. Whenever she mentioned it, I resorted to leaving. I would walk around until I cooled down, or she would call me to apologize. After revealing the small chink in Sophia's armor, the jealousy in her flooded out uncontrollably—it was off the charts. I was left regretting the trip home with almost every fiber of my being—every fiber, that is, except for the ones whispering "this would have come out eventually."

Sophia became more insistent and needy when it came to our love life, so we continued to argue about it. Thoughts about my taking a passive role in our love life were prominent in my mind every time the subject arose. Maybe there was something wrong with me, but I didn't feel like there was, so when Sophia suggested I see a doctor to get myself "fixed," I began avoiding her altogether.

I stopped spending time in our room, attempting to avoid arguments, and spent more time working on the clubs I was involved in. I had decided the previous year that I wanted to have a larger part in the LGBTQA club anyway. We had done some co-op events between RAVPA and LGBTQA and wanted to contribute some new ideas to the LGBTQA club. I had been elected secretary, giving me a voice in club planning.

I met with all of the other elected officials and instantly form a bond with the Vice President. We were kindred spirits in whispered snarky remarks, or rather I whispered and he thought I was funny. All it really took was for someone to find me funny, then it was all downhill from there. We spent most of the meetings sniggering and making suggestions, only half of which were remotely serious.

We planned the events to turn LGBTQA from a small club to a campus-wide explosion. We wanted to be out in force and available for anyone who needed a place to belong. Anyone with any sort of artistic skill was recruited to chalk the sidewalks of the campus to announce our first meeting, which was also a mixer. There would be a competition for a gift card to 10AM Somewhere at Chuck E. Cheese halfway through the semester, the children's games making it all the more fun. I suggested a few collaboration events but mine were more like volunteering at a crisis hotline than fun things like bed races.

In the aftermath of Sophia's suggestion to "fix" myself, I volunteered for every extra project in need of help. I was ashamed to admit to Noah that I was failing in my relationship, all due to my libido no less, so I kept my problems from him.

I began to spend a lot of time with the vice president of LGBTQA, Hugh, who also signed on for the extra projects, trying to live his junior year to its fullest. Hugh was a miracle to me; he was kind and funny. All of my ideas for the club paled in comparison to his notion of Asexual Awareness Week in October. I was embarrassed to admit I didn't know much about asexuality. I had never been taught anything about sexuality other than men were supposed to be with women. Even my attempts at thoroughly educating myself about sexuality had failed to tell me about asexuality. I lost a little faith in my ability to Google properly.

Hugh and I began working together immediately, as we only had about a month to get everything sorted. We met as often as we could manage, usually two or three times a week in the library. We probably could have finished the planning fairly quickly if we didn't get along as well as we did. Since he thought I was funny and I was an unbearable procrastinator. We worked intermittently but spent most of the time talking.

It took me a week to gather the courage to ask him about asexuality. I assumed, since he had suggested the event he at least knew about asexuality, if not someone who was. I swallowed my pride and asked.

"Hey, Hugh?" I asked as I slid into the bench seat across from him at the library table where we met regularly.

"Yes?" he said, smiling as I sat down.

"I'm a little embarrassed by what I'm about to say, but... I don't know anything about asexuality."

"Don't be embarrassed." He laughed. "It's actually really common for people not to know. I'm assuming you want to be educated, whereas some people can't be bothered. An asexual person is someone who does not experience sexual attraction. That doesn't mean, however, they don't experience love, and it doesn't mean they *can't* have sex."

I exhaled a breath I didn't know I'd been holding. From working on the project, I had gathered general information about asexuality but to hear a point-blank answer from his lips telling me I was part of a larger community of people who felt like I did about sex took a large weight off my chest. Despite how much I had tried to convince myself Sophia was acting crazy, a secret part of me was worried I was the crazy one.

"I thought they made drugs for that?" I responded, not wanting to get my hopes up. "I mean, you see them all the time—drugs to enhance sexual arousal or whatever."

"No, Penelope. Asexuality isn't something people should throw drugs at, trying to "cure" something that isn't broken. I'm asexual and it's completely natural. It's also a sliding scale, just like sexual attraction. It's not black or white, on or off, sexual desire or no sexual desire. Sure, people can identify at one end of the spectrum or the other with great certainty, but not everyone. I've helped many people who were actually on the asexual spectrum but still felt some desire. They, like you, thought there was some magic drug to fix them, but it turned out they were gray-sexual."

"Gray-sexual?" I asked, intrigued.

I found myself leaning across the table, trying not to miss a word. I wasn't alone. I wasn't an anomaly.

"It's a term for someone who falls into the in-between category on the sexual scale. They could feel arousal but almost no desire to have sex, or they have a desire for sex but only rarely. The thing about sexuality and all its many facets is all of the names we have for them are simply labels for you to own and use to describe yourself. It's not something you choose. It's not like someone can make themselves asexual just by calling themselves it often enough. For many people, it clears confusion and gives them a group to belong to. Once you know what something is called you can begin to understand it and learn about it. If you identify as asexual, it becomes easier to find people like you, and it can help you with aspects you find difficult. No one is alone, and no one should have to feel like they are."

I sat back in my chair, shocked into silence. I loved Hugh so much in that moment I could have cried. He was understanding and patient in explaining the answers to my ignorance, but more than that, he was telling me about me, and he was telling me I was okay. I didn't need to see a doctor. I just needed to know myself and the new words I could use.

We didn't work on the project at all; we just spent the whole night talking. I told him about the problems I was having with sex. This segued into how my relationship was starting to be torn apart by my lack of sexual desire for my girlfriend. Hugh listened quietly while I poured out everything about Sophia and how mad she got and how jealous she was being.

"It sounds to me like the possibility of you being asexual isn't the only problem," he said, looking at me with a mix of concern and attentiveness. "Trust is essential to every healthy relationship, especially if the relationship isn't aided by sex. People tend to underestimate the value sex can have in a relationship. It can enhance feelings of love and closeness with your partner, even if only superficially. Truly, sex cannot fix anything, but if it is coupled with the involved people working to make the relationship better, it can help to side-step a pothole. This is not something asexuals have. In a way, asexuals are forced to really be open and honest with each other, talking often and gaining that sense of closeness in other ways. It's not necessarily more difficult, just different."

"If you don't mind my asking, do you have a partner?"

"I don't have a partner. I'm aromantic as well as asexual."

A singular eyebrow shot up as the other one dipped, the inquiry clear on my face.

"Many asexuals define their romantic preference as well as their sexual preference...which, for me, is no in both cases," he said, chuckling to himself.

"So, I would be asexual, bi-romantic?"

"That's the correct terminology, but whether the words are true is something you have to figure out for yourself. It took me most of high school, even after having a sex ed teacher who was amazing, to figure out what I was feeling.

"The improper education of today's youth is one of the things I'm here to fight against. I want to become a teacher or a speaker so that I can help kids in situations like the one I faced in high school. Many parents think if you don't present children with any other option, then they will all be straight and wait to have sex until marriage. Yet the reality is if children aren't taught something, they go figure it out for themselves.

"I went through high school watching people go through things I couldn't even grasp. They were falling all over each other, and a guy would watch a girl walk by then talk about her in ways I just didn't understand. It wasn't until I found an asexual forum online called AVEN that I felt okay with myself."

I scribbled down the name of the forums and made a mental note to look them up later.

"But if I have sex to please my partner, can I still be asexual?" I asked after a few moments of contemplation.

"It's not like asexuals are an exclusive club where you must present your v-card at the door." He laughed. "Remember, it's a sliding scale. You need to do what's right for you, but having sex just for someone else's pleasure doesn't sound good to me."

"Yeah," I said, wrestling with myself internally about many things.

We didn't leave the library until very late. Hugh walked with me, as I didn't want to walk alone in the wee hours of the morning, but we didn't talk anymore. My mind was reeling. I felt like I had found out a secret about myself that I wanted to share with everyone and was hoping would redeem—if not completely then at least a little bit—my relationship with Sophia.

I imagined myself walking into Sophia's and my dorm room and explaining to her what Hugh and I had talked about all night. I would tell her I was asexual and that I loved her but didn't want sex, and she would take me into her arms and tell me it was okay and we would work it out. Over and over again, I fantasized about what would happen when I walked through the door. Half the time, the scenario would end tragically with her throwing my words back in my face or not believing me.

For this reason, I decided I would keep my feelings to myself until we had Asexual Awareness Week, and afterward I would explain better. The idea of telling her seemed easier once the seed was planted by someone else. Then she would have a base knowledge of asexuality and maybe the pieces would start falling into place without me even saying anything. My hope ran high while my expectations were pretty low.

Chapter Thirty-Eight

I ARRIVED home to a fuming Sophia. She was pacing when I opened the door and strode over to me in two steps. My mind flew into a panic, wondering how she knew already, logic not having time to filter through.

"Where have you been?" she seethed.

"I told you before I left that I was going to work on LGBTQA stuff with another officer," I told her, puzzled by her anger.

"If that *is* what you were doing, why didn't you answer any of my texts?" Her face contorted into a snarl.

My brows furrowed in confusion. I pulled my phone from my purse. Sure enough, there were ten texts waiting for me. I opened them and read the progression of Sophia's patience and mood.

"I'm sorry," I told her. "I got caught up in conversation with Hugh, and I didn't hear my phone."

"Seriously? Ten times! What if something had been wrong? What if I had needed you to come home?"

"I already said I'm sorry. And you didn't need me to come home—you wanted to make sure I wasn't out cheating on you. Are we still limiting this to Summer, or do you think I'm just giving it to everyone but *you?*"

My temper, so close to the surface from our almost constant fighting, boiled over. I hadn't moved away from my mother to be bossed around by someone else. My revelation for the night was wiped from my mind as I reared back to defend myself from the coming onslaught.

"I don't know, you tell me. *Are* you giving it to everyone else? Obviously someone enjoyed the show you gave them for the two of you to have been out so late. Or was that just a rehearsal before you take your show on the road?!"

In a snap reaction which took into account little to nothing about the consequences of the action, my hand came up from my side, almost of its own accord. The sound it made was deafening as it struck its mark. I had never slapped someone other than Clayton, and I hadn't stayed around to watch the aftermath when I had hit him. Sophia's face lit up with shock. Her hand flew to her cheek to grasp the place where a red hand print was already rising up in the wake of my hand. She stepped back from me, and I stood there glowering at her, unable to move to help her or escape her and completely unsure I wanted to do either.

After the initial surprise wore off, Sophia dropped her hand from her face and squared her shoulders, an emblazoned replica of my hand shining on her face.

"Are you proud of yourself now?" she spat at me.

"You have completely lost yourself in this war you insist on waging against my libido. When you can find the decent, self-controlled human being I began this relationship with, then and only then, can you call me." I turned and left.

It was around four in the morning. I had left the library about an hour ago. I didn't know where to turn, so I walked back to the library.

I was woken rather roughly around 9 am by campus security.

"If you're not here to study, then it would be best if you went home," said a gruff voice by my side, a hand on my shoulder.

I woke groggy and confused about why this person was in my room until I remembered I was in the library, the memory of a few hours earlier resurging. I got up and headed toward the elevators. I didn't have class for another couple of hours, so I headed down in the elevator. It stopped a couple of floors below, and I hoped security had already walked through them. I went to a book shelf, pulled some books out and placed them on a table. I laid my head down for some more sleep.

I awoke two hours later to the sound of voices and laughter, books being plopped on tables. I sat up and checked my phone for the time. I had class in five minute across campus then another class right after, consuming three hours of my day. Heaving myself up out of the chair, I walked toward the elevators.

I'm not even sure why I bothered to trudge to class. I hadn't slept enough, and my mind was not up for following what the teacher was saying, even if I had slept. I contemplated leaving class and going back to the library but knew it wouldn't fix anything. While staring blindly toward the projector screen the teacher was using for the lecture, I knew I only had two options. I could call Noah, or I could call Summer. Calling Noah would be the smarter choice, the choice to not selfishly involve someone who was already hurting due to a mess I kept her circling around simply to make myself feel better. But I hadn't been feeling particularly smart as of late. I knew to call Noah would mean a discussion about how I had shut him out of the most recent decline of my relationship, and I felt guilty. I knew I would call Summer even as I ran the list of reasons I shouldn't through my head.

After I was released from the second class, I called Summer. It was the first time I had spoken to her since we parted ways earlier in the month, about three weeks ago. For Summer and me, this was a comparatively short amount of time to go without speaking to each other.

Summer answered on the second ring.

"Hello?" Her voice was higher than normal, strained.

"Hey, what's going on?" I asked, my eyebrows coming together in concern.

"What do you mean? You called me," she said, her voice struggling to return to normal.

"You sound strange—tense. Is everything okay?"

"Yeah, everything is fine. What's up with you?"

"I need a place to stay," I blurted out, not wanting to talk about the fight, just wanting the situation to go away.

"You what?" Summer asked as I heard a loud clatter followed by laughter from the back ground.

"What was that?"

"I fell out of bed."

"If you were in bed, then who was laughing?"

All noise on Summer's end of the line stopped.

"Hello?" I said, irritated and feeling jealous on top of everything else.

"Yeah?"

"What is going on?" I questioned, my voice clipped.

"Nothing," she answered, her voice too short to be normal.

A realization dropped into the pit of my stomach.

"Are you with someone right now?"

"I told you this was going to happen. You knew very well this was a possibility," she explained calmly, seemingly bored with the conversation.

"I thought you were just saying it to make me jealous."

"Well, if saying it made you jealous, I knew actually doing it might bring you to your senses."

In the background I heard a female voice ask, "Is that her?"

"Shut up," Summer said in answer to her question.

"How could you? I needed you, and now you've blown that apart too!" I cried, my voice straining and faltering.

I began to feel the prickle of tears in my eyes, the day kept getting worse and worse.

"I'm sorry," Summer began, the gravity of the situation finally reaching her. "Listen, it's just my roommate. She came in to bring me the laundry, and you happened to call at the same time. What I did was childish, and I'm sorry."

"That's really not cool," I said fighting off my tears.

"I know, I'm sorry. I thought it was just a social call," she said.

I sucked it up. I knew what she did wasn't right, but she was the lesser of two evils right now.

"I need a place to stay," I said again.

"Why? What happened?"

"I'll tell you, just say I can come there."

"Of course you can, is that even a question?"

Chapter Thirty-Nine

I WALKED up to Summer's place about forty minutes later, the transit dropping me about a five minute walk from her place. She met me outside at the end of the walkway.

"This isn't an apartment," I told her. "This is a duplex."

"I know. Nice, hunh?"

"Yeah. How's the inside?" I asked nonchalantly, checking out the building.

"It's good, but I don't care about that right now. I care about you. What happened?"

I shrugged my shoulders and gave her a weak smile. "Can I get away with saying nothing?"

She gave me a scorching look and crossed her arms. "You tell me."

"But—" I whined.

She gave me a look which told me it didn't matter how much I whined. I recounted the previous night for her, the suppressed rage growing on her face as I did.

"And she just called you a whore in so many words?" Summer seethed through gritted teeth.

"Yeah, I guess," I mumbled, feeling fairly low at that point and wanting to crawl into bed and fall into oblivion.

"And this just came out of nowhere? She's never acted this way before?" Summer probed, her eyes tinted with skepticism.

"Well, not exactly." I looked down at my toes which had suddenly become incredibly interesting.

"Penelope." Her tone, so like my mother's, I felt foreboding tingle up my spine.

"It kind of started over the summer. At first, it was little comments I didn't pay attention to, but a week before we left, she accused me of cheating on her with you. It's starting to make me wish I had. I mean, if I'm going to get blamed for it, then I should at least have done it, right?" Keeping my eyes down, I avoided Summer's gaze.

When minutes passed without Summer saying anything, I raised my eyes to find her staring out of focus at the building behind me. We stood this way for about five minutes until I reached out and took her hand. This brought her back, and she pulled me toward her place. She opened the door and led me inside, closing it behind me. She deposited me in a chair in the kitchen and went to the refrigerator. I knew the look in her eyes. She was pissed and determined to take action. I was simply left wondering in which direction she was going to explode.

After I was fed, my mind still exhausted, Summer led me to her bedroom and sat me down on the bed. I began to protest weakly, but one look from her made me lie down without further complaint. Once I was under the covers, it was only a few minutes before I felt her climb in beside me. She pulled me to her and began petting my head. This was the straw that broke me.

I burst into sobs which racked my whole body. Summer held me tighter and tried to soothe me. I turned over into her embrace. In my misery, my shining beacon was the one person I had held at bay for months. I had never stopped wanting her. If Sophia was going to accuse me of cheating, I might as well. I found Summers lips with mine, but she moved and crushed me against her chest.

In a tight voice, Summer said, "Not like this. I don't ever want to be your revenge. I deserve more than that."

In a moment full of self-pity and utter selfishness, I felt rejected. My cheeks burned with the pain and the shame of what I had tried to do. She was right. Somehow, while I had been so wrapped up in my own problems, Summer had become someone I was surprised by. I cried harder from the quasi-rejection and from being ashamed until I sniffled myself to sleep.

I woke alone in Summer's bed after the sun was gone. Taking a moment to gather myself, I made sure I wasn't going to cry again. It seemed I was all cried for out the time being. I swung my feet out of bed and onto the floor then shuffled my way to the door before I heard voices in the other room.

I began to dismiss it as Summer and her roommate until I recognized Sophia's voice. I went back to the bed in search of my phone, but it was no longer there. Knowing Summer had gotten her number from my phone, I began to panic. I was not ready for this conversation. I was *not* ready to be mature and work things out. I wasn't ready to face Sophia and the mark I'd left on her face. Something inside of me twinged with regret at the image of the red, swollen hand print staring at me from the side of her face.

I coughed, hoping Summer would hear and come to me unaccompanied. I heard a bit of movement in the other room, but it wasn't followed by Summer's steps coming down the hall. I waited a bit more, but I knew I would have to go out there alone and face whatever was waiting for me.

I crept down the hallway, definitely not handling things like an adult. I peeked around the corner from the hallway into the living room area but only saw Summer sitting on a chair, reading. She would consume any form of the written word. I stuck my entire head into the room, looking around like a deer caught in headlights, still seeing only Summer.

"Where is she?" I asked, wary.

"Where is whom?" Summer asked, not looking up from her book.

"Sophia. I heard her voice."

"She's not here. I called her—the conversation was on speaker phone."

"Why?" I asked, stepping into the room, still ready to run.

"So I could continue cooking," she stated like it was the only logical answer.

With the mention of food, my stomach gave a loud, audible protest to the fact that it was empty again. Summer smiled at me, got up and walked to the kitchen. She had cooked for me again, and it smelled delicious. How had I missed the aromas as I was slinking from the bedroom to the living room? I chalked it up to unadulterated fear.

I followed her silently to the kitchen. She was busy dishing up plates, so I slid into a chair at the table to watch her. I liked watching Summer do things. She had a way about her, an easy grace which she would never acknowledge. She placed a plate in front of me and sat across from me. Dinner was quiet, but I looked at her often. When she would catch me staring, I would look away, but I glimpsed her smiling and shaking her head when I did. After dinner, we watched a movie in Summer's room, cuddled up like so many times before. The feeling was more natural than anything I had felt with Sophia. There was no expectation with Summer's cuddling; she simply wanted to be close.

When the credits began to roll across the screen, Summer said, "It's time."

"Time for what?" I asked, feigning innocence but dreading the answer.

"Time for you to go back and face Sophia," she said.

It wasn't the answer I expected or wanted. I thought there would be a lengthy conversation happening, sure, but I never imagined Summer would tell me I had to go back to Sophia. I stared at her incredulously. How did she expect me to go back? I looked into her eyes, so green even in the dim light, and there I saw the reason. I was causing her pain by being here. Her normal, even expression was failing, and I could see what I was doing to her.

"I don't want to," I whined sullenly and picked at the blanket covering us.

"Yeah, but you need to. You have to go back, either to fix things or to end them."

"Why? You never would have sent me back before," I replied, my emotions raw from the past few days.

"Because I have a chance at a new start here," she said, staring at the wall, avoiding my gaze. "I didn't realize how much staying at home to go to school held me back. I feel free here, and I want to be someone I'm proud of, not just someone who is chasing after things she can't have, disregarding who she hurts. And I may have been talking to Noah a lot over the summer to try and sort things out because this situation with you had me all messed up. I wasn't even sure if I wanted you or if I just didn't want other people to have you. I know it sounds stupid, and I probably shouldn't tell you, but you need to know the truth. I need you to know the truth."

"So you don't love me?" I whispered. I felt numb.

"No, that's not what I said," she replied, looking at me and taking my hand. "Of course I love you, but I wasn't being fair to you or considerate of what you wanted. I was being selfish, and the situation made me confused. I'm more myself now, and I wanted to be prepared for the moment when I could have you. So neither of us would have any regrets."

I was shocked again by how much I had missed of her personal growth and how quickly it had seemed to come. I nodded and started to rise from the bed. How is it she could have outstripped me in the maturity department? Of course, I hadn't been acting up to my normal standard recently, either.

She pulled me into her arms as we waited outside for a taxi. She said it was too late for me to walk to the station even if the buses were still running.

"I know this will be hard for you no matter what you decide to do, but please know I want your happiness above my own. Please, don't think of me when you're choosing."

She squeezed me once as the taxi pulled up, and then her warmth disappeared from around me. I hadn't made a choice about what to do. I hadn't gotten that far; I didn't want to do this.

Chapter Forty

A MERE twenty minutes later, I was standing outside the door to my room, dreading what the next few hours would bring. I had spent the car ride trying to decide what I wanted, and honestly, I couldn't see myself ever excusing Sophia for calling me a prostitute, but I couldn't see myself giving up on us either. Just as confused as ever, I knocked on the door before entering to give Sophia a warning. I opened the door to see her sitting on her bed, which we had mostly used for storage, waiting for me.

"Glad to see you're not dead," she remarked.

"Glad to see your attitude hasn't improved any." Things were starting well.

"I'm not doing this. I don't want to fight with you. Please, sit down."

I crossed the room and sat in the chair next to the bed.

"I can't do this anymore. Receiving the call from Summer earlier was a complete slap in the face and not just because you were there—I expected that. But she told me you tried to kiss her. The rage I felt made me understand crimes of passion. She and I talked about how this couldn't continue, and she's right. I don't trust you because I know you love her. Even though I logically believe you haven't cheated on me, I can't think logically when I'm around you. I'm not normally a jealous person, so when I started feeling crazed with a need to possess you, to keep you from her, I was completely unable to handle it.

"I think I need time to reconsider what I want and with whom, and I think you need to do the same. It's time for you to choose completely. I want to be with you, but I can't do that if you are going to maintain any type of relationship with Summer. I know it's not fair to make you choose, but throughout our whole relationship, you have been unfair to me"

"Do you seriously think I'm going to stop being friends with Summer?" I asked, my voice quiet and my eyes on the floor.

"No, I've been stupid in some of my expectations, but I'm not completely dumb. That's why I filed for an emergency dorm change today."

"So you've already decided?" I asked, looking up from the floor to her face.

"No, you did, and I can't take feeling this way anymore. I love you, and I'm sorry," she said looking me in the eyes.

My eyes fell from hers to the place on her cheek where my hand print had been. I sat in the chair dumbfounded, staring at my hands.

How did we get here? Did my relationship really end like that? Why have I been trying so hard to hold on to this when she was going to throw it away. I guess it doesn't matter now that I think I'm asexual. Should I tell her anyway? Would it matter?

I couldn't bring myself to tell her of my discovery. What would it matter if she was leaving because of Summer, anyway? She might have even thrown it back in my face, and I didn't want another argument. After a time spent in complete silence, Sophia got up and left. She didn't say anything else to me; she just walked out. I didn't move to stop her. I didn't have a leg to stand on.

I couldn't grab her and tell her everything was going to be okay and I would go wherever she went because it wasn't true. Things wouldn't ever be fine again because she had told me I would have to choose. I couldn't choose between the two of them, and that was where it had led us. Though the choice had been made for me, I still fought with myself over what to do.

I loved Sophia before summer happened, and I knew we could have that again but at the cost of Summer. Or could we? I was so easily dismissing the arguments over our sex life, assuming she would readily accept my sexuality discovery. The truth was she probably wouldn't accept it. Sex was so important to her. She equivocated sex and love, which I simply couldn't fathom. With the memories of our awful fights circling in my head, I crawled from the chair into the bed and refused to think anymore.

When the next morning came, I ignored it. Sophia hadn't returned, so I lay there staring at her empty bed, faintly thinking that was how she must have felt when I left. I hadn't slept much, just cocooned myself in my sheets and let my mind go a hundred miles an hour while I tuned in and out of its rambling every so often. I exited the comfort of my bed only to use the restroom and grab a bit of food from the small stores we had stashed.

Sophia returned once, during a time I should have been in class. She paused at the door when she noticed my lumpy, occupied bed but persisted, grabbing her clothes and school things. I lay in bed pretending to be asleep, sneaking peeks at her through barely cracked eye lids. When she was done gathering her things, she left without a word. I stared at her now empty side of the room until the sun had set again. Somewhere in the night, time lost to me, I fell asleep.

I didn't dream—I didn't even realize it had happened until I woke and the sun was shining again. I still had no intention of moving even though my phone kept going off. I had ignored it the previous day by putting the phone on vibrate, but the stream of information being fed to it was such that it vibrated itself off the table and onto the floor where it could be heard scuttling around.

I continued to ignore it, imagining it was a mythical beast which would die if touched by human hands, like the elusive beast called uncomplicated love. I ran out of food at some point, still refusing to look at the time but progressing to looking out the window at the people roaming around campus. I made up stories to myself about the horrible tragedies in each of their lives, slowly making myself feel not as alone in my misery. I knew I was wallowing but couldn't care less.

I was playing out a particularly horrible drama where the boy in blue was sleeping with his girlfriend in green's mom—she had found out from her friend in black only five minutes ago. I was distracted by a knock at the door, one I fully intended to ignore, annoyed by my characters walking hand in hand to the edge of my field of view. The knocking continued, accompanied by the growling of the phone monster under my bed. After the third series of knocks I made my way over to the door and cracked it open.

It was Summer, and she looked none too amused. She pushed the door open and by proxy me away from it. She barged in, thankfully carrying something which smelled amazing. I began stalking toward her like a feral animal and pawed at the bag until she swatted at me. I retreated to my bed and buried myself in the covers once more.

"If you weren't so cute, I would spank you for your behavior," she said, lifting the edge of the blanket and sliding in a bag of food from a fast food joint. The edges of her displeased frown twitched upward, the only hint she wasn't deeply angry with me.

I grabbed it hungrily and began to tear away at the paper in order to get to the food. I didn't want to be civilized or "normal." Maybe if I acted crazy, I could live in my bed, and people wouldn't expect things from me. I wouldn't be blamed for my failed relationship, and I wouldn't have to admit I still couldn't choose, even in the end.

I had thoroughly shred the bag before I started in on the actual food, pushing the dismantled paper bag, dotted with spit, back out of the covers and onto the floor.

"You know that's not the part you're supposed to eat, right?!" Summer chided me.

I just grunted and stuck my hand out for a ketchup packet.

Knowing me all too well and having been through this kind of scenario with me before, she put them in my hand before I even had to snarl to inform her I was waiting for something. Truly, there was something to be said for someone who knows you so well.

It was fun telling Sophia about parts of my past but, in retrospect I knew I had only shared with her the nice parts—the parts I was proud of. Summer knew everything; she was there when things were bad, and she had lived through some of my toughest days with me. We shared so many things in common and so much history.

When I was done eating and had ejected the rest of the trash from my lair, I heard Summer fishing for the mythical beast inhabiting the underside of my bed while she called it with hers.

She emerged, apparently successful, and asked, "Who's Hugh?"

I only grunted, smelling a ploy to remove me from my plushy cave until I remembered we were supposed to meet to go over more stuff for Asexual Awareness Week. I flung the covers back from my head, my eyes closed, and groped for my phone to no avail. When I finally opened my eyes, Summer was across the room and looking through all of my missed calls and texts. I was not up to chasing her down for it so I just flopped onto my pillow and began making noises like I was dying.

Over the sounds of my garbled wailing, Summer said, "I texted him and told him to come to the dorm. You might want to make yourself presentable and maybe smell better."

I scowled at her but raised my arm to smell myself—she had a point.

"Also, Noah called."

I hadn't talked to him in a long time. I felt bad but wasn't prepared to do anything about it. Summer wasn't the only one bad at communication, and I was embarrassed by how stupid it was not to call him in the first place, which expounded with the shame of continuing not to call him. I thought longingly of calling him but could only focus on one thing at a time, and I apparently needed to get ready to have company.

I tucked in my arms and rolled off the edge of bed and onto the floor, narrowly missing hitting my head on the desk. I didn't want to see anyone, but I obviously didn't have a choice. I knew calling Noah would mean reliving the tale, and I wasn't ready to do that either.

I heard Summer gasp, but she didn't move to help me or say anything else. I knew I was being ridiculous, but it helped me to cope, pretending I was slightly less than human, more wounded animal maybe. I did have to remove myself from the floor and walk upright to go to the showers down the hall but only begrudgingly.

Chapter Forty-One

I ARRIVED back at my room to sounds of Summer and Hugh's combined laughter. I paused at the door to put myself in check. I was not going to go in there and make a spectacle of myself. No more beast lady until Hugh left. Then all bets were off, and I would return to the fluffy caves of Bedfordshire.

"Hey, sorry about not answering earlier," I said, walking through the door, trying for light and easy but missing the mark. "It's been a rough couple of days."

"Yeah, your friend Summer was just telling me about you and your girlfriend. I'm sorry our talk didn't help you explain things to her," he said, the obligatory look of polite pity on his face.

I just shrugged, completely not ready to dissect the situation with anyone.

"So what do we need to work on tonight?" I asked, eager to change the conversation.

"Tonight I thought we would take care of paperwork. We need to make flyers and pamphlets plus whatever else we can think of." He made a gesture to indicate his laptop, shrugging a little.

"Okay, cool," I muttered, grabbing my laptop so I could get started.

"So what are you guys working on?" Summer asked.

"We're preparing for Asexual Awareness Week on campus, hosted by the LGBTQA club," Hugh informed her.

"Oh, that sounds cool. I think asexuals are one of the least talked about subsets of the broad spectrum of sexuality, so I'm glad someone is doing something," Summer intoned, smiling.

I turned to look at her, pretend disgust covering my face.

"You Internet too much," I mocked her. "I had to have Hugh explain it to me because I was clueless, and here you are all knowledgeable and spouting dictionary-like."

Summer just looked at me and cocked her head to the side, blinking innocently. I tossed a small bit of the fast food paper bag left on the floor at her. She laughed and pointed to my laptop, telling me to work.

We got all of the "paperwork" done quickly, and Hugh said he had to go. We set up plans for the next week to get started on setting up speakers and events for Asexual Awareness Week. There would be daily events through the week, culminating in a party on Friday night to celebrate and raise awareness.

After Hugh was gone, I made to change back into my pajamas to become one with my bed again, but Summer grabbed my hand.

"You are not climbing back into bed," she insisted, holding tight to my arm.

"Why not?" I wailed throwing my head back and stomping.

"Because I'm here, and we're going to go out. You're not going to sit here and wallow in your misery. You've had the better part of two days in bed, and now you no longer smell like toes, so you're not climbing back in there." She pointed a disdainful finger at the mass of plush on my bed and pulled me toward the door to underline her adamancy.

I rolled my eyes but didn't try to jerk my hand out of hers—as bad as it was, I wanted to touch her. I wanted comfort, to be close to her. She pulled me out of the room and shut the door. We made our way onto campus and over to the businesses which thrived on the influx of students. We walked down the street past 10AM Somewhere. I immediately rejected going in and kept going past some clothing stores.

We strolled further and found the frozen yogurt shop. Summer pulled me toward it. I protested feebly, but there was no stopping her, the "scent" of frozen goods in her nose. I walked in and remembered how Sophia had tasted of chocolate and strawberries. I noiselessly forbid Summer from getting either addition to her bowl by standing in front of them. I didn't know if she even wanted them but she swept passed me to add sprinkles and candy orange slices. Once she had an over flowing cup of frozen yogurt in hand, we walked further before Summer prodded to me to speak.

"I can tell you're not going to do this of your own accord, so let's have it," she said, her face expectant.

"Have what?" I feigned ignorance.

"You know what. You need to talk out what happened with someone. I'm here for you."

"I don't *want* to talk about it. I really don't. She ended it because I drove her to the brink of madness." I raised my arms then let them fall at my side in a gesture of defeat. "If talking about her and dragging the truth from me is all you had in mind, I'm going back to bed. I'll talk about anything but that."

"How did you get hooked up with Hugh on this project?" she asked, changing the subject so easily I did a double take.

I sighed in relief. "I ran to be an officer in LGBTQA last year. He's the Vice President and I'm the Secretary."

"Oh, you're a secretary are you? Does the title come with an outfit?" she said suggestively, wiggling her eyebrows at me.

"Ha!" I barked, the laugh ripping from my throat, escaping the prison I had put all of my happy feelings in.

The conversation about Hugh brought a resurgence of my desire to tell someone about what I had learned, even if it wasn't Sophia. The moment dawned on me—this was my chance to test the waters with my feelings of asexuality.

"Hey, can I tell you something?" I asked quietly, oddly feeling shy or maybe self-conscious.

"Of course you can. Since when is that a question?" she asked, a scowl masking her concern.

"I don't know." I rolled my eyes at her. "I talked to Hugh a lot when we were busy not working the other night. It was really cool because he wasn't annoyed by my thousands of questions or by us not getting any work done. The conversation we had made me think about myself and my desires, and I think I might be asexual or at least gray-sexual."

I hid my face as much as I could behind my hair. I didn't know what to expect. After all the fighting with Sophia, I was prepared for everyone to be all but riotous about the subject of sex. Summer and I weren't ready to hit the sheets, but we both knew the other one was interested in a relationship.

"I'm not surprised," she murmured between a mouth full of frozen yogurt. "I've known you long enough, and please don't forget we shared a boyfriend at one point. There were many times you could have done something with me, but you wanted to hangout or hold hands instead. Granted, I thought some of it was you being a little bit of a prude, but I can't say I didn't consider other possibilities."

I felt a mix of relief and annoyance rise within me. How could she know better than me what was going on inside my head? I looked at her, and she turned to look into my eyes. I saw nothing there but acceptance and understanding. All of my annoyance faded but left a little bit of anger in its wake, changing my expression to one of barely concealed snark.

"What?" she cried, chuckling. "I'm sorry I knew before you did. I mean, you knew I loved you before I could admit it to myself. This makes us even."

"I did not!" I said, throwing my hands up.

"Yes you did. You wouldn't have risked our friendship if you weren't sure I was going to return the sentiment. I know you better than that. Give me some credit." She gestured to her heart, affronted.

"Well, I didn't know it consciously," I said, shaking my head a little.

"Well, neither did I about your asexuality. It just made a lot of sense when you said it." She bit her bottom lip, making her so cute and innocent I couldn't be mad.

"Bah!" I cried at her.

She laughed as we continued to walk up and down the streets surrounding the campus. After finishing her frozen yogurt, she took my hand in hers. We were walking down the street hand in hand when I thought of Sophia, hoping she wasn't around seeing us. I didn't want to cause her more pain, depression nagging at me. I had begun to feel unencumbered, but not anymore. With the return of her to my mind, I remembered how I was afraid to tell her about my new self-discovery and wondered if it would have made a difference.

"Summer?" I asked tentatively.

"Hunh?" she replied, absent mindedly.

"Would you still want to be with me? I mean obviously not right now, but does my being asexual make you change your mind about...?" I trailed off, afraid of the answer and upset about something I had no control over.

"Not for a minute. Matter of fact, I would be totally fine with 'right now' except I know you need time. When we do *finally* make this official, it's going to be forever. I don't want to mess it up with leftovers from Sophia," she said, pulling me into a hug.

Tucked into her embrace I felt like a kid. "Hey," I whined. Summer ignored my feeble complaints. "So you're not worried about my not wanting to have sex with you and stuff?"

"No, I'm not worried. We've had a mostly happy relationship thus far without sex, so if it's what you want, then I'll do it with you. I'm not saying I won't think about you naked, and I'm not saying I won't want to touch you, but your asexuality won't be what stops us from being together."

I stared at the ground, tears welling in my eyes. She was willing to accept me just the way I was, no questions asked. It was how love should be. She released me, but we stood close to each other even after letting go.

"Thank you," I croaked. "That means a lot to me. I don't know what I'll want when I'm ready, but sex became a big deal with Sophia and me. She thought I was having sex with everyone but her, therefore I didn't want it from her. That's when she started getting really jealous, and then the night of explosion," I explained. "I didn't even get to tell her what I had figured out because the night I stayed out late talking everything over with Hugh is the night I ended up at your place."

"She doesn't know what she's talking about. If she knew you, she would know you would never do that. Plus, she was jealous before, but she didn't have a reason. When she found one, she clung to it for dear life. I won't say I'm not at least a little thankful for the time she has given us apart. It has let me work on myself to become someone who I think deserves you, and it obviously let you figure out some things about yourself. I know it's hard, and I'm not saying I'm happy for your suffering, but I know now that whatever relationship we end up in, we have to give each other room to grow and change without it destroying the relationship. Otherwise, there is no point."

"Can I say something without you getting angry?"

"Depends." A fleeting look of worry skittered across her face.

"How did you get so smart?"

"Noah." She smirked. "And maybe a therapist."

"Wow, that therapist must have been quite pricey," I chided her jokingly.

"I wouldn't know," Summer said, holding her chin high. "I never saw a bill. She was excellent, though, and I owe her a lot for where I am now."

"Her?" I asked with a silly pang of jealousy.

"Yes, *her*. And don't do that," she said, poking me to make me giggle.

I stuck my tongue out at her and huffed. As the sky started darkening, we made our way back to the dorm room. I was in a much better place than I had been before our outing, and I thought maybe I could get out of my bed again the next day. That was how I was going to take things—one day at a time until everything made sense again.

"So, tomorrow is Saturday," I began when Summer and I were back in my dorm room.

"Indeed it is," she replied, looking out the window.

"So, do you maybe want to have a sleep over?" I asked, trying to be coy and innocent.

"Don't think I'm tricked by you," she said with disgust, but I could hear the smile in her voice, though her back was to me.

"Trick you? I would never dream of such a thing," I replied, pushing my act over the top and feigning offense.

"Hahaha. Yes, I will stay with you, but you are to stay in your own bed," she said, turning around to face me and pointing to my bed, which still slightly resembled a cave.

"Fine," I said, rolling my eyes at her.

She left the room to go take a shower, and I knew it was time to bite the bullet and call Noah. We were soon going to have to work together a lot for Asexual Awareness week, and I missed him. I climbed on top of my bed, crushing the cave, and dialed his number.

"Hello?" he answered.

"Hi!" I layered on the enthusiasm in preparation for his anger.

"Hey, *Penny*. How are you?" His use of my hated nickname deflating my fabricated bubble instantaneously.

"Noah," I whined, switching tactics.

"No, no bull from you."

"But—"

"No! You left me high and dry while you waded your way through your mess without so much as a pity call. I had to hear from a guy in

LGBTQA who has History of Architecture with *her*. I wanted to be there for you, and you shut me out."

"I'm sorry, Noah." My true feelings of remorse flowed through my voice.

"That's it? You're not going to argue with me and defend yourself?"

"Nope."

"I can't stay mad if you're not going to defend yourself. I won't fight an unarmed lady."

"Well, good for me then. I don't have any fight left in me."

"Do I need to come over with ice cream?" His voice took on a proper amount of concern.

"No, not tonight. Summer's going to stay the night."

"Be careful, Penelope," he warned.

"I know, I will. I'll call you tomorrow so we can catch up?" I said, hopeful we could mend what I might have messed up with my foolishness.

"You better." I could hear his smile and smiled in return.

We hung up, and I felt much better. I wasn't sure why I had psyched myself out so much, but Noah wasn't a jerk, my brain was. I would meet him tomorrow at 10AM Somewhere and fix everything.

Chapter Forty-Two

I saw Summer off in the morning as I headed to the diner to meet Noah. We greeted each other with hugs and apologies on both sides. We sat, and I told him the rest of the story starting from our last conversation during the summer to the night I had spent alone staring at Sophia's empty bed. He told me he was sorry for my relationship ending but was more concerned with my not confiding in him.

"Why would you hide what was happening from me?" The hurt he felt was evident on his face.

"I don't know." I planted my forehead on the table. "I was afraid of failing, with Sophia, and I assigned that inner voice to you. It was unfair and led to my being stupid. Please forgive me?"

"Of course I forgive you. As long as you know I would never hold it against you for leaving someone who was making you so miserable."

"Yes, I know," I said, feeling small and ashamed.

We spent the day together, further preventing me from slinking back into my plush cave and taking one tiny half-step toward recovering my shattered sense of self and mending my torn heart.

I nursed my wounds slowly. My relationship with Noah took flight like I had never grounded it. Between him and Summer, I was rarely alone if I didn't want to be, which I didn't. I was content to immerse myself into any world but my own, reluctant to deal with my feelings head on. I tried to ease my pain by attempting to convince Summer to kiss me, but since I had made my asexuality clear to her, she told me if we started in on kissing, we wouldn't have anything to look forward to. She never said it with a tone to make me feel like kissing was all she was looking forward to, though.

Asexual Awareness Week came in a blur of time. Things were planned to the T thanks to Hugh. I often told him he should have been the Secretary and the Vice President of LGBTQA, as I was unfit in comparison. The week started with a general meeting inviting everyone on campus and sped forward from there. The meeting was open to all so we could spread awareness and educate people about asexuality. Hugh led the meeting and shared his story after a bit of general educating. Then he invited others to speak out about their experiences with sexuality as a whole.

I shared my story, starting a year ago and progressing through my indecision about asexuality. I loved the acceptance permeating not simply the meetings but the club as a whole. No one stood up and told me I didn't belong if I had questions, nor did they say it couldn't be true because otherwise I would've known. It was an amazing feeling to be accepted at face value without anyone telling me what I could or couldn't feel. Part of me wished Sophia had been there, so she would finally understand I hadn't been lying. Yet even without her understanding and acceptance, I had learned who I was and how I was different and that it wasn't bad to be so.

Tuesday, we had a bake sale with LGBTQA and RAVPA combined. The profits went to abused women's homes, and with each item the customer got a pamphlet about asexuality. I wasn't delusional enough to think everyone would read it, educate themselves, and be more considerate of others in the future, but even if only one of those things happened for one person, it would still be worth it.

On Wednesday, we had guest speakers come in, a prominent figure for the AVEN forums, and some others who had stories to share. Thursday was a sexual violence prevention class, again combining the two clubs I was in, led by an officer from the local police station. Before I knew it, Friday was upon us. The party started at 8:00 pm, and I had invited Summer to come with me. She showed up at my dorm around 6:00. I opened the door and felt the familiar dropping of my heart to the bottom of my stomach. I pulled her to me, but she turned her head as I made to kiss her.

"When are you going to let me kiss you?" I asked harshly.

"When you make an honest woman out of me!" she cried like a girl from the old south.

"No really," I demanded.

"When this doesn't hurt anymore," she said, watching my face. "Sophia."

I frowned then scowled, and she just looked at me. My eyes betrayed my sadness and undealt with emotions.

"Fine," I said, irritated. "Let's go or we're going to be late."

"Yes, madam secretary. You're the boss," she said, ignoring that I was bothered in any way.

"Yeah right!" I retorted as I opened the door for her.

The party was amazing. Hugh and I had really outdone ourselves, though realistically it had mostly been Hugh. He had gotten some of the local shops involved, and they donated food and decorations in exchange for their names being displayed on the skirt of the stage. They got to advertise and set up a booth to sell things if they wanted to, but to us it was nothing for what they had provided.

Set up took about an hour, and then I got changed for the party. I walked back into the big ballroom to find Summer swaying to the music. I had forgotten in the time we had been apart exactly what that girl could do to me on a dance floor. She wasn't particularly an amazing dancer, but her body moved so sensually it rendered me stupefied in an instant.

I stalked toward the dance floor, her back turned to me, and began to dance with her. If ever there was a more blissful way to spend four hours, I didn't know it. I could have stayed on the dance floor far past the music stopping and the decorations being removed, but at some point we were the only ones left and Hugh turned the lights on, breaking the spell I was under.

I took a step back from Summer but held her hand in mine, not wanting to lose the magic completely. I left break down to the other members who hadn't been there to set up while I took Summer to 10AM Somewhere. We had both worked up quite an appetite on the dance floor.

"Thanks for inviting me," Summer enthused as we waited for our food. "I had a really good time."

"The pleasure was all mine," I assured her, blatantly staring.

Her smile, always making me weak, could melt me completely. I reached across the table for her hands, oblivious to everything and everyone else.

"I want to know if we both agree to give this the shot we have both been holding our breaths so long for," Summer probed, looking down at our joined hands.

"Are you asking me to be your girlfriend?" I asked, chuckling, my thumb rubbing the back of her hand absently.

"No, I'm not," she said, more forcefully than I expected. My smile faded. "I'm just making sure we're on the same page and that neither of us is taking the other for a ride we don't intend to bring back to the station."

"I have no intention of leaving you hanging. I want to be with you, and I think this is as good an opportunity as any," I urged, more than ready to move on and be with Summer.

"Good, but we're still going to wait until you have your emotions sorted. As someone once said to me, 'I deserve to be more than your rebound,'" she said with a joking air of superiority and a knowing smile.

'Yes." I looked into her beautiful eyes. "Yes, you do deserve so much more."

I released her hand and returned mine to my lap. I had, up to then, been trying to bury my sadness over Sophia in my love for Summer, but I wouldn't do it anymore, and for me that meant no physical closeness.

I looked at her one last time then changed the subject. I had work to do, but it was work I would have to do without her in order for things to end well. I loved her, and I wanted that for us.

We returned to the dorm, and since it was so late, Summer decided to spend the night. She told me she was going to take a shower and I joked about going with her, but she gave me a "like hell" look. I laughed, watching her walk out. I called Noah almost as soon as the door clicked shut.

"I saw you on that dance floor, Ms. Van Buren. Are you calling me from the hospital after they surgically separated your pelvises?"

"Ha. Ha. Ha," I snarked, less than amused.

"Okay, what's wrong?"

"I'm ready."

"Ready for what?" he asked, his curiosity so evident I could see his eyebrow rising.

"Ready to fix it—for you to fix me."

"What?" He sounded dismayed.

"Noah," I whined. "I know you did some Jedi mind trick stuff on Summer to help her, and now I need you to help me. I want to get past Sophia so I can be with Summer." I felt the corners of my mouth pulling downward.

"I love you, Penelope, but changing isn't something you do for someone else. It's something you do for you. And I surely can't do it for you. All I did over summer break was talk to Summer because *she* called *me*. She changed herself. I was simply a sounding board."

"That sounds like hard work." My frown deepened, even though I knew he was right. I was being hard headed because I wanted a quick fix.

He laughed and said, "It probably is. I wouldn't know because I'm perfect."

"Oh *right*." I rolled my eyes and shoved as much sarcasm into my voice as possible.

"You can do this, Penelope. While I say you have to change for you and not her, she can still be a good motivator, just not *the* reason."

"Too many rules," I claimed. "I'm out."

As the words left my mouth, Summer opened the door and strode into the room, and my breath caught in my throat. I was bewildered as to how I had suppressed my feelings for her while I was with Sophia. I probably owed a lot of it to anger.

"Lies," I hissed once I could speak. "I lied. I'll do it."

Chapter Forty-Three

As October pushed toward November, Noah was in full Halloween mania when he called me after Asexual Awareness Week. His parents had consented to a raging Halloween party at their house, and he recruited to help make it a night no one would forget.

Noah made me agree to his passing out flyers for the party at RAVPA and wanted me to talk to Hugh about having them in the LGBTQA meetings as well. Since it was a come-one-come-all kind of invitation, no one seemed to have a problem with it. I called Summer to invite her, and she asked if she could bring along some people. I explained the general premise of the "no jerks" rule and told her to bring anyone who would fit in.

Summer and her friends arrived early, Summer dressed as the Last Unicorn. Noah freaked out when he saw her, and they jumped up and down for a moment in pure glee. I was Sabriel, a character from my favorite book series, and had received no such admiration from Noah—probably because he hadn't read them. Noah was dressed as a pirate for reasons he said I wouldn't understand, and Alyssa was a princess ninja hybrid.

I hadn't met any of Summer's school friends before, and it was a little weird to immediately put them to work after saying hello, but Noah's idea of a fun Halloween party also included descriptors like:

complicated, elaborate and award-winning. Even with the extra help, we only barely had everything ready to go by the time everyone started arriving.

I helped welcome people to the party for a while, talking in snatches to Noah between answering the door. While it had only been a few weeks, I was ready to be done with grieving over my failed relationship—ready to move on and not rehash every conversation. Noah was adamant about how not analyzing the past was horrible and allowed mistakes to be repeated. No matter how right he was, I refused to let him know I thought so.

After a few pokes at Noah's plan, I hung out with Summer and her friends for a while. They kept to themselves, so I drifted from her group to mingle with my friends. I was surprised by the dichotomy of how hard and easy being away from Summer was. It was hard because I wanted to be beside her even though I knew better and easy because I knew she wasn't going to get mad or cause a scene about it.

I was dancing with some people from LGBTQA when Summer found me to say she was leaving. It was around 1 am, and she was going to head out with her friends.

I frowned. "You can stay with me tonight if you want to," I said, batting my eyes sweetly.

She laughed and caressed the side of my face.

"I would love to, but not now. I'll see you later. You make an amazing Abhorsen, in case I didn't tell you before," she said, smiling at me.

I smiled back and walked her out to the car, saying bye to all of her friends.

I didn't see Summer after the party for what seemed like an eternity. Noah said it was for the best and had warned Summer to stay away. I knew deep down he was right, but I didn't have to like it. Without the distraction of trying to make her swoon, I was left alone with my thoughts far too often. I called Noah in the quietest moments so he could drown out the litany of voices in my head telling me I was going to be alone for a long time, telling me I didn't deserve to be happy. I talked my old relationship out over and over again, trying to figure out where it all went wrong and trying not to blame myself.

There in lay the problem. I did blame myself. I blamed myself for not being able to choose, for forcing Sophia to interact with Summer, and ultimately for not being able to be the sexual creature she wanted me to be. Logically, I knew I was being ridiculous, but I really felt like the failure of my relationship rested solely in the hands of my not wanting to sleep with her.

I hadn't heard from Sophia since the night we had broken up. She quit both of the clubs I was involved in, and we didn't have any classes together. I even received a new roommate. She was a mid-semester transfer who kept to herself and went to bed way too early.

I tried to sort things in my mind, to be confident in myself and who I was. I couldn't change the fact that I was asexual any more than I could change the fact of my being bi-romantic, but I couldn't stop hearing Sophia telling me I needed to be "fixed." Her voice, once reassuring and sound, now dogged me in quiet moments. Even though I knew she would never want that, I couldn't stop it.

Noah told me some things would simply take time. He came over, and we watched musicals like we had in the beginning of our friendship. I slowly but surely began to feel a knot in my stomach loosen. He told me almost every day how proud he was of the person I had become since he'd known me. At first I blew him off, but then I began to think of reasons to be proud of myself. I started to feel like maybe I deserved happiness.

In late November, I received a frantic call from my mother.

"Hello?" I answered. We talked every few weeks when she called to make sure I was still alive.

"Thank God. Are you okay?" she blurted, panic lacing her voice.

"Calm down, Mom. What's going on?" I asked, trying to relax her while feeling my own breath quicken.

"Haven't you heard? There was a gay man attacked in Seattle and beaten to death!" she screamed into the phone.

"Mom, despite my sexuality, I am *not* a man," I cried, thankful to be outside and not in the library.

"I know"-inhale-"but it could"-cough-"have been you."-moan-"I can't believe I've been so stupid!"-sigh of frustration-"I don't care who you love."-sob-"I just need you to know I love you!" she said, barely able to get the words out.

"Mom, please calm down. I can barely understand you," I said, trying to placate her.

I heard my mother force herself to take three deep breaths before beginning again.

"It was like a slap in the face—a wakeup call, and it wasn't about what the neighbors said or what your grandparents thought. It was about how much I love you and how much I've been trying to make you behave when I should just let you live. I knew I couldn't control you after you left, but I wasn't ready to let go," she said between moments of barely contained sobbing.

I felt a small flicker—a glow—begin to warm me. My mother had never praised me as a child, never told me she was proud of me. I love yous were saved for events which never came. Her breaking down and telling me all of this was more than I could have hoped for, but I was skeptical and unable to stop years of conditioning myself not to show I needed her love.

"Mom, I hate to be the bearer of bad news, but both grandma and grandpa know I like women. They both told me in no uncertain terms they don't care and they love me no matter what."

"*What?*" she shrieked. "Your grandparents know?"

"Yes, Mom, they told me last year at Christmas. And much to everyone's shock, I'm sure, they did not keel over. Grandma also told me she knows you and my aunts try to keep things from her, but she's not yet deaf or senile."

I heard my mother's huffing and puffing on the other end of the line, undoubtedly having a mock argument under her breath which she would never actually have with my grandparents.

"I'm sorry you were worried, Mom. I'll be home in a month, and I'll hug you then," I said, mostly patronizing.

Having not experienced the shock my mother had and still vividly remembering her condemning most of my actions, I didn't feel too sorry for her.

"Don't patronize me." she began to cry again. "I'm trying to say I'm sorry. I'm sorry for the way I treated you"-sob-"and Sophia when you brought her home." Sob. "I promise if you bring her with you for Christmas then I will be nice." Sob.

"Mom, Sophia won't be coming home with me for Christmas," I said, beginning to pace.

"Oh no!" she wailed. I imagined her melting into an armchair. "I made her never want to come home with you again, didn't I? Are you staying there for Christmas? Oh, please don't stay there! I want you to come home."

She got the words out but only barely as she sent herself into hysterics.

"Mom!" I shouted at the phone. "Please calm down. Sophia and I broke up, and you had nothing to do with it." *Though I wasn't truly confident of that point.* "Things between us just didn't work out."

"Okay," she whined, miserable and pathetic.

"Mom, please go lie down and get some sleep. You know I'm fine now. I'm completely safe on the campus, and everything will be okay," I said, trying to rein her in.

She continued to sob on the phone for a little while longer, but eventually hung up after she had crawled into bed.

While I was touched by my mother's seemingly heartfelt apology for her behavior, I was more concerned with not having heard anything about the story before her. At the very least, I should have heard about it from someone in LGBTQA. I got on my phone immediately, enacting a web of people which would stretch to cover most of the campus in about an hour or so.

Two hours later, I was no better off. No one had heard a thing, and now I was getting bombarded with questions. I figured news like that warranted breaking the near silence between Summer and me, or I liked the excuse to call her. When she answered, I could hear the smile in her voice. I tried to calm the butterflies in my stomach to see if she knew anything, but they wouldn't be stifled. I felt confident Summer would have heard of the story, being the technophile she was. If she didn't know then no one would. However, she also had no answers for me. I tried to come up with reasons to stay on the phone and listen to her voice, but she had work to do and got off the phone rather quickly.

I set my mind back on the task at hand. I began to think my mother had made it all up. Maybe she had watched a documentary and thought it was current news. I was distracted from my contemplation by my phone ringing again.

"Hey, buddy, what's up?" I asked my brother upon answering.

"Did you like your early Christmas present?" he replied, the devilishness apparent in his voice.

"I didn't get anything. What was it?" I asked, nonplussed.

"The call you got from mom was it." He sniggered.

"*What?*" I cried, almost dropping my phone.

"Well, you know she believes everything sent to her in an email, so I made a fake email address which looked official from your college and emailed her about this gay guy who found unfortunate circumstances." He was obviously proud of his masterful plan.

"That's so not cool, man! Now there are about a million people here who are wondering what the hell because I've been calling everyone trying to find out what happened!"

"What? I didn't hurt anyone, and there was no way I could watch anymore of the painful parade that was you, Sophia and her over the summer. I didn't think you could call the whole school so quickly."

"It's called I phone tree, duh." My emotions were mixed. On one hand, it was brilliant. On the other, I had a ton of people to call and explain the situation to. "I appreciate where you were coming from, but you have to tell her it was fake. Otherwise, she's going to be talking to people everywhere, and they're going to think she's stupid."

"Yeah, well, that's just an added bonus for me." He chuckled again.

"No, seriously, you have to tell her."

"Fine! I'll tell her tomorrow, but you have to admit the results were pretty amazing!" He was openly laughing then.

"So, you miss me that much." I prodded him to see what I could him to admit to.

"I wouldn't go *that* far."

I laughed with him, for his denial and for his well-meant prank on our mother. I gave him props for his ingenuity but still disapproved of his methods. It was a testament, whether he wanted to claim it or not, to how much he loved me and wanted me to be happy, wanted me to continue to come home on my breaks from school.

Chapter Forty-Four

NOVEMBER ROLLED into December. As my heart healed and I got my self-love back in place, I oddly wished I could see Sophia again. Even if it was only from a distance, we could wave at each other in a sort of well wishing. I wanted her to know I wished for her happiness and forgave her for all the things she had said to me. Regardless of her absence, though, I had put a lot of effort into moving past it, putting the hurt behind me.

Noah, as usual, had been right about keeping my distance from Summer so I didn't hurt her in the process. When I felt moderately whole again, Noah suggested I sit down with Summer to discuss what we each needed to make our relationship work. Summer and I would only have one shot at making us a couple, and we both knew it. I called her, and we agreed to meet on the waterfront so we could talk without interruption.

I was standing with my back to the street looking out at the Sound when I felt a tap on the shoulder. I turned around and there she was. She was beautiful, even in the gray blur of the day. Her red hair moved gently in the slight wind. She was bundled up against the cold; I had forgotten how easily she was effected by it. I felt bad for recommending we meet outside until I reminded myself she had agreed.

I held out my arms to hug her, momentarily afraid she would refuse until she stepped into them, smiling. She nestled her face into my neck, and joy flowed through my veins filling the spots left empty by our near two months of silence. Her scent overwhelmed my senses even though we were outdoors—she smelt like home. I knew our not talking hadn't been her fault, but it was all too reminiscent of my first year at school for my liking. I hugged her tight and told her I had missed her. She said she missed me too into the warmth of my neck then asked if we could go inside somewhere.

While the original point of meeting at the waterfront was to be where we wouldn't be interrupted or overheard, she was shivering so violently when I released her from our hug, I couldn't refuse her the warmth of a place indoors. We found a small coffee shop a couple blocks away which was mostly empty. We both ordered hot drinks and sat at a table opposite each other.

I laid my hands on the table palms up, saying with a gesture what I was afraid to say with words. I knew I didn't have the right to ask for couple-like affection while we lived in a limbo-type relationship while I put myself back together, but I did it anyway with actions instead of speech for fear of rejection. If I didn't say it out loud, I could pretend she might not have known what I wanted exactly.

I sighed mentally when she placed one of her mitten-clad hands in mine. It was a small thing, but it was the baby step I needed to let me know we were both still on the path of us being together.

"I'm glad you came out today," I said, sounding oddly formal. I was nervous, which was weird. She was my best friend, yet we were sitting across from each other almost like strangers. "I'm sorry, that was weird. This is weird."

She smirked and retracted her hand. "It is a bit weird, isn't it? But I don't know why. I mean, we've known each other forever, but now we're planning to traverse the unknown together."

"Maybe it's the waiting and the silence. It's not like we haven't gone without talking before, but I don't think it's ever been such a conscious effort for me to *not* pick up the phone and dial your number."

"I know what you mean. I've never wanted to talk to you as much as I did when I couldn't. Maybe that says something about me as a person, but it's the truth."

She wasn't alone in her feelings. Even when we had been far apart and our conversations halted, I was never under the impression I wasn't allowed to talk to her, which was how the situation felt. I smiled at her, wishing we could just go back to before everything got messed up, back before I went away to school. But to do that would undo all the lessons we had both learned along the way.

The barista called out our number, and Summer went to retrieve our steaming drinks. When she sat back down and scooted mine across the table, I asked, "So, you're still waiting for me?"

"I told you I would, and I meant it. I sit at home and eat ramen and shun the people at school who try to bridge the gap."

"Well, you don't have to be lonely. You can make friends."

"I have friends. You met them. What I need is you."

I smiled down at my hot tea and breathed in the fragrance of it. "I'm working on it. I promise I am."

"I didn't say it to rush you. I only wanted to reassure you of my commitment."

"It means a lot to me." I smiled as I looked up into her eyes.

We didn't need to have a conversation about what the other one wanted, not now. It was enough to see her face, and in it I found the answers. She wanted me, me and her as we had always been, but more. We had enough conversations over our years of friendship to fill a book with things we knew about each other. I simply needed a reminder. I let the silence stretch between us as we sipped our drinks, but it was comfortable and familiar.

As she sucked the dregs of her hot chocolate from the cup, she asked, "What did you need to talk about?"

"Nothing—everything. I just needed to see you to bring me back to myself."

She beamed at me, the full Summer smile. I couldn't help but smile back as we got up to throw away our trash and head back out into the cold.

"I think I need more of this," I told her, gesturing to the two of us.

"Done listening to Noah then?"

"He doesn't know everything, and I don't think he realizes I'm not me without you."

I reached for her hand as we walked but she pulled it away gently.

"I want us back on speaking-every-day terms, but are you ready for more than that?"

"I think so."

"I need you to know so before we go there."
I nodded.

Summer and I talked every day after our outing to the Sound. I would be lying if I said no part of me was waiting for her to drop off the face of the earth again, but every day when I received a text or a call, it filled the hole made long ago with love and an understanding that she was trying as I was. The days of thinking about Sophia had passed long before I felt whole again. I forgave her for the things she had said and made peace with my asexuality.

I had put myself in counseling to rectify the feelings I had about sex, Sophia and Clayton. By mid Decemeber, I understood why I felt like they were the same. Clayton had tried to force himself on me. Then when Sophia would be so adamant and push sex on me, I would sometimes zone out while it happened because my mind had associated the two. It explained the panic I felt and the eventual need to make her understand I didn't want to, which ultimately ended our relationship.

It was finals week again before I knew it. I felt sure of myself once again, but I didn't know if I was ready for another relationship. I couldn't be sure if my feelings of completeness were because I was healed or if it was the stress of finals pushing everything else from my mind. I kept the idea to myself, not wanting to get Summer's hopes up. Winter break was coming, which would give me plenty of time to assess things properly.

Finals week passed, and even with the rough semester, I got good grades. I was excited to be going home. I wanted to see if my mom really had changed and maybe start a positive relationship with her. I missed my brother and the rest of my family. Christmas was everywhere as we rode the shuttle to the airport. Summer and I flew home together, her sleeping on my shoulder for most of the flight.

Summer's parents picked us up from the airport, eager to see her since she had been away so long. Summer and I didn't discuss protocol or anything like that about returning home. I knew her parents respected her privacy, but more so, we were who we had always been. No need to make a big deal out of something we had been doing forever.

They dropped me off at my mom's house. I was sad to leave Summer but grateful to have a bit more time to evaluate things before I fell into her again. We were set to see each other in a week. It would give each of us time to see our families before consuming each other for the whole of the winter break.

After waving goodbye, I walked up the walkway. My mother rushed out the door, grabbed me up and crushed me against her, apparently not dissuaded by Cooper telling her the story was fake. I was hoping it hadn't changed her mind.

I dropped my bags to hug her back, and in my ear she whispered, "I love you."

I had waited years for this. What kind of child waits nineteen years to hear I love you from their parent? I guess this one. We stood holding each other in the front yard without concern for the minutes spent there. In fact, we stood there so long Cooper came out of the house to issue his greeting.

"Hey, how was the flight?" he called to me, walking from the house.

"Good," I called back, not breaking the hug.

His monster arms encircled us both. This caused my mother to burst into tears. We didn't let go until she had stopped crying. After a few minutes, I felt the rumble of my bother chuckling silently. When she felt sated, my mother straightened herself and looked at me and my brother.

She smiled and turned to walk into the house, calling over her shoulder, "Don't think this means you're ungrounded."

I looked at Cooper, who rolled his eyes, his grin dying on his lips, and I burst out laughing. Even though I loved Seattle, I had a feeling being home wasn't going to be so hard this time—maybe even enjoyable.

Epilogue

It had only been a week since my parents dropped Penelope at her door, only a week since I had watched her walk into the welcoming arms of her family. From the greeting she received from her mother, I could tell the idea I gave Cooper had worked. I wanted no credit. It was not up to me to fix her family, but if I had it in me to make Penelope happier, then you would be hard pressed to find a way to stop me.

I saw her car turn onto my street. I began bouncing on the balls of my feet with excitement. It had been several months since Penelope and Sophia's relationship had ended, and as patient as I wanted to be, I was ready for her to be ready for me. I knew that sounded convoluted, but it was true whether or not it was right. She pulled up to the curb, and I bounded to the car, hopping in happily, ready to make sure things went well.

"Where do you want to go?" she asked, turning in her seat to give me a quick hug.

"I don't care," I said, releasing her to put on my seat belt. "I'm just happy to see you."

The amused grin she wore when I bounced into the car turned into a breathtaking smile I would kill people for. She meant so much to me. I wondered if the mere sight of Penelope would ever *stop* taking my breath away; I decided probably not. I marveled, as I often did, at how

I could have been so stupid as to not see how much she meant to me before my world had blown apart.

I reached over and pulled a hair out of her eyes, her face leaning into my hand. I longed to caress her and pull her to me. If she still wasn't ready to be with me, this break was going to seem longer than I thought, but I would be supportive even if it killed me.

"Well, you have to pick." She chuckled as we pulled away from my house.

"Why do I have to pick?" I protested, not caring as long as we were together.

"You just do. That's the way these things work," Penelope stated, giving me a disapproving look with a smirk.

We ended up at the mall with no real plans and nothing exciting to pass the time except sitting in the food court watching people walk by. We were people watchers. Penelope's favorite thing to do was make up stories about them. I could always tell her mood or what was going on in her mind by the type of stories she told. Today's stories were all of love, not of getting over someone or struggling with depression. I felt hopeful for the outlook of our winter break.

"Hey!" Penelope shouted then quickly turned to face to me, a blush creeping up her cheeks. She had obviously not meant to yell. "Look at the cute old couple over there!" she whispered excitedly at me.

I turned my head in the direction she had nodded, and sure enough, there were two old men sitting together on a bench, their hands clasped together between them.

"They are quite the heart-melters," I told her, amused by her excitement.

"Do you think we'll be as adorable when we are old and walking through the mall holding hands?" she asked me turning to look at the couple once more.

My eyebrows shot up in the air. Was she thinking about us growing old together already? I stretched my hand across the table and took hers in mine, snapping her mind back to focus on us. She looked down at our hands then ever so slowly up to my face. In the same tempo, the amazing smile crept across her face. I liquefied into a puddle in the chair.

"I think we should start our legacy now," I suggested, motioning with my head to the pathway around the mall, hoping beyond hope I wasn't making a mistake.

We got up from the table and strolled around the mall. She never lost her smile, and I couldn't stifle my grin. We walked hand in hand, getting dirty looks from some people as we passed, but neither of us cared. We rounded a corner and ran into the old couple who had been on the bench. They were walking the opposite direction as us. I smiled when one looked our way. He took it as an opportunity to strike up a conversation.

"How are you ladies doing?" he asked politely, steering himself and his partner closer to us.

"We're doing just fine," I told him genially, looking to Penelope.

"Good, good. I just wanted to say you girls have the right idea. We hid our love for what seemed like an eternity and we both regret it to this day. You stay true to yourselves and don't let everyone else tell you how to live your life," he said.

"Thank you," I said. "That means a lot to me. I like to think that if we all stick together, we can maybe make some headway against the bigotry which lays waste to the intelligence of good people."

Both men's eyes looked a little shocked but amused as their faces broke out into almost identically lopsided smiles. "You ladies be careful now, you hear."

"You too," Penelope and I intoned together.

They continued on their walk, and I turned to Penelope and smiled. She was staring after the old couple and squeezing my hand. After they turned the corner, we too continued walking. As the day started to darken, I turned to Penelope, my curiosity and lack of straightforward conversation driving me crazy.

I asked her, "So, how are you doing on the whole emotional recovery front? Well, I hope." I nodded to our clasped hands.

Penelope turned to me with a knowing smile but said nothing. She hadn't shied away from the mention of her past relationship. I had let my hope win out, but she hadn't taken any of the ample opportunities to tell me how she was feeling. Maybe she was hiding her pain, or if she was ready to move on maybe she no longer wanted to do so with me. Penelope had confided her asexuality to me in October, but she hadn't acted like that was going to stop her from being with me. Maybe she'd changed her mind.

I gazed at her expectantly, but she just began humming along with the Christmas music playing throughout the mall. I hated Christmas music, but I loved the sound of her voice. We were walking past the main entrance for the second time when Penelope began to pull me toward the doors. I protested because of the cold outside, but she pulled me persistently and wrapped me up in her embrace. We walked outside, my back cuddled up against her, into a courtyard centered with a huge Christmas tree.

"Why are we out here?" I was still protesting, the cold making me cranky as I shivered.

"Why do you always have to ask so many questions?" she complained and pushed me with her entire body toward the tree.

"To drive you crazy," I retorted, my curiosity piqued despite my teeth beginning to chatter.

The only time Penelope withheld information was when she planning something. I was confused as to how, since the mall plan had not been a plan at all. Nonetheless, she was giving off I'm-trying-to-be-sneaky vibes. I tried to turn to look at her, but between the diming light and her head being on my shoulder, face next to mine, I couldn't make out her expression.

Penelope pulled me tighter to her and whispered in my ear, "I love you."

My chest exploded in relief and bliss. How long had I waited for those words? I nestled into her and snuggled against her neck.

"I love you too," I crooned at her, my heart soaring around and over the Christmas tree.

She turned me around to face her, and her lips met mine as everything around us lit up. I pulled back in surprise and looked around at the newly lit splendor. The tree went from a normal evergreen to a twinkling pillar of lights. At the top was a beautiful star with draped lights going to the buildings close by, creating a lighted canopy over our heads. A nutcracker and a ballerina had come from inside and began dancing around the tree to music being played into the circle. It was like someone had flipped a switch and made the world magical.

"How did you do that?" I asked in wonder, looking around at everything.

Penelope laughed. "You were too curious last time I planned something big, so I had to be nonchalant about it this time."

"But you asked me where I wanted to go. What would you have done if I'd had a plan?" I asked, looking into her eyes, completely enamored.

She simply laughed and pulled me in to kiss her again. I pecked her lips in return but pulled back again. I wasn't done asking questions.

"Does this mean you—" I was silenced by her lips as she kissed me again, shushing me all the while.

About the Author

In the hours between corralling her circus of animals and feeding her husband, Stacy breathes life into the characters running rampant in her mind. Born in the south with a proclivity for travel and the nerd life, Stacy rests her head in the clouds and daydreams of equality. When not writing or working, she loves to craft, and spends many a night curled up with her hot glue gun. An avid Chipotle fan, she hopes to eat at one in every state and country lucky enough to have one.

267